I0596454

Other Books by Christina Edgar Olds

Giving Up Grace

The First Summer

Everything Will Be Okay

Christina Edgar Olds

ISBN: 9798993365800

This book is a work of fiction. Names, characters, organizations, places, and events are either the product of the author's imagination or are used fictitiously to benefit the storyline. No part of this book may be used in any form without the permission of the author.

First Edition, October 2025
Printed in the United States of America

christinaedgarolds.com

For Holly, Emily, Lauren, and Rob—

How a family comes together
isn't as important as how it stays together.

CHAPTER 1
Ella

"May I have your attention? The Felicia Carmichael show will begin in ten minutes."

The announcement from deep within the old auditorium preceded the sound of three magical chimes, sending theatre patrons scrambling for their seats.

Ella Daley and her closest friends slipped into the seventh row. Lively chatter surrounded them, and the air reeked of floor cleaner and old wood. The renowned Norris Center for the Performing Arts appeared locked in a time warp with its rich red stage curtains and old-fashioned balcony boxes. Its elaborate decor only added to the evening's mystique.

Ella stayed close to Marcy, Sondra, and Lisa when they all landed in the Twin Cities after graduating from college. They regularly met for drinks or dinner, but birthdays called for a bigger celebration. Ella's hectic life had kept her from joining the girls for a few months, but her milestone birthday offered a temporary distraction from her responsibilities, and she was grateful for it.

"How did you snag tickets to Felicia Carmichael?" Ella asked.

"You're turning thirty tomorrow, so we needed to do something special," Marcy insisted.

Well-known for her psychic capabilities, Felicia Carmichael starred in her own television show. During their days at the University of Northern Iowa, the friends got together every Friday night to eat pizza and drink beer while they watched *Felicia Feels You*. The famous medium hosted small groups from her Georgia home as cameras televised their paranormal experiences. Ella never really bought into the eccentric star's supposed powers, but watching the program was one of her favorite memories of college life.

The readings often started with surface-level insights and gradually exposed more as people unwittingly opened up about their lives. An extraordinary number of family members wanted to make a post-death appearance on TV, and Ella thought this fortune-telling smacked of a scam. Her lack of faith in Felicia's telepathy didn't take away her excitement to see the celebrity in person. And sometimes Felicia revealed a unique tidbit, making her ability to speak to the dead seem plausible. On those occasions, Ella questioned her skepticism of the clairvoyant, and the uncertainty kept her tuning in each week.

Ella relaxed as two pre-show Cosmopolitans started to take effect, allowing her to push everything else out of her mind. She looked good in the dark skinny jeans and black silk top she'd chosen to wear for the night out. Her husband, Jordan, had already given her a pair of camel-colored booties for her birthday, and they completed her ensemble.

She'd recently gone to the salon for a balayage highlight on her shoulder-length brown hair, which had done wonders for her well-being. Ella appreciated getting compliments on her stylish looks, but other things had taken priority lately. She hadn't pulled herself together in any fashionable way in a long time, and it felt good to feel good.

"I can't believe we're here," Marcy said. "It better be as much fun seeing Felicia Carmichael in real life as it is to watch her on TV."

"I see four gorgeous women celebrating, and one of them is going to get lucky tonight," Lisa imagined with her eyes closed, imitating Felicia's southern drawl.

"Oh, I hope it's me," Sondra said as her hands folded into prayer.

"Ladies and Gentlemen . . .the Norris Center is pleased to welcome the one—the *only*—Felicia Carmichael!"

The announcer held each syllable of the entertainer's name longer than necessary to add drama to the introduction. Colorful spotlights circled the room, mimicking the start of a professional sporting event. The atmosphere intensified as Felicia strolled onto the stage, wearing a sequined jacket and waving to spectators like she was the Queen of England.

"Well, heeellooo Minneapolis," she said to the crowd's roar, stretching each syllable of her greeting.

Ella and her friends were sitting close enough to see Felicia's heavy pancake makeup, false eyelashes, and dark concealer. The artistic application of cosmetics made the performer appear younger than seventy. An asymmetrical gray bob framed her face in a trademark look sometimes turned into a caricature for marketing purposes. Glamorous as any Hollywood actress, Felicia carried herself with the poise of a star.

Marcy bounced in her seat, and Sondra and Lisa cheered and whistled. Their enthusiasm brought a smile to Ella.

"Okay, my darlings," Felicia started. "I can already feel the souls reaching out to me. The dead have a way of making things right in the afterlife. Whether you are willing to help them find the peace they deserve is up to you. So, let's not waste another second. Close your eyes as I call out to the spirits."

Ella glanced at the girls, whose eyes were shut tight in strict obedience. She faced forward again, joining them in dark anticipation. The vast space held its breath except for Felicia Carmichael's loud humming and histrionic calling to those beyond the grave.

"You may open your eyes now," she said after a few moments of suspense. "The dearly departed have entered the building."

Sondra snorted, and the other three women tried to keep from laughing at her outburst. It took Ella back to when she'd played with a Ouija board at a middle school slumber party. She remembered squirming in discomfort as the pre-teens dabbled in the mysteries of the occult, ignoring their fears.

Felicia walked through the hall where attendees clutched teddy bears and pictures of relatives they hoped to contact in the hereafter. Without any problem, the entertainer located a person with a mystical tie in each quadrant of the playhouse. Ella rolled her eyes at the convenience of it all. Did anyone really believe in such hocus pocus? She didn't want to allow herself to lean into the absurdity.

Felicia connected with the loved ones of more than a dozen people, revealing their private secrets to everyone in the room. The prevalence of fiery crashes and long-lost lovers seemed unusually high in this group desperate for answers. Even if Ella didn't trust Felicia's improbable abilities, the touching stories confirmed plenty of heartbreak in the world.

"I'm getting a reading on someone who's celebrating tonight," Felicia said, making her way toward Ella and her friends.

"How much did Jordan have to pay for this little coincidence?" Ella whispered, fearing her husband may have involved himself in the evening's antics.

Felicia stopped next to their row, and Ella froze.

"It's our friend's thirtieth," Sondra blurted out as Ella looked on with dread.

"What's her name?"

Ella nudged Marcy, saying under her breath, "Felicia's the psychic. Should she need a hint?"

Ella knew she couldn't be the only one marking a birthday and hoped someone else had doled out the cash for an individual shout-out. She'd never liked unwanted attention, and having hundreds of eyes staring at her made her want to disappear.

"It's Ella," Sondra said, pointing at her reluctant friend.

Maybe her old pals were in on the surprise, identifying Ella so Jordan got his money's worth. He'd probably found an address and emailed Felicia's staff with personal details, making it all seem legit.

"Ella . . . Ella . . ." Felicia pondered. "What a pretty name for a beautiful woman."

Felicia motioned for a blushing Ella to stand before she continued.

"Thirty is a joyous time of life, yet you're apprehensive about what's ahead."

Ella didn't know if she should respond or stay silent. She could hardly say, *Well, yes, Felicia. My mother has Alzheimer's disease, and I'm an only child caring for her. My husband is pushing me to get pregnant, but I'm distrustful of marriage and am afraid he will eventually leave me. I feel lost and alone, and the stress and sadness are killing me.*

"I see the recent loss of a man in your life," Felicia said with her eyes closed. She turned her head back and forth, trying to figure something out. "I'm confused because a woman urges the gentleman forward, but he's hesitant. Do the initials 'J' or 'C' mean anything to you? No. Sorry . . . forget the 'J'. It's not a letter—it's a hook pulling the woman away from the man. The 'C' is coming in much clearer now. The man has been deceased longer, and he has a stronger spirit. An eagle flies above him, which in many cultures represents fatherhood."

Ella *had* lost someone, but she didn't think twenty-five years constituted recently. Maybe it was all relative in the world of seances. She didn't want to admit it, but the reference did pique her interest because her father's name happened to be Charlie.

"I see an empty heart, signifying people who aren't close. I don't feel an estrangement, but I do sense a distance between the two of you."

Yeah, that happens when you've got a deadbeat dad who took off when you were a kid and never came back, Ella thought, without looking at Felicia.

"You come from a big family, but you don't have the support of your siblings. Perhaps you've had a falling out? I see you floating on a raft in the middle of a large body of water, which lets me know there is a rift separating you from them."

Felicia stood close to Ella, and the performer's perfume nearly choked her.

Ella hadn't spoken to her dad since the day he packed his bags. The part about brothers and sisters could not have been more inaccurate, and Ella kept reminding herself it was all an act.

Felicia wanted validation before moving on, but Ella didn't flinch or give the story an ounce of recognition. Finally, the analysis concluded with a flourish of insignificant disclosures.

"I'm envisioning a cake and lots of candles in your future," Felicia joked, ending her time with Ella to thundering applause as she moved to the next section of the venue.

The number of deceased coming forward lasted two hours, exactly the timeframe listed on the ticket as the length of the show.

CHAPTER 2
Maggie

Cameron Mason Sanders, 64, of Spencer, Iowa, died at home on May 16. He was born March 14, 1958, in Sioux City, to Mason and Hazel Sanders. He married Margaret (Maggie) Marie Anderson on May 4, 1979, in Cedar Falls. Cameron worked for Midwest Energy Corporation his entire career, retiring in 2015. He was a member of the First Lutheran Church and the Clay County Rotary Club. In addition, Cameron volunteered for several community organizations, including the Northwest Iowa Humane Society. Survivors include Cameron's wife, Maggie, of Spencer; son Mason (Jenny) of Des Moines; daughters Mallory (Tom) Martin of Ankeny and Erin (Tessa Lloyd) of Albuquerque, New Mexico; five grandchildren: Anna, Daniel, and Henry Sanders; Callie and Brenna Martin. He was preceded in death by his parents and a brother in infancy. Services will be held at 11:00 a.m. on Saturday, May 21, at First Lutheran Church in Spencer, with visitation one hour before. Thayer Funeral Home is assisting the family.

Maggie's hands trembled as she set the obituary aside and took a drink of coffee from a Styrofoam cup. Was it too much to ask for a regular mug when they were paying thousands for a funeral?

"Where did Erin go?" Joe asked.

Joseph Thayer took over the business after his dad retired, and he'd done an excellent job helping with Cam's arrangements, if you didn't consider how they served their coffee. One of Mason's friends growing up, Maggie still viewed Joe as a gangly teenager. She would never have imagined him supporting their family so professionally when he played basketball in the driveway with the neighborhood boys.

"Erin couldn't handle reading the obituary. She's waiting for me in the car."

The day Maggie discovered Cam's body, her youngest daughter and her wife flew in from New Mexico. Erin and Tessa helped fill the quiet space in the house after everyone left to get clothes and attend to commitments before returning for Cam's funeral.

"Does the wording meet with your approval, Mrs. Sanders?"

"Yes, it's fine," Maggie answered, as if *fine* were good enough.

You couldn't portray the essence of a person in two hundred words or less. Something lengthier would mean spending an obscene amount of money on a newspaper advertisement. Maggie didn't think taking out an ad promoting Cam's demise, like a Fourth of July sale at a car dealership, felt appropriate.

Maybe no one cared that Cam liked his tapioca pudding warm, cried at Christmas commercials, or insisted on making popcorn on top of the stove instead of using the microwave. Everyone knew Cam loved the Chicago Cubs, even when they were losing. They had a dog named Wrigley, for God's sake, but there wasn't room to include such a vital piece in the short inventory of his life.

Did anyone else need to know that Cam spent hours studying topics of interest on the internet? The Sanders rarely paid for repairs when Cam could Google how to fix the ice maker or replace the car's headlight. He'd wasted so much time investigating irrelevant subject matter when he should have been researching ways to stay alive.

Maggie had leisurely walked the aisles at the Hy-Vee grocery store as the last moments of her husband's life ticked away. Could she have saved him if she'd hurried or driven straight home instead of stopping to get lunch for the two of them?

Ever since Maggie found Cam on the garage floor, a range of emotions had overwhelmed her. Her throat hurt from a combination of crying and holding back tears. Once she handled all the particulars, there would be time for *feelings*. For now, losing control was out of the question.

Three days earlier, Maggie had sat in her favorite chair, surrounded by her books and a snoring dog at her feet. She heard Cam puttering around on the dock at the lake house and smiled at how content they were. The possibilities of a new day and the plans for a weekend at Lake Okoboji made her feel as if life didn't get any better than theirs. Now, Cam was gone, and she had the responsibility of mending the pieces of her family's broken hearts.

Cam's early retirement had offered him and Maggie a fresh start. Their lives had taken an abrupt turn that year, and the heartache caused by what happened served as the catalyst for how they would live the rest of their years together. They'd already indulged in a European riverboat cruise and bought the house on the lake. Sadly, the slip of paper listing the unfulfilled dreams on their bucket list would now deteriorate in the back of the kitchen junk drawer.

Thank God Cam rescued his canine best friend before he died. Maggie never wanted an inside pet. She'd lived on a farm as a child, where animals knew their place, and it wasn't on the furniture. Cam adored dogs and volunteered at the Humane Society every Wednesday. He'd done so much to make Maggie happy that she couldn't refuse him when he brought home a five-year-old golden doodle, surrendered to the shelter by an elderly man going into a care center.

Wrigley grew on Maggie within a few days. He'd bolted into the house, knocking over a potted plant as he defecated in the foyer, and he captured her heart anyway. Softening to the idea of a dog exemplified the changes Maggie had made to adapt to a marriage she'd only fully understood in the six years before Cam's death.

When they'd taken a flight to Las Vegas back then, their kids had no inkling they would be renewing their vows at one of those cheesy wedding chapels on the strip. And they certainly didn't know why it was necessary. Maggie imagined her children giggling at their mom and dad's later-in-life spontaneity, never realizing the family's stability stood in jeopardy.

"Why don't we take another look at the casket you chose?" Joe suggested. "Are you set on the oak finish rather than the mahogany?"

"I suppose it doesn't matter, does it?" she asked.

"It's my job to ensure you're satisfied. I want you to have a sense of peace as you lay Mr. Sanders to rest."

Maggie knew Joe must have practiced his undertaker script a hundred times. The darker wood selection cost more, and the pressure to give Cam the perfect heavenly sendoff weighed heavily on her. It seemed silly to incur extra expense when the oak casket would suffice, even if it wasn't quite as beautiful as the other.

Maggie made her way back to the showroom to solidify her choice for the right box to forever cradle the man she loved. She thought of Cam lying in his too-tight suit while their friends trotted past in a line of respect.

Should she make the trip to Smithfield Men's Wear and buy Cam a pair of black trousers in a larger size, so he'd be more comfortable in eternity? Ridiculous notions like this kept cramming their way into Maggie's newly widowed head. Obsessing over the memorial service was easier than dealing with the big questions concerning what would come after the funeral.

"Let's go with the mahogany one," Maggie said, yielding to Joe's sales pitch.

CHAPTER 3
Ella

The Alpine was packed for a Thursday, but the girlfriends lucked out and snagged a booth. The bar's proximity to the Norris Center made it popular for after-show gatherings, and Ella recognized other patrons from Felicia's audience sitting near them. The nightclub featured smoked cocktails and scrumptious desserts, and a jazz trio entertained in the corner. Ella had a soft spot for the place because it was where she and Jordan met for their first date.

The four women hadn't been together since Lisa and Seth's wedding. There were pictures to peruse from their Hawaiian honeymoon and a recap of the reception shenanigans. A commotion had ensued when the bride's mother, Delores, danced into the tiered cake after drinking too much during the social hour. The raspberry filled torte didn't look as elegant spread across the floor in front of the head table, and the mood had taken an ominous shift.

"I hate that your mom left the party early . . ."

They all giggled, including Lisa, as they recalled the chaotic scene.

". . . but Ed says if we ever get married, he wants to invite Delores to make sure everyone has a blast," Marcy finished.

Marcy and Ed had been dating for over a year, and they all assumed she would be the next one to marry.

"Mom doesn't drink much," Lisa said, excusing the lapse in judgment. "The open bar, combined with trying to calm her nerves about hosting such a large event, was a recipe for disaster."

"It's too bad she footed the bill for the night, and she didn't get to enjoy it," Sondra said. "Well, I guess she had a good time for a while."

"Did you know Jordan is paying the tab for us tonight?" Lisa asked Ella, changing the subject and sparing her mother from more humiliation.

"When I told him I got the tickets, he insisted on covering everything else," Marcy added.

"Really? I thought Jordan might have been in on Felicia's reading until I realized he would *not* have divulged something so private about my dad to her handlers."

"Of course he wouldn't. You've got the greatest husband," Sondra praised, draining her gin and tonic and motioning to the bartender for another.

As a third-grade teacher and a Minneapolis firefighter, Ella and Jordan watched their spending. After his mom died, he and his brother received a small inheritance. They finally had a place to call home when they'd used some of the money to put a down payment on a townhouse. Ella appreciated the financial breathing room, and covering the expense for an evening out was another advantage of a healthier bank account.

"I'm still stuck on what we just witnessed. Can you believe a train hit that lady's son, and Felicia heard a whistle and smelled diesel fuel?" Marcy questioned.

"Are you serious?" asked Ella. "I'm sure they take the list of names off the ticket roster and run an online query for news stories. The lady said it happened last year, so Felicia's team likely found it on the internet and pointed her toward the poor gal through an earpiece. That's just too specific. Felicia even knew he drove a blue car."

"Maybe it was a lucky guess," Lisa suggested.

"My reading was way off, aside from this," Ella said, pointing to a towering slice of chocolate cake the server was delivering. "And she bombed that prediction too. There's only one candle on this thing."

"You never talk about your dad, so how do we know if Felicia got *any* of it right?" Lisa asked, taking a bite of the decadent dessert.

Ella didn't like discussing her father. The topic brought self-doubt and a concern that others might pity her. She was used to hiding the truth about her past, and having Felicia Carmichael open those wounds in front of friends and strangers unnerved her.

"The lady with the hook? Come on, what could that mean? And my dad is not dead as far as I know—even if he's dead to me. He and my mom split up years ago, and I haven't seen him since."

Ella tried to act as if her father's desertion didn't bother her.

"I'm sorry, Ella. Don't you ever wonder what happened to him? What if he *did* die, and Felicia Carmichael got it right? Wouldn't you want to know?" Marcy continued probing.

"I don't have any interest in a father who doesn't want to be one."

Ella said nothing else on the subject, but she *had* decided to do a Google search for an obituary for her dad, Charles Meyers, as soon as possible.

***

Ella didn't feel any different than she had twenty-four hours earlier. Thirty always seemed like it would usher in wisdom and a feeling of peace, making sense of everything in her life. The first few moments of a new decade didn't bring any special clarity, and Ella felt foolish for thinking it might.

"Good morning, beautiful," Jordan whispered, kissing Ella's shoulder as she turned to face him. His hair stuck to his scalp on one side, and the stubble on his face grazed her skin. "Happy thirtieth."

"Thanks. What time is it?" Ella asked.

She'd taken her birthday off from work, so there'd been no reason to set an alarm.

"It's nine. I didn't want to disturb you. Do you want to know what we're doing today?" Jordan asked.

"Yes, tell me. Although you're in for a challenge to beat what the girls pulled off last night."

Ella enjoyed her night out, even if it brought up unresolved issues with her father.

"I'm up to the task," Jordan grinned.

Ella had allowed her husband to plan the festivities without her input. She also gave her word that she would refrain from visiting her mother. She hated not seeing the most important woman in her life on her birthday, but she'd promised, and the break would do her good.

"Since your mom's diagnosis, you've been the best daughter. Two years of worry and now daily trips to the care center mean you've earned a well-deserved retreat from everything. And I'm the guy to make it happen."

"That sounds intriguing," Ella said.

"First, we're having coffee and croissants on the deck."

"The chocolate ones from *Fleur's*?"

"Are there any others worth eating?" Jordan asked, feigning indignation.

"Yum. And then what?"

"Well, in case you forgot—you said we could start working on making a baby after you turned thirty."

Ella stiffened at the suggestion. Jordan began nudging her to start a family once they had some money in the bank. With a type A personality, Jordan adhered to a strict timeline for how things should unfold in his life. Having kids was next on the list, and Ella didn't want to listen to his belaboring of the point on her special day.

She wanted kids, but she didn't feel in a rush to have them. They'd been married for three years, but the fear that Jordan might walk out the door still terrified her. They'd discussed her misgivings many times, but no matter how hard he tried to reassure her, Ella's uncertainty prevailed.

"Let's not debate the pregnancy topic today," she insisted, pushing back on his proposition.

"I'm teasing," he said, pulling her closer. "Even if we aren't officially trying, I can't see the harm in practicing. And we'll get that opportunity because we're going away for the weekend."

"You mean until Sunday?"

"Yes. The weekend does include Sunday," he joked.

"You have time to pack after breakfast, so throw some things in a suitcase. An Uber is scheduled for noon, and he'll take us to the airport to catch our flight."

A getaway sounded wonderful to Ella, but how her mother would fare caused concern. Staying away for more than a day didn't sit well with her.

"Oh, Jordan. I shouldn't leave Mom for so long. What if she needs something?"

"That's why she has round-the-clock care. The staff can handle Jillian."

Jordan's grand gesture took Ella by surprise, and she knew there was no getting out of the mini vacation.

"Where are we going? I'll need to know what to bring."

"We're taking the short flight to Chicago and checking into the same hotel as our first getaway together. I've got tickets to a show and dinner reservations at two of the top restaurants in Chi-Town. I'm pampering you for three whole days."

Jordan was a thoughtful and loyal man. He'd never done anything to betray Ella, but the ache of rejection from her childhood made it impossible for her to believe in the longevity of *any* relationship. Hopefully, the next chapter of her life would bring a new mindset, and she vowed to try to give Jordan the trust he deserved.

CHAPTER 4
Maggie

"Let's go home and get you something to eat," Erin said after the funeral arrangements were finished.

Erin always took care of those around her. When Maggie called her daughter to share the devastating news about Cam, she hadn't hesitated to book a flight home, even though she and her wife had been back earlier in the month to celebrate Erin's birthday.

Maggie needed her youngest daughter more than anyone. After all, it was Erin's pursuit of living honestly that set the course for the most pivotal time in her parents' lives. The fact that she wasn't aware of how she'd changed their marriage didn't make it any less powerful.

Erin's teenage years had been difficult, and Maggie cherished their closeness as adults. She'd never considered that one of their children might love someone of the same sex. The disclosure sent Maggie and Cam reeling, but the upheaval had nothing to do with Erin being gay.

As they left the funeral home parking lot, Maggie noted what required immediate attention at home.

"I need to run to the store for a few things," Maggie said, making a mental list.

She knew they weren't hosting a party, but even a funeral called for preparations.

"We'll do it, Mom."

"I'd rather go myself. There is an organic chocolate milk that the twins like. And Anna will want Gatorade, but she only drinks the blue kind."

"And the boys? Is there something special for Daniel and Henry too?"

"I do like to have the puffed Cheetos for the grandsons. I think it would be easier if I did the shopping myself."

Maggie wasn't giving in. She'd always shown her love for the grandchildren by providing their favorite snacks.

"Write it all down, and Tessa and I can run the errands. When we get home, I'm going to make you a sandwich and pour you a glass of wine. You need to relax after all you've been through today."

Erin was insistent, and Maggie knew she should let others help. She found it hard to hand over the reins when everything else was spinning out of control.

Maggie remembered her graying hair needed a trim, and her nails looked atrocious. Lately, she'd felt like the mid-sixties woman she'd become, and she carried twenty extra pounds to prove it. Everyone of importance to the Sanders family would gather to honor Cam, and Maggie hated to look so frumpy for the somber occasion. She'd always struggled with self-esteem, and a public spectacle would expose her vulnerabilities.

Maggie had purchased a black dress when she found one on sale after the holidays. She'd bought it for the impending funeral of a close friend's mother, never imagining she would wear it to Cam's instead. Still, knowing it hung in the closet made one less detail to fret over in an already demanding week.

Cam used to keep his wife from getting too anxious by saying, "Everything will be okay," when things got crazy. She doubted his words held validity this time.

Maggie would get through the next few days and tackle the rest after everyone left.

***

"Mom, would you like a chair for the visitation?" Mason asked.

"I don't need one. Thank you, honey."

"Let me know if you change your mind, and I'll grab one for you."

"I'm fine, sweetheart," she said, hugging him.

Maggie hoped her kids wouldn't start treating her as if she were a delicate flower. She'd always kept things going for her family, and she didn't plan to stop because of Cam's death.

They all took their places near Cam's open casket and prepared to receive those who would embrace them with love and friendship. They were arranged by seniority; Mason and his family by Maggie's side as the oldest, followed by Mallory's crew. Erin and Tessa stood last in line, which put them first to greet people.

Maggie watched as friends and relatives fell into Erin's arms like they were seeking her out for their *own* comfort. Maggie wished she'd taken their spot in the lineup, shielding them from the emotional brunt of those initial contacts. She hadn't mulled over who should stand where, and she blamed herself for letting something slip her mind during the orchestration of Cam's funeral.

21

By the time people reached Maggie, they'd pulled themselves together. Thoughts and prayers were a common thread of consolation for the family. Not many in Maggie's circle were outwardly religious, and she bristled at their words. She doubted they spent much time in prayer to begin with, so the promise to lend support in that way seemed insincere.

Maggie's friends passed by with their spouses, wearing expressions of gratitude that they weren't yet facing life alone. She didn't wish her devastation on any of them, but their sympathy didn't change her uncertain future.

After a while, the grandchildren began to get restless. Mason's wife, Jenny, and Tessa removed them, using their roles as in-laws to help out. Mallory took her father's passing the hardest, and she couldn't keep it together for more than a few minutes. Tom stayed close by and looked thankful when Tessa took their twin girls to the bathroom.

Maggie appreciated the successful and happy children she and Cam raised. Their significant others and the grandkids rounded out the family perfectly. She would need them in the coming months, even if she didn't want to depend on them.

Maggie had relished the role of being Mrs. Cameron Sanders. Now, she was just Maggie, the woman who lost her husband too soon and had to reinvent herself in the last quarter of her life. He'd left her with so many years to share, and she was angry about it.

***

Solemn chords from the pipe organ filled the church with the melody of "Amazing Grace." The instrument wasn't played often; more contemporary music had become the norm. The commanding voice was still summoned for rare occasions—like funerals and weddings. Its overpowering presence reminded Maggie that the day marked something sacred. She wanted to stop time, because each moment that passed carried her further from the life she shared with Cam.

The sermon droned on longer than Maggie would have liked, but she'd zoned out anyway. Reflections about the fragility of life and the highs and lows of her marriage to Cam overwhelmed her. They'd only allowed the outside world to see the traditional and simple existence they chose to portray, even though it wasn't exactly the truth.

Maggie and Cam were sharing their best years when he died. They'd mended past resentments, burying the hatchet deep enough that it didn't seem likely the blade would come back and slice them in the heart. An acceptance of wrongs and a commitment they would stay together *despite* the ways they may have hurt each other had brought them true happiness and an intimacy having nothing to do with sex.

Maggie heard a car horn outside the church, and it took her thoughts to the day before her and Cam's 1979 wedding.

Cam honked in front of Maggie's childhood home to let her know he'd arrived.

"Can you believe we're getting married tomorrow?" she'd asked her fiancé, scooting closer to him on the bench seat.

His dad's new Chevrolet Impala shimmered in the sunlight, cleaned and polished for the following day.

"That's why I have a surprise for you," Cam gushed.

"What is it?"

As they pulled away, Maggie intertwined her fingers with Cam's.

"We've got a busy twenty-four hours ahead, and we can't lose the specialness of the wedding for you and me," he said.

A hopeless romantic, Cam would do anything to make Maggie happy.

"Mom wants me back as soon as possible to finish the attendant's gifts. We still have rice bags to tie, and I've got to get ready for the rehearsal dinner. We better make this quick, or Mom is going to have a cow."

Maggie didn't know why Cam insisted she go on a car ride with so much left to do before their big day.

"This is important. Close your eyes, and don't look until we get there," Cam said from the driver's seat.

"Can I open my eyes now?" Maggie asked when they stopped ten minutes later.

"Yes. You didn't peek, did you?"

It took her a minute to realize they were at a park. Cam popped the trunk and pulled out a basket of food and a blanket. He handed Maggie a bottle of champagne, and they headed into the woods. After walking a short distance, they came to a clearing, and Cam set everything up for an impromptu lunch.

"A picnic?" Maggie asked as Cam motioned for her to sit.

"You wanted an outdoor wedding, and your mother wouldn't allow it. So, I took matters into my own hands. I want us to marry each other with only the forest looking on. I'll give you my promises for the rest of our lives, and then you can share yours. God will already consider us married when we get to the church tomorrow."

The champagne cork released with a thud, and the cold liquid overflowed the plastic cups Cam packed. Sunlight spilled through the trees, and birds sang in different pitches of melody. The aroma of lilacs filled the air of an unusually warm May. The spring fragrance reminded Maggie of growing up on the farm.

"You're the best," Maggie said, slurping the bubbly beverage to keep it from spilling onto her shirt.

Cam started, "Margaret Marie Anderson, I pledge to honor, protect, and uphold you. I will do everything I can to make you happy in our life as husband and wife."

Cam's love made Maggie forget that her ankles were chunky and her hair too curly. She'd always felt passed over for prettier girls or those who offered better personalities. Once she and Cam got together, it didn't matter what all the other boys thought. He was the man she wanted.

Cam waited for Maggie to recite her vows. He'd spent time preparing his speech, but Maggie had to improvise.

"I can't imagine marrying anyone as wonderful as you, Cameron Sanders. I will love you until the end of time."

Maggie's words were brief, but she meant them with all her heart.

"Till death do us part," Cam added.

"Till death do us part," Maggie repeated as they toasted each other.

Cam's funeral came to a conclusion as the final phrase of "How Great Thou Art" faded. Maggie touched the wedding ring on her left hand and felt Cam's death parting them.

***

The women of First Lutheran Church knew how to put on a luncheon. The tables looked pristine, covered in white linens with spring blossom centerpieces adding color to the room. Members of the ladies' circle served the abundant spread, allowing everyone to grab a bite while talking with family and friends.

Maggie tried to thank each person who showed up to remember Cam. She smiled and chatted casually as if she hadn't just lost the love of her life.

Mason followed behind his mother, filling in the gaps with people and giving his own life updates. He stepped in as a buffer to ease Maggie's role as hostess, and she was grateful for his overprotection.

"Mom, why don't you get some food and sit?" he suggested.

Maggie couldn't eat anything. Tessa had cooked breakfast that morning, and scrambled eggs and bacon had given her energy for the day.

"I'm fine. This is a good time to say hello to people. I'll have to face them at the grocery store or the dry cleaner when all I want to do is get home if I don't do it today. You take a break. Jenny might need you."

Maggie saw Mallory struggling with Callie and Brenna. One of the twins protested about getting green Jell-O, and the other lifted her dress above her head, exposing Paw

Patrol panties. Maggie tried to will Tom to hurry in the food line and get back to help his wife.

Tessa sat by herself while Erin visited with a friend. The look on her youngest's face told Maggie that Erin didn't know how to end the conversation and return to her wife.

She glanced at the wall clock and wondered how long people would stay. The funeral acted as a placeholder between life with Cam and everything after. Maggie didn't want to go on without her husband by her side, but she looked forward to getting past the purgatory of the previous few days.

***

The Sanders spent most of Sunday together until the kids started to pack their cars and contemplate resuming their lives with the added burden of grief.

The house seemed strangely still in the absence of Cam's big personality—no board games, no bags set up in the yard, no spontaneous ice cream runs.

Maggie's duties as the unpaid executive assistant to her husband's exuberance allowed Cam to benefit from her organizational skills while remaining the preferred leader of the family. None of the children gave it a second thought when Cam announced an outing to the bowling alley or a last-minute weekend at the lake.

Maggie was the one who would call King Pin to ensure they could bring a group on a Saturday night and would stay up until midnight baking cookies and throwing lasagna together. Motherhood had been thankless much of the time, but looking back, Maggie realized how much she'd loved it.

"Mom, why don't you come to New Mexico soon?" Erin asked as she became tearful.

"That's a great idea," Maggie said.

She had no intention of planning a trip out west, but pretending it was a consideration might appease Erin enough to get her back to Albuquerque feeling hopeful.

"We'd love to have you," Tessa added, moving to give Maggie a hug before she and Erin squeezed into Mason's van for a ride to the airport.

"Take care of my girl," Maggie whispered to her daughter-in-law.

"You have my word," Tessa promised.

***

Alone for the first time since Cam's death, Maggie could finally exhale. She climbed onto the bed with Wrigley. He licked her hand, and his eyes became heavy as she rubbed behind his ears. The house fell silent except for the steady drip of a leak in the bathroom sink. For weeks, Maggie had hounded Cam to fix it, but he kept putting it off as if time were of no concern to him.

She pulled Cam's pillow close, and the smell of his cologne made his loss inconceivable. How long would his scent linger if he didn't exist anymore? It proved he'd been there, and she didn't want this last part of him to evaporate.

After days of roller-coaster emotions, Maggie drew a hot bath. Once she immersed herself in the soothing water, she allowed the tears to flow.

CHAPTER 5
Ella – Fall 1997

Daylight peeked through the slats of Ella's bedroom blinds, and she heard muffled voices and angry outbursts. It scared her when she woke up to the frightening sounds of her mom and dad fighting, and lately, it was happening all the time. She took the decorative pillow with the pink and white flowers on the front and put it over her head. She wasn't supposed to use that one, but it was all she had to drown out the arguing.

She needed to get up, and she hoped her father would be the one to take her to school. He liked to stop for donuts, and she loved choosing one with sprinkles on top and crawling back into his truck to have breakfast together.

Her mother, Jillian, cooked eggs or oatmeal for her. She complained when Ella ate sugary treats and frothy hot chocolate from a machine at the gas station. Ella learned that sometimes keeping a secret, like what you ate when you were with your dad, didn't hurt anything.

Ella brushed her teeth and slipped on the Mary Kate and Ashley T-shirt and matching navy-blue leggings her mother had laid out for her the night before. She had jobs to do each morning, and she'd already checked off two by dressing herself and taking care of her teeth. She grabbed her purple tie-dye backpack and headed for the kitchen.

"Good morning, sweetheart. How did you sleep?"

Her mother looked tired and grouchy as she drank her coffee, though she tried to act cheerful.

"Fine."

Ella didn't want to tell her mom that she'd heard them again.

"Let me get you a bowl of cereal."

"Where's Daddy?"

"He's at work, but he'll get you from school today. Don't forget to look for his truck instead of the Camry."

Ella adored her father and any time she got to spend with him. He hardly ever picked her up from kindergarten, and Ella liked the change.

"Are we grilling hamburgers tonight?" Ella asked.

She looked forward to their family barbeques when they sat on the brick patio and enjoyed the evening air.

"I don't think so, honey."

Ella thought her mother might cry, and she wondered why asking a question about supper would be so upsetting.

***

The bell rang at 2:30 p.m., and Charlie Meyers's truck held the first spot in the pick-up line.

"Hi, Daddy!"

"How's my girl?" he asked, helping her into her seat.

"How come you're getting me today? Did you get off early?"

"I did. Want to get an ice cream cone?"

30

"Yes!" Ella exclaimed, giggling with excitement.

They drove to the Dairy Queen, and after collecting their order, they went to a nearby park.

"Let's sit for a bit," her dad said, pointing Ella to an empty picnic table.

The trees were beginning to turn orange in the autumn sunshine, and the October air still felt warm in the late afternoon.

"Guess what?"

Ella licked wildly at the melting chocolate dripping down her chin.

"What?" her father asked, handing her a napkin.

"I'm the student of the week starting on Monday, which means you and Mommy can visit my class and even have lunch with me. Can you come on the same day? That way we can all eat together."

"I doubt my boss will let me off over the noon hour, but I'm sure your mom will be there."

"Can we go play when I'm done with my cone?" Ella asked, watching some children vacate the swings.

"I want to talk with you first," her dad said.

His face was red, and there were tears in his eyes. It gave Ella an uneasy feeling in her stomach.

"About what?"

Ella looked past her dad to a group of kids on the slide.

"I'm leaving after we get home tonight."

"Where are you going?" Ella asked, turning her attention back to the conversation.

"I'm moving to another town because I got a new job at a bigger grocery store."

Ella's dad tried to hold his mouth still, but it wobbled anyway.

"You know how I work a lot of hours? Well, I'm a manager now," he continued.

"We're moving?"

"Not exactly. You're staying here, and I'm going alone. Your mom and I aren't getting along, and we've decided it's best for all of us if we get a divorce."

At five years old, Ella still knew it would *not* be best for all of them if her parents got a divorce. A few kids in her class came from families who weren't together, and she understood what it meant.

"When will I see you if you live in a different town?"

She threw the rest of her ice cream to the ground. Her dad scooted closer on the wooden bench, putting his arm around her.

"I don't know. It's complicated. Never forget how much I love you, and nothing will ever change that."

***

Two months passed, and when Ella and her mom decorated their tiny Christmas tree, their life seemed almost routine again. Ella hadn't heard from her father, and when she asked about him, her mother always changed the subject.

Ella thought he would show up on December twenty-fifth, and when he didn't, she figured he must be too busy with his new job. Easter, her birthday, and the Fourth of July all slipped by without seeing him, and Ella continued to make excuses in her heart. It made her sad, but she knew he'd take her for a weekend at the lake or to see her grandparents as soon as he could.

Ella didn't have to hear the fighting and slept better, even if missing her dad often kept her up late into the night. Her mom worked two jobs, and sometimes Ella would have dinner with the neighbors and sleep on their couch until she got off work. Eventually, they decided to move downtown where the rent was cheaper, allowing Ella's mother to quit her second job.

"Did you go through your toys and decide which things you want to take to the apartment?"

Ella could tell her mother was trying to act enthusiastic about moving.

"I want to take it all."

Ella didn't want to leave her home and change schools, let alone part with any of her belongings.

"Sweetie, the new place is much smaller than this house, and we won't have room for everything."

"Does Dad know we're moving? What if he comes to pick me up, and we're not here?"

"It's just us now, baby," her mom said, taking Ella's face in her hands as she knelt beside her. "I know this is hard on you, and I'm sorry."

"Why don't I get to go to Dad's? Kiley's parents are divorced, and she gets to see her dad every other weekend. Can I start staying with him after we move?"

Ella was not giving up.

"No, honey. I'll explain more when you get older. For now, know that I love you, and I'll take good care of you."

"But doesn't *Daddy* love me anymore?"

"Of course, he does. Everybody loves you. Sometimes, things happen between adults, and you'll understand better when you are a grown-up. Get your overnight bag because you're sleeping at the Monroe's tonight."

Jillian's good friend, Donna Monroe, lived next door. She had a little girl, and the two children got along well. Ella didn't mind spending the night there while her mother got them settled, and by the time she arrived the following day, her mother had promised she would have everything unpacked.

***

The new apartment wasn't like a real house. Ella liked her room with the colorful bedspread and matching pillow sham she'd picked out at Walmart, but the high-rise building seemed like a hotel rather than a place where they would spend the rest of their lives.

"Can I invite Daddy to my party?" Ella asked when her seventh birthday came around the following year.

She repeated the question when her mother didn't answer.

"I heard you. But we've talked about this . . ."

"I miss my dad. Why can't I see him?"

"Lots of other people will be there. I even invited your Aunt Eloise to come from Des Moines, and she's bringing two of your cousins."

"Can all the girls from my class come too?"

The possibility excited Ella.

"Of course. We'll make out the invitations, and you can take them to school next week."

Ella wanted to go to Chuck E. Cheese, and she jumped for joy when her mother agreed. Two weeks later, ten of Ella's classmates showed up at the pizza restaurant. They played games and exchanged tokens for cheap trinkets as if they were gold.

No one noticed Ella looking at the front door every few minutes to see if her dad would join the celebration.

When Ella woke up the next morning, her cousins were still asleep in their makeshift beds on the floor. A pile of presents rested against her closet door, and she couldn't wait to play with everything.

The voices of Ella's mother and aunt from the kitchen were louder than usual, and it reminded her of the way her parents used to argue. Aunt Eloise told her mom she should get something called child support. Ella wondered if child support meant seeing her dad again.

"This is not your problem. Let me handle my own life," Ella's mother said.

"Jillian, it's been eighteen months since Charlie left, and you're struggling to raise your daughter in a fleabag apartment. You could use the help from that jerk," Eloise disputed.

Ella hated hearing them speak about her dad negatively.

"Charlie is not the terrible guy you're describing. Things didn't work out, but I'm not hauling him into court. I'm doing fine."

"Is that why you borrowed money from me to pay for your daughter's party?" Eloise asked.

After the voices quieted, Ella got up and joined them. She didn't want anyone to think bad of her father, and she wanted to put an end to their cruel words.

"Good morning, birthday girl," her mother said. "Are you ready for pancakes?"

The rest of the day was dedicated to celebrating the new seven-year-old by attending a production of "Annie" at the Norris Center. Later, when she blew out the candles on her second cake that weekend, she made a wish to see her dad again.

***

Ella grew up well, despite not having a father to depend on. Love filled Ella and Jillian's lives, but material things didn't come as easily.

It wasn't long before Ella realized that Charlie Meyers had walked out on her and her mom, but she never stopped hoping he would make a surprise appearance. Every holiday without him made his daughter miss him more, but as Ella got older, her understanding of her father's choices soon changed her feelings to anger.

When he didn't show up for her high school graduation, Ella finally wrote him off. Her mother had done an excellent job of raising her, and she had a bright future. She didn't need a dad to turn out well, even if she'd wanted one.

CHAPTER 6

Maggie – Fall 1976

Maggie sat on the front steps of the brick fraternity house and waited for her boyfriend to bring her a beer. She didn't like this kind of party, but they'd been dating since August, and she couldn't make excuses indefinitely.

Maggie thought frat life entailed too many rules and regulations. Why would anyone want to follow guidelines set forth by a group of people with their own interests at heart? If she dated a boy involved in the Greek system at Iowa State, she would need to get over her insecurities and accept his unfamiliar world.

"Here you go," he said, handing Maggie a can of Old Milwaukee.

"Thanks."

He started to walk away, oblivious to her discomfort. Maggie liked going out with someone in college, but she already knew she wouldn't be with this guy for long.

"Where are you going?" she asked.

"I told you—the pledges have responsibilities at these parties. I can't hang out here with you all night. Come inside, and I can talk to you when I'm not schlepping beers for the upperclassmen."

"But I don't know anyone."

Maggie felt unwelcome in a place where only one of them belonged.

"You know me," he said with a wink. "Come on, there are other girls in there."

Maggie followed him and took a seat in the living room. The stench of cigarettes transported Maggie back in time to her grandparents' house. They'd smoked like fiends, and ashtrays adorned every table. She wasn't fond of the smell of Marlboros, but it reminded her of people she missed. The wave of nostalgia made her homesick, and she wanted to escape to her dorm room and watch Starsky and Hutch.

"Aren't you Maggie?" asked a blond girl with a perfect nose and a headband matching the print on her argyle sweater.

"Yes, didn't we meet a couple of weeks ago at the football tailgate?" Maggie asked, seeking common ground.

"I remember you because you weren't wearing any letters. We live in the sorority across the street," she said, referencing three coiffed co-eds sitting beside her. "Are you in a house?"

If you didn't identify with one of the many groups in the ISU Panhellenic system, you were an outsider.

"No. I live in the dorms. They plan outings, and I don't have to pay any money to participate in them."

Maggie didn't mean for her response to sound as condescending as it did, but the young women didn't notice.

"My boyfriend is a GDI too."

The friends laughed at the proclamation, and Maggie looked on, feeling stupid.

"What's a GDI?" she asked.

"It's a God Damn Independent," the sorority sister scoffed as if everyone should know the acronym. "That's him over there," the girl said, pointing to an attractive guy standing in the doorway. "I got him an invitation to this party, hoping he might want to join during spring recruitment."

He gave a half-smile, and his girlfriend said under her breath, "I'm getting him into this fraternity if it's the last thing I do."

As the sisterhood turned their attention to dress choices for an upcoming formal, Maggie watched the girl's boyfriend as he leaned against the wall and drank his beer. He sighed and looked at the clock above the stone fireplace. Maybe the minutes ticked away as slowly for him as they did for her.

Maggie sat for more than an hour, occasionally making small talk, before searching for the guy she came with.

"Let's get out of here," Maggie suggested when she found him filling a cooler.

"Aren't you having fun?"

"No, it's not that. I'm not feeling well. I'm probably catching a cold," Maggie fibbed.

If she faked illness, it would give them an excuse to leave early.

"That's too bad. Why don't you take the CyRide back, and I'll call you tomorrow?"

Suggesting Maggie hop the free university bus, instead of delivering her to the dorm himself, didn't seem very considerate.

"I thought you said we only needed to make an appearance and then we could go do something else."

"I need to stay here and make sure we have enough help from the pledge class to clean up later. And since you're sick, you should go home anyway."

"Oh, okay."

He'd made it clear to Maggie on several occasions that she could not compete with his frat brothers. The fact that she didn't care if she spent the rest of the evening alone spoke volumes.

"Dork," yelled someone from the sun porch. "Get over here with a mop. There's beer all over the floor."

The boyfriend looked at Maggie apologetically and pecked her on the cheek. He grabbed a rag and ran toward the spill like an obedient child. He had no problem doing whatever it took to influence the opinion of those who pulled rank to his lowly recruit status.

Maggie retrieved her jacket from a dirty-looking sofa and walked a half-block to catch a ride. She approached the bus stop and saw the other God Damn Independent waiting too.

"Hi," she said, taking her place in line next to him.

"Hello," he responded. "You're leaving kind of early, aren't you?"

"About as early as you," Maggie replied. "It's not my scene."

Her feeling of unease began to subside.

"Me too. I assume your boyfriend can't leave the party yet?"

"Nope, he's a pledge, so he's got *responsibilities*," Maggie mocked, making quotation marks in the air.

"Are you in a sorority?"

"No, I'm a GDI," Maggie said, knowing where she fit in the Cyclone social hierarchy.

"Well, you certainly know the lingo for a GDI."

"Your girlfriend is the one who enlightened me."

He looked like a young Paul Newman, and he carried himself with confidence.

"You and that guy serious?" he asked.

"Well, I'm not going to *marry* him."

His smile put her at ease.

"Good, then I should introduce myself. I'm Cameron Sanders," he said, extending his hand. "Want to go for a drink up on Welch?"

Everyone went to Welch Avenue to hang out, and Maggie had been there several times. In Iowa, a person could buy alcohol after they turned eighteen, so most students could go to the bars when they got to college. The fun of meeting new people while enjoying music and socializing could also bring danger if you weren't careful.

"I don't know."

Maggie had a boyfriend, and she barely knew this stranger.

"I promise to get you home safely," he assured her.

Cameron Sanders seemed perfectly nice, and his sincerity calmed Maggie.

"All right, we can have one drink. It's getting late," Maggie said.

"It's only 9:30, Cinderella. Everything will be okay."

Maggie appreciated being rescued from a night of boredom, and his fairy tale reference didn't go unnoticed. They began walking downtown as the bus pulled up, and a dozen people got off, heading in the direction of the party.

***

"So, you live near Cedar Falls but didn't go to school at the University of Northern Iowa?" Cameron asked as the server put two cocktails in front of them.

Music blared from large speakers secured above the bar with bungee cords. Most of the rowdy crowd, dressed in red and gold, were ready to celebrate after a big football win over Kansas State earlier in the afternoon.

"Too close to home," Maggie answered, stirring her slow gin fizz with a swizzle stick.

"True. It would have also made it impossible for you to meet a great guy like me," Cameron bragged.

"And a humble one too."

"Touché."

"Where did *you* grow up?" she asked.

"Northwest Iowa. But my life story is boring. I want to hear all about Maggie Anderson. What makes her tick, what does she do for fun, and why is she dating such a dolt who takes her to terrible parties?"

"Hey, you were there too. But you do have a point."

"That idiot let you leave without him, and another guy met you at a bus stop and invited you out on a date. In my opinion, he's not taking very good care of you."

"I can take care of myself, thank you. And what makes you think this is a date?" Maggie asked.

"A boy and a girl meet at a party, and they hit it off and go someplace else. What do you call that?"

"Two people getting to know each other."

"What constitutes a *proper* date to you?" he asked.

"Flowers, dinner at a fine restaurant, maybe coffee and

dessert after . . .”

Maggie had never been on such a rendezvous, but it sounded perfect to her.

“I can buy that. What are you doing next Friday night?” he asked. “That gives you five days to get rid of your current boyfriend so you can start dating your new one.”

“And what about *your* girlfriend?”

“That’s the reason I left the party. I broke up with her when I saw her flirting with another dude. I have been officially single for over an hour,” he touted, looking at his watch.

“Here’s how you can get a hold of me,” he said as they stood outside Maggie’s dorm at the end of the evening. “I’ll be back at 6:00 o’clock on Friday, unless you chicken out.”

Cameron took a pen from his pocket and reached for Maggie’s hand, writing his number on her palm.

“I’ll be ready. Give me a call when you’re here, and I’ll come down to meet you,” Maggie promised.

“That means I need your phone number too,” he said.

She held onto his hand for a few seconds after giving him the information he needed.

“I’ve had a wonderful time with you tonight. I’d love nothing more than to kiss you goodnight, but I don’t make out with other guys’ girlfriends. So, if you want to stay with the frat boy, just let me know. I’ll understand. Not everyone wants to be swept off their feet by the man of their dreams.”

Cameron’s charismatic manner convinced Maggie to take a chance on him.

CHAPTER 7
Ella – Fall 2017

"Class, please be quiet so Bianca can introduce her guests from the Fire Department," Ella requested.

The Lakeview Elementary students obliged their teacher and found places to sit on a semi-circle of carpet squares.

"This is my dad, Captain Marcus Jones," Bianca said, beaming with pride. "Oh, and his friend, Jordan."

It wasn't every day that a girl got to have her father speak to the class, but Fire Prevention month provided the opportunity, and it made Ella happy when Captain Jones accepted her invitation.

"Hey, kids. Thanks for having us today. This is my partner, Lieutenant Jordan Daley. We work together at station fifteen, and he's the best there is," Bianca's father boasted.

The men acted as a team, educating the children about fire safety and ways to flee from a burning building. Any time a student raised their hand, their questions were answered with expertise.

Jordan Daley looked as good as Bradley Cooper. Besides being handsome, he interacted thoughtfully with her class, and it impressed Ella. She noticed the lieutenant wasn't wearing a wedding ring. Ella's last relationship had been over for months, and the attractive firefighter intrigued her.

"What happens if your house starts on fire?" one of the third-grade boys asked.

"Your family needs to have a plan. It's too late once your house is in flames. Do you all know what a fire drill is?" Captain Jones asked.

The kids nodded their heads and added a variety of comments.

"My mom put a rope ladder in my bedroom. My brother and I practiced hanging it out the window and climbing down."

"That's a good idea," Lieutenant Daley agreed. "Remember, you need to stay low to the ground to keep from breathing in the smoke."

"My dad says we can only have fake candles because once the dog knocked over a real one, and it burned a hole in the living room carpet."

"My grandma and grandpa had a fire in their kitchen, and they got new cupboards because the others turned black."

When you gave kids a chance to talk, they never held back.

The presentation lasted thirty minutes, and the children soaked in every word. Ella thanked both men for making the appearance while her pupils washed their hands and got ready for lunch.

Captain Jones moved toward the line to hug his daughter goodbye, and Ella didn't mind time alone with the lieutenant.

"Can I leave some of our firefighter trading cards for the class?" Jordan asked.

Ella could smell his masculine aftershave and wondered what scent he was wearing.

"Oh, you have fire swag?" Ella ribbed, giving Jordan a hard time regarding his celebrity status.

"It might be weird, but the City of Minneapolis's marketing team insists on it. And it gives me street cred with my brother's kids."

"I'm joking, the children will love them. Set them on my desk while I get them off to the lunchroom. Thank you again for being here today. We all enjoyed it."

Ella shook Jordan's hand, doubting that anyone *enjoyed* the presentation as much as her.

Ella never had enough time for her midday break. After her class went to the cafeteria, she was lucky if time allowed her to go to the bathroom. With only fifteen minutes, it became an important ritual to take a few quiet moments for herself.

She unwrapped her turkey and cheese sandwich as the sounds of recess floated through an open window. She noticed the stack of cards Lieutenant Daley left, and one had a note written across the front.

Drinks at The Alpine on Friday at 7:00? If you don't show up, I'll understand.

Jordan

Ella could not stop smiling when the class returned after lunch. She'd have to cancel dinner plans with the girls if she went out with Jordan, but they wouldn't care.

***

Ella arrived at *The Alpine* a little early. When Jordan waved her over and confirmed he already had a table reserved, his brown eyes and friendly demeanor reminded her of why she'd agreed to meet him.

"I thought I might get stood up tonight," he said. "I worried the school might frown on this kind of thing, but I took the risk anyway."

"There are no specific rules about having a date with someone who comes to your class to speak."

"Well, good. Because I want to get to know you better. I heard the kids calling you Miss Meyers, so I figured you weren't married."

"I noticed you didn't have a wedding ring on either. But sometimes men with dangerous careers don't wear jewelry to work. I was excited to see you again when I saw your note."

Jordan smiled from across the table and sipped his bourbon. He'd chosen a spot tucked in the corner of the crowded bar, and its location made it feel as if they were the only two people in the place.

"Tell me about Ella Meyers."

Dates rarely wanted to hear Ella's life story before sharing all the pluses on their own dating resume, and his interest flattered her.

47

"I grew up here in the cities. My parents divorced when I was young, so Mom and I survived on our own. We didn't have much, but we loved each other, and we're still very close. She lives in Des Moines now. I went to college at the University of Northern Iowa and returned to Minneapolis after graduation. I taught at another school and then landed at Lakeview. I adore teaching third graders, so when this position opened up—I was thrilled."

"It impressed me to see how you corralled your students when they got out of control. I enjoy doing classroom gigs because I might encourage a student to become one of us when they grow up, but sometimes they're pretty unruly."

"Oh, believe me, several of my kids want to go into the fire service now."

"That's great," Jordan said.

First dates always brought an unavoidable awkwardness. Jordan's eyes held Ella's attention a little too long, and the conversation stalled before she broke his stare and started asking her own questions.

"And you? Give me the skinny on Jordan Daley."

"I'm from north of here, and I have one brother, Wes, who farms. His wife's family owns hundreds of acres, and he lucked into the successful agri-business. My dad died a couple of years ago, and Mom moved to a house near Wes's land. He keeps busy with the crops and livestock but also watches over her every day. Since I work twenty-four-hour shifts, with forty-eight off in between, I get to see my mother often. I try to take her to doctor's appointments and make sure she has groceries, so my brother doesn't have to do everything."

"That's nice for your mother. Did you ever want to be anything other than a firefighter?"

"Nah . . . I'm living my dream."

Jordan seemed happy with his career choice. He carried himself with unassuming assurance. Ella didn't know where things would go with this person, but she was drawn to him.

Drinks turned into dinner, and when they ordered dessert and coffee at a cozy restaurant near *The Alpine*, Ella knew she wanted to see Lieutenant Daley again. He put her at ease, and despite her usual mistrust of men, she felt a pull toward Jordan that couldn't be ignored.

"Well, I can't remember a better first date," Jordan said as they stood beside Ella's car at the end of the night.

"I had fun too. Thanks for a wonderful evening."

"Do you have any plans for next weekend?" Jordan asked.

"You mean Friday or Saturday, or what?"

"I mean the entire weekend. I'm sorry, I know this must sound forward. Actually, I'm *not* sorry. You are fantastic, and I want you to come to a wedding with me in Chicago. I'll get you your own room, and you can be my plus one. What do you say?"

Ella wasn't sure if she should consider such an offer from someone she'd just met. Still, she didn't want to pass up three whole days with the new man in her life. Something in her gut told her to take a chance on him.

"Okay," she said, ignoring any misgivings.

When they checked into their hotel on the Magnificent Mile, Jordan kept his word and charged more than a thousand dollars for two rooms. It was a shame, because they only used one of them.

***

Ella and Jordan dated for a year before they were engaged, and the wedding quickly followed. Being suspicious of men was a hard habit to break, and Ella still found it difficult to trust the one man who never disappointed her.

"You look pretty, Eloise," Jillian said as she touched the tip of Ella's veil, and the photographer snapped a photo.

"Mom, you called me by your sister's name again."

"Oh, I did? Silly me."

It was the second time her mother had addressed her as "Eloise" that week. Ella hugged her, brushing off the slip as an insignificant mistake.

"How can I ever thank you for all you've done? You took such good care of me, and I'm old enough now to realize your sacrifices. I'm so sorry Dad turned out to be a loser."

"Don't say that, Ella. There's no reason to disparage him."

Ella couldn't understand why her mom always defended Charlie Meyers. Their dismantled marriage wasn't the only relationship he left in shambles. He abandoned them and never looked back, yet Charlie's actions didn't seem to bother her mother.

"After everything that's happened, I'm grateful I have you by my side," Ella said, dismissing thoughts of her father.

"I love you, sweetheart. There is no place I'd rather be. Having me walk you down the aisle is a little unconventional, although it's symbolic of our lives. Now you have Jordan, and I'm happy and proud of who you've become."

50

"Let's head up to the chapel," a tearful Ella said, taking her mother's arm.

Ella and Jordan didn't have the money for a lavish wedding, and her mom certainly couldn't afford to host at an exclusive venue.

The only attendees included their mothers, Jordan's brother and his family, and Ella's maid of honor, Marcy. After the ceremony, they returned to Jordan's mom's home for dinner and dessert.

When the couple arrived at the farmhouse, candles flickered softly, and the scent of garden peonies filled the dining room. A small cake covered in lavender sugar roses provided the focal point on the table, and the simple occasion reflected the pure love Ella and Jordan shared.

CHAPTER 8
Maggie – 1980's

Maggie and Cam moved to Northwest Iowa after Cam accepted a job with Midwest Energy Corporation. The couple's first apartment in Spencer was no palace. The windows were single-paned, and cold air seeped in when the wind blew. There was one comfortable place to sit, and it had a broken leg, and the original color of the carpeting remained a mystery thanks to a surplus of stains.

Maggie was due to give birth in a few weeks, and the couple decided she would stay at home with the baby the first year. It didn't excite Maggie to delay the accounting career she'd studied for, but it seemed like the best option for a young family living in a new town.

"Can I get you anything?" Cam asked as he stabilized the foot of the chair to prevent it from collapsing.

That's what they got for shopping at Goodwill.

"How about a spicy burrito to start my labor. How can you stand to look at me?"

Maggie's ankles were swollen, and she was plagued with pregnancy acne.

"You've never looked more beautiful to me. Two days past your due date means it won't be long now. Want me to rub your feet again?"

Cam relished his role as an expectant dad, but Maggie's trepidation concerning motherhood overwhelmed her. Cam embraced whatever life handed him with his laid-back personality and philosophy of acceptance, while she doubted herself and longed for composure.

Maggie had gotten pregnant during the couple's last semester at Iowa State. They'd married the previous summer and thought they would have the luxury of two incomes following graduation. Maggie dreamed of eating more than popcorn and macaroni and cheese for dinner three times a week, and a baby meant any additional money would have to go to diapers and formula.

When Cam heard the news, he'd bought cigars and champagne they couldn't afford. He shared them with everyone in student housing. Even the guy who lived below them, who didn't speak much English, lit up a stogie and patted Cam on the back in an understanding of joy that transcended cultures.

They'd redecorated the second bedroom in their tiny Spencer apartment, turning it into a nursery. Maggie's mom gave them an old rocker, and they painted it white before placing it in the baby's room. Maggie spent part of every day pondering the future while taking whiffs of baby lotion and folding pastel onesies. Hope for how the child would improve their lives replaced Maggie's fears as their little one's arrival drew near.

***

"Are you ready to push?" the physician asked as if Maggie had a choice.

"Let's do this," she said, thrusting her first little one into the world with a strength she didn't know she had.

"It's a boy!" the doctor exclaimed.

"A boy?" Cam asked as if he thought the obstetrician was messing with him.

The look of awe on Cam's face made all of Maggie's discomfort worthwhile. She knew the greatest gift she could give her children was having him for a father.

"Yes, Mr. Sanders. You have a son. Do you want to cut the umbilical cord?"

"Of course," Cam said, tears streaming.

A nurse appeared from somewhere beyond Maggie's bent legs and led the new father to his first parental task. Maggie watched her husband move away from her and toward their little boy, symbolic of the changes to come.

***

The early years flew by for the Sanders. Cam thrived in his career, and Maggie tolerated her vocation as a homemaker. She never got her first real job and only used her bookkeeping skills to balance the budget and figure out how to make fifty dollars of grocery money stretch for a week.

Two years after the birth of baby Mason, a little girl came along. With a son and daughter to love, their family seemed complete. Maggie didn't know the pink bundle of joy they named Mallory would come with contentment she hadn't experienced with Mason. Maggie's new focus became raising the most intelligent humans to ever grace the Earth, and she forgot all about her professional aspirations. Sometimes, Cam's needs didn't make the list either.

Cam earned good money as he climbed the corporate ladder, so having Maggie stay at home continued to make sense. Eventually, he traveled several days a week, and Maggie and the children got into a routine. She knew she'd signed up for the responsibilities of parenthood, but at times, Maggie barely made it through the exhaustion.

***

Maggie had survived another twenty-four hours alone. Mason spiked a fever due to strep throat, and Mallory's incoming teeth kept her up most of the night. Maggie dragged her body down the stairs at 6:30 a.m. Her knee cracked on the third step, and she froze. The kids could sleep through a thunderstorm but were also prone to rising for the day at the tiniest sound. Maggie wanted to savor a few more moments of silence, and she clung to her hope of quiet like a life raft.

Safe in the glaring light of her cheerful yellow kitchen, Maggie hit the button on her Braun Aromaster and slumped at the table. She'd been tired the night before and hadn't cleaned up supper. Dried spaghetti coagulated on a colorful plastic plate near the microwave and in every crevice of Mallory's highchair. Coffee would provide the magic potion she needed to start her day.

She added cream and took a sip of the only thing she looked forward to in the morning. She tidied up the mess and tried to adjust her attitude for the day ahead. She had to keep going because no one was coming to save her.

Just as she put the last of the dishes away, she heard Mallory calling out from her crib. If she hurried, she could swoop in and bring her little girl downstairs before she woke her brother.

Maggie ascended the staircase and opened the nursery door.

"Shhh . . . Good morning, little miss. Let's get you up so Mason can sleep a while longer."

"Mama," Mallory said with a wide grin.

Maggie scurried to change the toddler's diaper, trying to be as quiet as possible. She rested Mallory on her hip, and they started toward the flight of steps.

"Mommy?" Mason yelled out from his room.

At 7:03 a.m., it was on.

***

The years rushed by as Mason and Mallory grew out of their baby stages. The days of sippy cups and nursery rhymes were replaced by the blossoming of school-aged children whose lives revolved around homework and extracurricular activities.

"I'm back," Cam hollered as he came in after another business trip.

The kids ran to greet their dad like a long-lost hero, and Maggie wished she could melt into his arms too, but something stopped her. Cam's weekends at home were a constant give and take, and Maggie often felt as if she did all the giving.

Cam tried to pour himself into a family who survived without him during the week, and Maggie needed to get out and let someone else take the pressure off. Two little people hung on Maggie nonstop while Daddy worked, and she wanted time for herself.

Although Maggie appreciated having another adult around on Saturday and Sunday, their day-to-day routine was thrown off. She knew it wasn't healthy to count the hours until her husband left again, and she hoped they were only going through an unpleasant marital phase. Surely, she and Cam would reconnect once they got through the tough years.

As Mason and Mallory got older, Maggie's duties shifted to driving a carpool and overseeing the PTA. She had more time alone during the day, even if single-parenting big kids brought a new kind of stress. She didn't tire as easily as when they were babies, but she looked to Cam for relief when he returned on Friday nights.

Cam liked to lounge in front of the television or nap on the covered porch on his down time. Maggie didn't want to have to tell Cam what he should do as an adult man who could see dishes piled in the sink from the comfort of his recliner. He seemed oblivious to the chores needing attention and preferred scheduling a round of golf with his buddies to hanging around all day with his family.

Cam got to do whatever he wanted while he was home, and it didn't sit well with Maggie. Weren't they *both* working full-time, even if Maggie didn't have to leave the house for her job? Resentment began to smolder when Maggie started to feel like Cam was a houseguest when he was there and not a romantic partner.

***

"I think I'll head out early this week," Cam said matter-of-factly.

He'd come home on Thursday for a change, and it had been another two days of passive-aggressive behavior between them.

"For what reason?" Maggie asked, anger tightening her breath.

"Kansas City is close, so I can drive in Sunday night. Then, I don't have to leave before dawn. I would enjoy it much more if I could take Monday morning to prepare for my meetings."

"Well, by all means. We want *work* to be as *enjoyable* as possible for you," Maggie snapped.

Cam traveled almost every week. He usually flew out of Des Moines on Monday, which never took away part of the weekend. Only five and a half hours from Spencer, Cam could easily make the drive to Kansas City.

"What's that supposed to mean?"

"I'm already doing all of this without your help ninety percent of the time. It isn't unfair for me to balk at you leaving a day early so you can get some downtime."

"It's not easy carrying the financial load of this family. Do you think I like being away from you and the kids all week, only to get back just in time to do my laundry, eat a home-cooked meal, and prepare to do it all over again?"

"Yes, I do think it's easy. You're working during the day, but what do you do on those business trips at night? I imagine you're ordering room service, watching a movie, or going out for drinks with your coworkers. Do you know what I'm doing? I'm busting my butt all day and sometimes most of the night, and I don't *ever* get a break. Who do you think does the laundry and makes your meals? You walk through the door, and I've got one more person to look after."

Silence replaced the oxygen in the room. Maggie saw hurt flicker across Cam's face as her irritation flared. The suggestion that he leave early brought her emotions to the surface, and there was no escaping her wrath.

"I didn't know you felt that way," Cam whispered.

"Yeah? You might understand how I feel if you asked me once in a while."

Maggie moved toward the sink and started filling the dishwasher. The plates and silverware clanked and scraped against each other as she indiscriminately stuck them into the plastic slots and slammed the door shut.

"I'm trying to give you everything, but if you aren't happy—I guess I'm not sure what to do. I'm an involved husband and father when I'm here, but all you do is push me away."

"I don't know what to tell you, Cam. If you think *involved* means showing up at a few of the kids' sporting events and then falling asleep in front of the TV before coming to bed at midnight, then we have different definitions of the word."

"You're always busting my chops. Sometimes it doesn't feel like you love me anymore," he said.

"Of course, I love you. You all mean the world to me. Is it unreasonable to need something else to get excited about too?"

Cam came to Maggie and tried to pull her toward him. She wanted to soften into his embrace, but his touch repelled her, and she didn't know why.

"I'm frustrated that you aren't a part of the most important years of our life," Maggie said.

Her feelings of loneliness were at the root of the problem, and she'd finally found the courage to tell him.

Cam let go and walked out of the kitchen. Maggie heard him climb the stairs and wished she'd handled the conversation better. She knew Cam loved her, even if she couldn't depend on him anymore. He brought home the paycheck, but everything else fell to her, and she didn't know if she could continue.

They didn't talk much the rest of the weekend, which passed quickly with family commitments and a pre-planned dinner with friends on Saturday night. On Sunday morning, Cam insisted that Maggie stay in bed while he took Mason and Mallory to breakfast. When she heard the garage door close, she rolled over, hoping to fall back to sleep. Tears came to her eyes, and the only thing she could do was stare at the ceiling.

***

The afternoon was coming to an end when Cam loaded his company car and hugged the kids, promising to bring them a surprise on Friday. Maggie could not believe that her husband had chosen to leave early for Kansas City after their heated discussion. She didn't ask Cam to let her know when he arrived at his destination or send him off with the loving words of a devoted spouse.

Cam had never gone against her wishes, and his blatant disregard for her needs made Maggie feel scared and alone. Maybe Maggie didn't know Cameron Sanders anymore.

Maggie seethed all week. When Cam called to check in, she answered his questions with succinct responses.

"Yes, the children saw the dentist. No, the plumber did not return my call, and the toilet is still leaking. I don't know if Mallory's soccer tournament is rescheduled after the rainout."

"Okay, then," Cam said. "I guess that covers everything."

"It doesn't even get us started."

Maggie's affect was calm, as if she were standing in the quiet center of an emotional storm. She knew if she allowed her emotions to gain strength, they could blow her world apart, and nothing would ever be the same.

"Do you want to talk about this now, on the phone from hundreds of miles away?" Cam asked.

"No. Sunday night would have been my preference. That's when you should have been with your family. Are you having an affair, Cam? Because something has changed."

Maggie doubted the unfaithfulness of her husband and didn't think he would remember how to pursue a woman anyway. A concerning distance was growing between them, but the involvement of another person seemed unlikely.

"Why do you have to make everything so hard? You used to enjoy staying home with the kids. Now, it's the last place you want to be."

"I'm happy being a mom. It's the responsibilities of a wife that are troubling me. How can I have a marriage with a man who would rather be elsewhere? You proved where your priorities lie when you left us early after I asked you to stay."

"I'm sorry. I wanted a few hours to myself. What's wrong with that?"

"Nothing, it's what I want too. Only, it's impossible for me because I don't have a wife. Honest to God, Cam . . . I need someone like *me* to take care of me."

"I'm doing the best I can, but I can try harder," Cam promised.

"Well, if you're doing your best, then I can't see your efforts making much of a difference. I will tell you that your *best* is nowhere near good enough."

Maggie couldn't help but push Cam further away. Her self-esteem had plummeted, and she wasn't even sure if she deserved better. It had been a long time since she'd shared a meaningful connection with Cam. Now, all she felt was regret for everything they'd lost.

CHAPTER 9
Ella – Fall 2019

The decline in Ella's mother started with minor things. A missed birthday blamed on a calendar mistake, a forgotten phone call brushed off as insignificant, and a misplaced purse found in a laundry basket. Jillian's cognitive lapses had become more frequent in her early sixties, and they ushered in a difficult conversation between mother and daughter.

Ella didn't want to accept that her mother could have a serious illness. It had always been just the two of them, and she'd never contemplated a life without her mom. Ella wanted to address Jillian's memory loss with an open mind. Maybe her mother suffered from age-appropriate forgetfulness, and there was no reason for concern.

After trying to dismiss her daughter's worries, Jillian admitted that something had begun to dull her senses. Doctor's appointments and tests to confirm the worst filled the following weeks. Jillian had Alzheimer's disease, and it was progressing. They'd lived in purgatory since the diagnosis, waiting for changes that would require more extreme measures. It didn't take long before that day arrived.

"I'm Ella Daley. I was notified that my mother, Jillian Meyers, is here," she said to the officer at the reception desk.

She'd received a call at school, and after the principal took over her classroom, she'd driven three hours to Des Moines to retrieve her mother from the police station.

"Let me grab Detective Barkley for you," the young cop replied.

The Polk County Law Enforcement building stood stark and cold, and the cement block walls did nothing to make the place feel less intimidating. It smelled like a combination of antiseptic and unappetizing food, and Ella couldn't wait to get out of there.

"Can I see my mom first?" Ella asked, imagining the woman who raised her in an orange jumpsuit.

"I'm sorry, ma'am. You'll have to speak with the arresting officer first."

Several people were waiting to conduct their own business, and Ella's imagination ran wild over what they had going on with the cops. After a few minutes sitting on a hard bench, a man appeared from behind the main desk and escorted Ella back to his office.

"Tell me about your mom," the detective started.

You could tell he spent a fair amount of time in the gym for a middle-aged man. His boot-black hair and neatly trimmed mustache added to his tough exterior. In his line of work, you could not afford to look weak.

"Yes, she's a wonderful woman, but she's having memory issues. My mother has never stolen anything before. She's been diagnosed with Alzheimer's disease, and it's the only reason I can think of that would cause her to shoplift," Ella explained, hoping for the officer's leniency. "How much did the purse cost? I can pay whatever restitution is necessary."

"Let's pump the brakes a little. I'm here to help your mother. I've already done a background check on her, and I see she doesn't have a record. She's scared, and given what you've told me, I tend to believe she can't remember taking the bag from Target. I can get the store to drop the charges if I have your word that you'll watch over her. I can't emphasize enough the danger for a person with your mother's impairments walking freely out in the community. Someone could recognize her condition and might take advantage of her."

Ella appreciated the officer's fatherly demeanor; a brush with the law could have turned out much worse.

"Yes, sir. I won't leave her alone again."

Life was about to change.

***

"This room should be comfortable for you, Mom," Ella said, putting the last of her mother's clothes into the guest room dresser.

She'd taken a week off work and spent it with her mom in Des Moines while they figured out a plan for Jillian's immediate care. It made sense to have her move into the townhouse with her and Jordan, so that's what they did.

"When am I leaving?" Jillian asked.

"Remember, we decided you'd stay through the holidays?"

Ella knew her mother would never live alone again. Still, the doctor encouraged them to take things slowly before they sprang the permanency of the living arrangement on Jillian.

"Oh, that's right," she answered. "You have a lovely home."

Having her mom close would make it easier for Ella to care for her, and she hoped her mother's health would stabilize over time.

***

Jillian lived at Ella and Jordan's for months without any problems. The restrictions of COVID-19 required Ella to teach remotely during isolation, and the global pandemic came at a perfect time for their family crisis. Teaching eight and nine-year-olds from an online portal while watching over her mother was challenging, but Ella had handled both responsibilities successfully.

It seemed like things were going well when Jillian's condition began to deteriorate.

"Would you like to go for a walk, Mom?"

A beautiful evening allowed Ella and her mother to sit on the deck, and they had time for a short stroll around the neighborhood.

"I would love to," Jillian replied. "It's getting chilly, so I think I need my sweater."

"I'll run in and grab us each something to keep us warm."

Ella stacked their dessert dishes and planned to drop them in the kitchen. She hit the bathroom and put a sweatshirt on before returning to get her mom.

When she opened the glass slider, the table sat empty.

"Mom?" Ella yelled into the house.

She searched again for Jillian, but her mother wasn't in her bedroom or the first-floor powder room.

"Mom?" Ella hollered again, this time louder and more urgently.

She unlocked the front door, hoping to see her mother waiting on the steps. Ella headed toward the sidewalk, continuing to call out to Jillian.

"Is everything all right?" her neighbor, Brad, asked as he took his recycling bins to the curb.

"I left my mom for a minute, and when I got back, she'd vanished."

"I'll get my bike and try to find her," he said, springing into action. "You head to the park. Maybe she's there."

Jillian loved the park, and they went often. A busy street and a pond at the end of the block intensified Ella's fears. She quickened her pace, repeating her mother's name and looking in every direction. Panic began to set in as dusk crept around her, and the chirp of cicadas reminded Ella of the fading sunlight.

She dialed Jordan's number on her cellphone.

"Hey, what's up?" he answered.

Ella rarely called him at work, and she knew it would alarm him.

"Mom's gone," she said, struggling to catch her breath.

"What do you mean she's *gone*?"

"We were going for a walk, and I went inside, and when I came back out . . . she'd disappeared."

"Have you notified the police?" Jordan asked.

Ella heard the concern in his voice.

"No, should I? I hoped I would find her. Hold on, I see Brad, and he has Mom with him. Thank God. I'll call you later."

Ella disconnected before Jordan could say anything else.

"Mom, where did you go?" Ella asked, pulling her mother into a desperate hug.

"I went for a walk."

Jillian seemed unfazed by the situation.

"Why didn't you wait for me? Thank you, Brad. I don't know what I would have done without you. I almost called the police."

"Glad I could help. I found her at the corner," he said. "You ladies have a good evening."

He shot Ella a sympathetic smile as he got on his bike and went back to his house.

"I waited for you at the crosswalk," Jillian offered.

****

There were a multitude of facilities serving the needs of those living with dementia and Alzheimer's disease in Minneapolis. Some touted programs and services beyond Ella's expectations. Others didn't come close to having the standards required.

Many of the accommodations under consideration had waitlists so long that Jillian might never get in. The cost eliminated over half, and distance took out another batch. Ella questioned if she would ever find the right place for her mom when she got a call from Hannah's House.

The nursing director for the brand-new facility happened to be one of Ella's friends from high school. They were taking resident applications, but it would be a few weeks before the first occupant could move in. Ella did not want to wait, but considering their limited options, Hannah's House became the only choice.

Ella could pick the location of Jillian's apartment and choose the paint color for an accent wall since final decor was still being decided. She took control and paid the deposit the next day.

When they moved Jillian in, Ella had made peace with her decision. They'd picked out a quiet room at the end of the hall with an extra window to let in the sunshine. It looked out into a secure courtyard, accessed by a door near Jillian's room. It appealed to Ella that she could give her mother some autonomy while eliminating the possibility of her wandering off.

The studio included a queen-sized bed, a small sectional with matching side tables, and a dining set. The white cabinets in the kitchen over a length of upscale granite made the space appear high-end. Ella would bring a few of Jillian's belongings from Des Moines to fill out the furnishings and make it feel like home.

It took ten minutes to get to Hannah's House, so making daily visits would be easy. The place gave Ella a good gut feeling, and when she and Jordan drove away after moving Jillian in, they celebrated by going out to dinner.

It had been more than a year since Ella sprung her mom out of jail, but the months in between had seemed endless.

CHAPTER 10
Maggie - Fall 1991

Cam didn't travel during Thanksgiving week, so he made himself useful by packing the car for the trip to Maggie's parents' house. She wasn't used to his assistance, but she appreciated the help. They loaded pies and sweet potato casserole into a cooler, and when they began their trek to Northeast Iowa early Thursday, the excitement about a few days away had everyone's spirits soaring.

Maggie's only sibling, Kimberly, had recently moved back to the Midwest from California. She and her husband, Dave, and their two boys were joining the family for the first time in years. Maggie couldn't wait to spend time with her sister and best friend.

After Cam's parents died, Thanksgiving in Maggie's hometown had become a tradition. It kicked off the holiday season and Maggie's favorite time of year, and it allowed the kids to get a taste of where their mother grew up.

On Friday, the sisters strolled the quaint streets of downtown Cedar Falls and started their Christmas shopping.

"Come on, let's get a drink before we head back," Kimberly suggested, leading Maggie into a bar on Main Street.

The smell of pine garland stirred childhood memories, and twinkling lights cast a magical glow over everything.

"I don't know. It's 1:00 p.m., and the kids have been with Mom all morning."

Left over dishes from the big Thanksgiving meal the day before still needed attention, and Maggie doubted the grandchildren had taken care of those chores.

"What's wrong with you? Mom wouldn't even invite us to Thanksgiving if it weren't for them," Kimberly joked.

"I'm just so tired. I can't figure out why, and my stomach is upset too. You order a drink, and I'll get a Sprite."

"No wine with your little sister? Are you pregnant or something?" Kimberly quipped, taking a seat at the bar and grabbing a menu.

"Yeah, right. Last time I checked, pregnancy would require a sex life."

It wasn't that Maggie and Cam weren't intimate at all, but things were strained, and those special moments didn't occur often. Cam's pulling away from their marriage happened gradually, and Maggie had been too busy raising the kids to mull over ways to nurture their relationship.

"What's going on? Do we need to talk about this?" Kimberly asked.

"We've grown apart, and our focus is always on Mason and Mallory. I never thought this would happen to Cam and me. I remember when he couldn't keep his hands off me. Now, our love life involves once-a-quarter guilt sex."

"Which of you is feeling guilty?"

"Both of us? Right now, all we have in common is indifference. The kids will get older, and it will improve when we have more time together. At least I hope that's what happens."

"Have you discussed this with Cam? Because you don't want to ignore such serious issues. Several of my friends experienced the same kind of marital woes you're talking about, and they're all divorced now."

Maggie could see the concern on her sister's face.

"Maybe splitting up wouldn't be the worst thing."

Maggie hated to admit that she'd begun romanticizing the idea of leaving Cam. Having her husband take the kids every other weekend seemed like a dream. She sometimes entertained the harmless fantasy while drifting off to sleep in her lonely bed.

Maggie imagined buying a condo for herself and the kids and furnishing it however she chose. She would buy an overstuffed chair for a cozy reading nook and devour a novel whenever she wanted to. Maggie surmised she would be a better mom because she'd have a periodic break from parenting. A chance to relax would be a positive change for everyone.

At least, that's how it turned out in her make-believe, post-divorce life.

Despite her discontent, Maggie had tried everything possible to get her heart in the right place again. An encounter with her friend, Rich, made Maggie realize she needed to do something drastic if she wanted to save her marriage.

Rich worked flexible hours as a financial planner and handled his family's schedules like Maggie did. He jogged past their house every morning, and Maggie had started taking her coffee to the front window so she wouldn't miss him.

With a pediatrician for a wife, Rich spent a lot of time alone. Maggie saw him at school functions and in the carpool lane in the afternoon, and he always waved and came over to talk to her. His flirtatious demeanor revived Maggie's libido. She began looking forward to the times they would interact, and she craved Rich's attention more than she allowed herself to need Cam's.

Things only got out of hand once, but the potential recklessness of the situation had jolted her back to reality.

Rich and his kids had stopped over after a flag football game—his wife at a conference and Cam in Houston on business. Maggie ordered pizza, and the children took theirs to the basement rec room while Maggie and Rich shared a supreme pie and a bottle of wine.

"Tell me how you do it," Rich asked Maggie after they finished their first glass of Pinot Noir.

"Do what?"

Maggie snatched a circle of pepperoni and ate it.

"How do you stand the loneliness when Cam's gone?"

"I guess I've gotten used to it," she said, wondering when having mediocre standards had become acceptable.

"I don't want to get used to it. I need excitement in my life and a reason to get up in the morning. I want a partner, a lover, and a best friend. That's not asking for too much," Rich said, his words charged with intensity.

The two friends had discussed their marriages before, but those conversations never crossed the line into more than minor complaints. Rich's admission caught Maggie off guard, and suddenly, she wanted the same things.

He moved close to Maggie and put his hands on either side of her face and kissed her. After the moment passed, they stood in the kitchen, deciding in which direction they would go.

Maggie flushed with embarrassment, and Rich made excuses for his actions, obviously regretting what he'd done. Maggie couldn't look her friend in the eye as he grabbed his jacket and yelled for his kids to get their backpacks.

"Why do we have to go?" his daughter asked as she came upstairs. "I'm not finished eating."

"I forgot, I have to call a client before it gets too late. You can bring your food along," he said.

Maggie took Rich aside once they reached the driveway.

"Hey, it's okay. Nothing happened. Two people feeling sad for a moment about their lives and finding comfort in each other isn't a crime."

Maggie's conscience did *not* agree.

"I'm sorry," he said as he got into the car and left.

Maggie *wasn't* sorry. She didn't want to risk her family's security with a guy from her kids' school, but his kiss reminded her of the missing spark in her marriage. Maggie promised herself she would do whatever it took to rekindle the feelings she and Cam once shared.

She never spent time alone with Rich again.

On Friday night, when Cam returned from Texas, Maggie farmed Mason and Mallory out to friends for the night. She made a reservation at a restaurant they usually booked for birthdays and anniversaries and surprised Cam with an overdue date night.

Dressing up for a fancy dinner made Maggie feel like a woman again. Cam opened the door for her and pulled out her chair as if they were dating. She hadn't realized how much she'd missed her husband.

When they got home later, Maggie and Cam connected in a way they hadn't in years, and it gave Maggie hope that not everything was lost between them.

Was Kimberly on to something? Had she missed her period last month—or had it been longer? She tried to remember the last time she'd bought tampons and came up blank.

Maggie felt awful the entire weekend, and on Sunday, she took the pregnancy test Kimberly had snuck out and bought at Walgreens. With only two toilets and lots of overnight guests, the bathroom was a coveted spot in the morning, but she needed a few minutes to take it without drawing suspicion.

A quick shower would give her the time she needed, so she followed the directions and then laid the test on the counter before she jumped in.

After she got out, she wrapped her hair in a towel and looked at the results. Adrenaline surged through her body when she saw the plus sign on the front of the stick.

Maggie had just turned thirty-four, and Mason and Mallory were practically grown at nine and eleven. Catapulting back into diapers and bottles did not make her happy.

When Maggie left the bathroom, Kimberly waited by the door with a bottle of vodka.

"Mom and Dad don't keep champagne in the liquor cabinet, so this is the best I could do. Are we celebrating?"

"We are *not* celebrating, and I will have to have milk instead of alcohol to drown these sorrows."

"Are you kidding?" Kimberly gave her sister a hug and whispered, "Congratulations!"

It didn't feel like congratulations were in order. It embarrassed Maggie to be pregnant when everyone would know she hadn't planned it. She took birth control but had forgotten her pills a few times when things got busy. Maybe she'd missed more than she'd realized. Because she and Cam weren't having sex regularly, she hadn't given it much thought. Regardless of how it happened, she was pregnant with her third child.

"Do *not* tell Mom," Maggie begged.

She had no desire to hear her mother's opinion on the subject.

"I won't tell anyone. But when are you going to talk to Cam?"

"I'll do it later. I need time in the car to decide what to say."

***

Maggie didn't want anything to do with another baby. She knew she had to let Cam in on the news, but she was angry that his life would proceed as normal. He wouldn't have to wake up in the middle of the night to breastfeed or stay home all day with a newborn. He'd leave every week and enjoy four nights in a hotel, just like he always did. It wasn't fair.

After an exhausting Thanksgiving weekend, Maggie walked into the family room where Cam was watching football and muted the television.

"What's up?" Cam asked, obviously bothered by the interruption to the game.

"We need to talk."

Maggie sat beside her husband and took his hand. She needed Cam to tell her everything would be okay. She hesitated to reveal her secret—the pause as pregnant as she was. The way they would move forward hinged on Cam's response, even if he didn't know it.

So much had changed. They were moving through the years of their marriage blindly, unable to see the danger ahead. Maggie had fallen into the habit of pushing Cam away, and he withheld his affection as punishment. They never did any of the work necessary to heal their relationship, clinging to the hope that the next stage of their lives would bring them back to each other.

Returning to the first phase of parenthood didn't seem like something they could repeat successfully.

"What's wrong?" he asked with concern.

"I'm pregnant."

Cam looked shocked. He didn't move toward Maggie and take her in his arms like he had the other two times she announced her pregnancies.

"You can't be," he said. "We've barely had sex in the past six months."

"Well, Cam . . . *barely* can get the job done."

He finally stood to hug his wife, and she sobbed into his shoulder.

CHAPTER 11
Ella

The birthday getaway to Chicago had been fabulous, but Ella couldn't stop thinking about what Felicia Carmichael revealed during her psychic reading. A scheduled day off from school on Monday provided the perfect opportunity for Ella to dig in and try to find more answers.

Jordan bit into a Honeycrisp apple, and the crunch drew Ella's attention away from her computer screen.

"How do you make a piece of fruit sound as loud as a gunshot?" she asked.

"Talent . . . pure talent," he joked. "Do you really want to do this? What if your dad *is* dead? How will that make you feel?"

"So, you do believe in psychics!"

Ella hadn't seen her dad for a quarter of a century. She first hunted for him on social media in 2008, and he finally popped up on Facebook in 2012.

When she saw his face appear next to his name after another random search, she was angry and heartbroken to find out he'd remarried, lived in Rochester, and had three more daughters. It made sense; he'd been raised not far from there. He'd returned to where his people were, even if he'd left one behind.

Why didn't Ella's mother insist he pay child support and

take an active role in raising his daughter? And why did Charlie Meyers want to share his life with his other children—her half-siblings—but not her?

"Maybe this feels so raw because of what's going on with your mom," Jordan suggested.

"This has nothing to do with her."

He had a point, but Ella didn't want to own up to it.

"I'm sure it's difficult when you don't have any close family. If it's any consolation, you've got me."

"Nothing could be better than having you in my life. I just want to know if this crazy medium lady from last week knows what she's talking about. I'm not lonely. I don't feel pressure or sadness . . ."

Jordan looked at his wife with a sideways grin.

"Okay. . . maybe I'm struggling a little," she said. "I'll admit, I need closure with my dad. It's time to address what happened since I don't have the fear of hurting Mom with what I discover."

"Why do you think she didn't tell you more?" Jordan asked.

"She was trying to protect me from the truth, but I'm going to find out what that truth is."

Jillian always promised to tell Ella why she and Charlie Meyers divorced, but she never got around to it. Mother and daughter had fallen into a silent pact as the years passed, and they never delved into the painful subject. Unanswered questions grew into secrets neither chose to address, and then Ella stopped asking about it.

With Jillian moved into a facility and Charlie Meyers taking center stage at the Felicia Carmichael Show, Ella knew she needed to unpack her emotional baggage.

***

After Jordan left for work, Ella poured herself another cup of coffee and began her investigation. A computer search seemed like the best way to start, but she spent the first few minutes online answering work emails and sending a birthday greeting to a childhood friend. Social media was great for staying connected with old acquaintances and creeping on fathers who'd cut you out of their life.

Ella entered the words "Charles Meyers obituary" into Google, and two pages of entries came up from across the country. She studied each face and age, easily eliminating most. She had no idea so many men—*dead* men—shared the same name as her father.

When death notices didn't give her any solid leads, Ella flipped over to Facebook. She usually browsed through Charlie's account late at night after a couple of glasses of wine. This often happened around the holidays when she vacillated between missing him terribly and hating his guts. It was like looking up an old boyfriend with equal parts dread and longing.

This wasn't an ex, but Charlie *had* been the first real love of her life.

Ella's research unearthed photographs of people she didn't know. Even though her father walked out of her life, why would her paternal grandparents have abandoned her too? None of it made sense.

Ella noticed her father didn't get on Facebook much, but if he'd recently died, his family would likely have posted something. She logged in and entered his name next to the magnifying glass icon.

80

His picture appeared, showing the middle-aged man dancing with one of his girls at her wedding.

At least Ella's mother had been an important part of her and Jordan's nuptials before her memory slipped away.

Ella scrolled through her dad's posts. Many older people didn't set their security settings to private, probably because they didn't comprehend that anyone, including daughters you'd forgotten about, could scrutinize your personal life on Facebook.

A friend had tagged Charlie in photos from a Minnesota Twins game the weekend before. He'd been less than five miles from her forty-eight hours earlier, and she hadn't even known it.

Over the years, Ella imagined a chance encounter with her father, where he would tell her that he'd been looking for her for years. Ella played this scenario out in a hundred different ways, and it always ended with the realization that she would have been easy to track down had Charlie Meyers wanted to find her.

Ella wasn't sure how long it took Felicia Carmichael to get insider information from the afterlife. If Charlie Meyers was watching baseball a few days before, it seemed unlikely that he'd be dead and already starring in psychic readings at the Norris Center.

Ella had seen most of the pictures on her dad's profile many times. She tried to visualize life with Charlie as an involved dad. The snapshots on his timeline showed images of a happy father with arms around his daughters, who gazed at him with adoration. Ella had idolized her dad the same way at one time, and she wished she had a similar photo to cherish.

Charlie was short, and his petite girls favored him. Taller and blue-eyed, Ella looked like her mother's side of the family. She searched the faces of the women in the photographs and questioned whether they knew about another sibling who yearned to know them.

***

"Hi, Mom. How are you doing?" Ella asked.

Visits to Hannah's House had become routine. Each time she entered Jillian's apartment, Ella wondered which version of her mother she would encounter. Sometimes she found a talkative and happy Jillian, at other times, her mom didn't say a word.

"It's almost time for Jeopardy. I'll turn it on for you," Ella offered.

Over the years, Jillian had always said that people who watched television weren't interesting enough to find something better to do. Now, she spent hours watching whatever someone else tuned in for her.

"Jillian, it's time for your medicine. Oh, sorry, Ella, I didn't know you were here. Don't you have school today?" the nurse asked after barging through the door.

Young and sweet, Amanda held the title of Ella's favorite RN on the day shift. She liked everyone at Hannah's House, but Amanda seemed to have an extra caring manner.

"We had the day off, and since I didn't see Mom all weekend, I wanted to spend some time with her this afternoon. Hey, how's your grandma doing after her heart surgery?"

Interacting daily with staff members meant learning details about their personal lives.

"She's doing fine. Thanks for asking."

The TV blared in the background as Jeopardy contestants took their turns.

"Board games for a thousand, please," a player asked.

"In the classic board game of Monopoly, properties such as Marvin Gardens and Boardwalk are streets in what American City?"

"Atlantic City," Jillian answered without hesitation.

"What is Atlantic City," the Jeopardy leader responded from the television as the total on his winnings increased.

Ella looked at Amanda and sighed.

"She can come up with Atlantic City, but she can't remember I turned thirty this week."

"Happy birthday!" Amanda exclaimed as if her belated acknowledgment compensated for Jillian's limitations. "She's in there, Ella. She loves you, but she just can't figure out how to show it anymore."

Ella made some tea and sat with her mother for more than an hour. She told her mom about the night out with the girls and discussed plans for the summer.

Jillian added an occasional smile and nod of the head. Ella would have given anything for her mom to offer an unsolicited opinion or disagree with something—like the old days.

"I'm taking off now," Ella said.

As she began to gather her things to leave, her mom reached for Ella's hand and struggled to say something.

"Happy birthday," Jillian said, finding her words.

CHAPTER 12

Maggie – Fall 1991

"How did it go?" Kimberly asked after Maggie answered the phone.

At ten minutes past eight, her sister already wanted a report on Cam's reaction to the pregnancy.

"I told him. He *said* he was excited, and then we went to bed. Not exactly marriage of the year material."

"Did he say anything this morning?"

"Cam seemed very preoccupied. He barely uttered a word before leaving and then kissed me on the cheek as if I were his elderly aunt," Maggie complained.

"Maybe the two of you need the week to collect your thoughts. The distance might be good for you."

"If we had any more *distance* between us, we wouldn't be living together."

"What are you going to do, sis?"

"I want to climb into bed and sleep until the kids are grown," Maggie confessed.

"Oh, honey. I'm going to say something, and I don't want you to take it the wrong way," Kimberly cautioned.

"These days, I'm taking everything the wrong way."

"That's why I'm not holding back. I've been mulling over whether I should bring this up to you or not."

"I can't stand anything Cam does, the kids are driving me nuts, and my friends are no better. Everyone smiles and carries on like their lives are perfect. That's not the way I feel anymore. So go ahead and let me have it. I'll add you to the list of people making my life miserable."

"Try to listen to what I'm saying, and don't dismiss it until you've really thought about it. Do you remember how mom always said, 'Whenever everyone else is at fault, you should take a look at yourself for the reason'?"

"Please don't turn into Mom right now."

"I think you're depressed. Maybe your doctor could prescribe something to help you cope. There—I said it. You can hate me if you want to, but I'm probably the only person who can get away with telling you what you need to hear. Even if your feelings are hurt, they won't stay that way forever."

The two sisters rarely argued. Maggie knew Kimberly was her biggest fan, which made her criticism more acceptable.

"How do you distinguish between depression and a crappy life?" Maggie asked, fighting tears.

"That's my point. You don't have a crappy life. You feel that way because you're looking through a different set of lenses than you used to. You're off lately, and I think it's your mental health causing the issues. You have a wonderful husband and two great kids, and you're having another child. People handle worse with far less than you, and you're getting a beautiful baby to love in the process. It's the most exciting news you can be given, and the fact you don't see it that way proves my point."

"It's easy for you to give advice when you aren't facing any of this."

"Maggie, I love you as much as anyone. You need to do something to fix these problems before you lose everything. I have nothing to gain from convincing you to seek help. I don't want you to be mad at me, but if I don't tell you the truth, who will?"

"I'll think about it, Kimmy."

Maggie knew she stood at a crossroads. She wasn't sure drugs were the answer, but she agreed with Kimberly. Taking control of her life again would require extreme measures.

***

Maggie's bag sat by the door, packed with what she'd need for two days away as well as the resolve to change her current circumstances. She'd stopped at the Harvest Inn earlier in the day and rented a room. Cam would have to take care of Mason and Mallory, along with a list of what needed to be done over the weekend.

She'd eat junk food, watch movies, and sleep. She'd missed rest the most, and she couldn't wait to close her eyes. Maggie had daydreamed about this for years, and the idea was finally coming to fruition.

Maggie hoped Cam would comprehend the seriousness of their situation if she left him, even for a couple of days. A baby was on its way, and Maggie decided she'd rather bring the child into a broken family than live another day in her crumbling marriage.

Maggie got the kids from school and started them on their homework. It would be good to get it done early so Cam wouldn't have to worry about it. It was hard to break the habit of being the caregiver for everyone around her.

For an hour, she waited at the kitchen table, clicking her nails on the Formica top. Cam arrived just as the pizza driver pulled away.

"Pizza tonight?" Cam asked, flipping through envelopes he'd collected at the mailbox.

"It seemed easier since you're just getting home," she replied, noting that he hadn't greeted her yet.

Cam took his place as the kids ran in from the family room to pile cheesy slices on paper plates, oblivious to his wife's plans.

"Mom, can we have pop?" Mallory asked.

"Sure," Maggie said.

She wasn't going to be there, so what did she care if they were hepped up on caffeine?

"Why is there a suitcase by the door?" Cam asked, continuing to separate the bills from junk mail.

"I'm going to be gone for a couple of days."

"Gone? Where are you going?" he asked.

When Maggie didn't answer, Cam looked at her fully for the first time since entering the house.

"I'm taking the weekend off. I'll be at the Harvest Inn if there's an emergency."

Maggie kissed the kids and collected her belongings as Cam stood by the refrigerator looking puzzled.

"Maggie, what's wrong?"

"Everything," she said.

✳✳✳

Maggie changed into her pajamas as soon as she got to the motel room. Bloated and cranky, the soft flannel felt good on her skin and comforted her wavering heart.

Guilt nagged at Maggie. Cam didn't seem to have a problem disappearing every week, so why should she? He had to earn a living for their family, but she did everything else to make their household thrive and deserved the time away.

Maggie pushed her feelings aside and watched television while eating some of the snacks she bought. As she settled in, the shrill ring of the bedside phone startled her.

"Hi," Cam said.

His voice was quiet as if he were afraid.

"Did I forget something?" she asked.

Maggie had left a list to help Cam cope with anything he might encounter during her absence. It cataloged the kids' activities, directions for cooking a casserole she'd made, and instructions for giving Mallory the antibiotic for her recent diagnosis of pink eye.

"Please come home," Cam begged.

"I can't—I need some time. This pregnancy has thrown me for a loop, and I've realized I'm not happy."

"You're not happy with us? Or do you mean you aren't happy as a stay-at-home mom anymore?"

"I'm not sure. That's what I want to figure out. You don't love me like you used to, and I don't know how to get *us* back. I would never have imagined feeling abandoned and alone when we first got married, and now I'm having a baby

89

I don't want. Can you believe that? I don't want this baby. What's wrong with me?"

"We'll get through this. We've grown apart, but it doesn't mean it will always be this way. Any couple at our stage in life is going through the same thing."

"We can't go on like this. At least I can't. Please let me have this weekend, and I'll be back on Sunday afternoon to talk."

"Don't give up on us, Maggie."

She was trying hard not to.

***

Maggie spent Saturday doing whatever she wanted. She slept in and then got breakfast at a diner downtown, where she ran into a friend who questioned why she was out for made-to-order omelets alone.

A trip to the mall allowed Maggie to window-shop while admiring the festive holiday decorations. She enjoyed devoting time to the mall's anchor store without the distraction of having at least one of the kids along.

After spending an hour in the fitting room, Maggie purchased a stack of maternity clothes. Years earlier, she'd donated her pregnancy wardrobe to a women's shelter, never anticipating she'd have a third child. Maggie hoped the shopping spree would improve her attitude.

Maggie piled pillows behind her head and settled into the king-sized bed on her second night away. Cam hadn't called again, and although Maggie couldn't fault him for doing what she'd requested, she wondered how they were getting along without her. She considered taking in a movie and eating an entire bucket of popcorn without dividing it into smaller portions for the kids, but she didn't want to leave the room.

A knock at the door came a few minutes after Maggie got comfortable, and the interruption annoyed her. Maybe the office manager needed her to move her car, or another guest complained about the volume of her television. Regardless, she'd have to get up and deal with it.

Maggie squinted through the peephole and saw Cam holding flowers and a sack of takeout food. She unlocked the deadbolt and slid the chain free on the door. His arrival perturbed her as much as it stirred a softness for the man she'd loved for so many years.

"Hi," he said, looking pained.

"What are you doing here? Where are the kids?"

"They're spending the night with the Maxwells."

Mike and Alecia Maxwell lived close by and had children the same ages as the Sanders. Maggie wondered what Cam told them to secure overnight childcare. She imagined their friends discussing the Sanders' marriage and criticizing Maggie's choice to take some time for herself.

"Can I come in? This chicken lo mein is getting heavy," Cam said with a smile.

Maggie loved Chinese food and Cam knew it. She invited him in, and he put the bag on a small table near the window and offered the bouquet to her.

"I should've given you flowers more often. I love you, and I can't make it without you."

Maggie took the roses from him and laid them on the bed. Cam took her in his arms, and they both began to cry.

"I need you," Maggie said, her rigid exterior giving way to vulnerability.

She hadn't realized until that moment that all she wanted from her husband was genuine validation.

"I didn't know you felt as disconnected as I did, and I'm sorry I didn't come to you sooner with my feelings," he offered.

"It seems like being on the road all week would be a dream, but I know it must be hard on you to be away all the time."

"You really don't want this baby?" Cam asked.

"I *really* don't want this baby. I know a mother shouldn't say such a thing. I'm more than a wife and mom, and I've lost what makes me happy, and I don't know if I can do it again."

"Are you considering an abortion?"

"Should I?"

Maggie knew the answer would indicate his level of commitment to their future, even if she'd never do such a thing.

"No. We both need to make our marriage and family a priority again. I already love him or her, even though this baby is unexpected. It's no different than when we found out we were having Mason. We hadn't planned for him either, but we figured it out."

"I have no idea how to get those feelings back," Maggie admitted.

"What if we started over and tried to rebuild our lives, making it better than before? I've made so many mistakes, and I'll do whatever it takes to make it right."

"Do you still love me?" Maggie asked.

She missed the romantic and optimistic husband Cam used to be.

"More than the first day I met you at Iowa State. I blame myself for not giving you what you need lately. I've been selfish, and I'm sorry. I promise to make it up to you if you give me the chance."

"Let's go home," Maggie said.

"What? Why would we leave? I brought your favorite dinner, and the kids are gone for the night. We can't waste an evening at one of Spencer's classiest motels," he teased.

"Cam, we have to make this work for the sake of Mason and Mallory. We owe it to them to put in the effort to stay together."

"They're important," Cam agreed. "But we have to find our way back to each other, and that's as crucial as what Mason and Mallory need."

"And this baby too," Maggie added, placing her hands on her stomach.

When they went to bed later, Cam pulled Maggie close. He rubbed her back without taking it any further. Maggie understood their reunion didn't depend on a revival of their missing sex life, or mostly missing, considering they had a little one on the way.

Before they fell asleep, Cam whispered life-changing words to Maggie.

"I'm applying for a different job with the company. I don't want to travel anymore. We'll have three children soon, and the big kids will need rides to activities. Hauling a baby around in the cold is never easy."

"There will be plenty of responsibilities for *both* of us. I want us to raise our family together. I don't want you to act like a weekend visitor in our lives. I could get excited to have a third child if you're serious about all of this," Maggie conceded.

Maggie had forgotten how life often shocked you into reality when you got too complacent. Maybe she hadn't been thankful enough for her blessings, and a higher power was lashing out at her for thoughts of leaving Cam. This baby would tether Maggie to what she valued, despite her sense of being trapped.

"Everything will be okay, because I'm never letting you down again," Cam promised.

Maggie knew he meant it.

CHAPTER 13
Ella

"I'm going to miss all of you so much," Ella said as her students filed out of the classroom for the last time.

It felt bittersweet to move this group on to fourth grade, but having time off trumped her need to keep them to herself.

"Lacie, what are you doing this summer?" Ella asked, pulling one of her favorite students aside.

Lacie's dad died in a hunting accident the previous fall, and Ella gravitated toward the little girl without a father.

"We get to spend July at our grandparents' farm. Mom says a change of scenery will do us good."

"That sounds amazing," Ella said. "You'll have a great time."

Ella became an educator so she could support children going through difficult times. She remembered how caring teachers had made such a difference in her life, and she wanted to pay it forward.

After the last student passed through the door, the school secretary popped in to talk to Ella.

"Your cute hubby has done it again," she said, pulling a bouquet of tulips from behind her back.

"Awww . . . he is so sweet," Ella agreed.

"The sweetest," the co-worker agreed. "Don't stay too long today, you've got time to close up your class for the summer."

Ella had several days left on her contract, and the bright-colored blooms would remind her that the future held some downtime. Jordan always treated Ella well. Considering how her father's absence affected her, he tried hard to make sure she knew how much he loved her.

Ella texted Jordan: *THX for the flowers. UR the best!*

He responded: *Happy summer!*

Ella felt uncomfortable reading his cheerful words, knowing how she intended to start her three-month work hiatus.

She'd been thinking about making the trip to Rochester to see her dad ever since the Felicia Carmichael show spun her into detective mode, but her final decision had only come in the last few days. She'd tell Jordan eventually, but Ella didn't want him to discourage her from going.

Ella hated to keep a secret from him. Trust had always been important to them, and hiding something so significant gnawed at her. Jordan would never suspect his wife of keeping anything from him. He had complete faith in Ella, even if she hadn't always offered him the same devotion.

Jordan's mother had been gone for two months when Ella started noticing her husband's secrecy. She tried to give him the benefit of the doubt. He'd just lost his mother, and Ella knew firsthand how tough losing the support of a parent could be.

Jordan was dependable and steady. Given Ella's history, he'd always taken his responsibilities as a husband seriously. His parents had been married for almost fifty years, sharing a solid and enviable relationship. It had been one of the reasons Ella allowed him to get close to her so quickly.

The sudden changes in Jordan's behavior seemed out of character. Could she have been wrong about him like she'd mistaken Charlie Meyers for a loving father? She'd always trusted her gut. She didn't want to believe Jordan would betray her, but he'd taken more than a few covert calls and cleared his phone when she walked behind him.

Ella couldn't ignore what was happening any longer. She'd tossed and turned through another sleepless night, wondering what the result of their conversation would be. She planned to get the answers she needed as soon as Jordan got home from his overnight shift.

"We need to talk," she began after he got home from work.

"What's going on in that beautiful head of yours?"

Jordan had no idea of his wife's suspicions. He was always charming, and Ella hoped he wasn't using that appealing character trait to hook up with another woman.

"I'm not going to sugar coat this. I've noticed your sneaky behavior lately, and I want answers."

A look of bewilderment spread across Jordan's face, and then he smiled. Ella had prepared herself to challenge any lies he might tell. Why would she have thought she could trust Jordan? He was probably like every other man she'd ever known, even if it had taken her a while to discover the truth.

"You're right, I've been taking a few private calls. But

I promise this is not anything you need to be upset about. I wanted to make sure I had all the details figured out before I surprised you."

If he was spontaneously making up excuses, he was doing a good job. Ella opened her mind to things that might be happening other than Jordan having an affair.

"Tell me what it is. I have to know."

"My brother and I are getting some money from Mom's estate. I should have guessed there'd be something there because she and Dad were very frugal."

"How much are you getting?"

"Enough to get us started on our dreams," he said.

"Oh, Jordan . . ."

Ella felt like an idiot.

***

"You're up early," Jordan said, joining Ella for coffee.

The peak of the Minneapolis cityscape could be seen from the kitchen window, and it stood at attention as the sun warmed the day.

"School's out, but my internal alarm clock hasn't turned off yet," she answered.

"What's on the agenda for your first official day of summer break?"

Jordan was ready to take on another shift at the fire station, wearing his uniform and a smile, and Ella hesitated.

"Um . . . I'm not sure," she fibbed. "I might do a little shopping after I visit Mom."

"Well, give Jillian a hug for me. I'll see you in the morning. I love you," Jordan said, heading out the door.

98

His words of devotion deepened the guilt she felt for keeping her travel plans secret.

***

Farmland raced by the window in streaks of green as Ella drove south. It would take an hour and a half to reach her father's home in Rochester, and as every mile brought her closer to seeing him again, she questioned if she was doing the right thing.

Ella had done her homework and double-checked her dad's Facebook page. She'd taken a screenshot of a recent photo of him in front of a house and then expanded it to check the number, and it matched what she found on Peoplesearch.com. Everything pointed to Charlie Meyers living at 612 Jericho, where he'd been for years.

After she arrived, Ella crept past her father's two-story colonial as if she were doing something wrong by driving down his street. Tall trees cast shade over the established neighborhood, their branches arching like a natural arbor of protection. It was the kind of place where you could raise a family well, and she wondered why she hadn't grown up there.

It was summer in Minnesota, and the home's porch showed off two pots of red geraniums. Ella's dad loved the hearty plants. She remembered going to the nursery with him to buy them for their brick stoop, before Ella and her mother had to move to an apartment where outside flowers were useless.

She circled the block and parked one house down and across the street. She had a good vantage point from there and would observe from a distance until she got brave enough to leave the safety of her vehicle and ring the doorbell. She knew from her father's social media account that he was retired, so she hoped he would be there in the middle of the day. It didn't take long for her to see the man she'd come to confront.

When Charlie Meyers got out of his truck, Ella recognized him immediately. His familiarity made her yearning stronger, but the reality of her dad standing feet away from her brought doubts. What if he reacted poorly and called the police on her for stalking? No matter what happened in the past, she didn't think her father would dare do something so callous as to involve the authorities, but she couldn't be sure.

Charlie went around to the back door and helped a little boy out of the Chevy Silverado. He took his hand, and they walked toward the house. A woman came out and made a big production of their arrival, and the child ran into her arms. He was probably their grandchild.

They entered the home Ella would never know, slamming the door on her courage.

She slumped in her bucket seat and started the ignition. Sadness gripped Ella at seeing the child with her father. She'd missed a life with her siblings, but her nieces and nephews were also strangers to her. It seemed like it was so much to lose for no reason.

With her mother locked in the world of Alzheimer's disease and her father absent from her life, Ella felt utterly alone. She had Jordan and his family to love, but it wasn't the same as having her own relatives. What she'd wanted her entire life was inside the house in front of her, but she had no way to embrace the people who shared her lineage, and it devastated her.

Ella didn't want to give up on connecting with Charlie Meyers again, but it would have to be another day. She'd lost her nerve, and the only thing she could do was go home.

***

"I can't believe you went to see your father without telling me. What if something happened to you?"

Ella wasn't good at omitting the truth, and she fessed up as soon as Jordan got home from work. She'd contemplated keeping it to herself, but after she stayed awake wrestling with her conscience again, she decided she preferred honesty to putting up with more insomnia.

"It's not like he's a serial killer, Jordan. He's obviously figured out how to have a happy life, so I don't think I need to be afraid of him."

The worries she'd had the day before about her dad getting the cops involved were nonsense, and Ella knew it.

"You don't know this guy anymore, and showing up unannounced will do nothing but blindside him."

"So what? I wanted to find out why he left Mom and me. I needed him to tell me why he started another family and never looked back, but I chickened out. Now all I can think of is driving down there again and finally dealing with him."

"I support you in seeking answers, but you need to be careful. Why don't you search for his phone number or email

101

address? You should contact him in one of those ways first, and then you can plan to meet if it gets that far."

"No, he doesn't get a say this time. I want to knock on his door and have him answer my questions without giving him time to think of excuses."

"What can he say that will take away the pain you've endured or change your relationship moving forward?"

"Oh, there's not going to be a *relationship*. This is about me taking my power back. I want my dad to know how he's hurt me. I'm doing this for Mom as much as for myself."

"What *do* you know of your parents' breakup? You've never shared the details," Jordan said.

"I don't *have* the details, that's the problem. I remember the arguments," Ella started. "They never fought in front of me, but I sometimes heard them from my bedroom. One day, my dad picked me up after school and told me he was moving. All his belongings were packed when we got home."

"Oh, Ella. I'm so sorry." Jordan hugged his wife. "If you're hell-bent on this, at least let me go with you. I can't tell you what to do, but I'm begging you not to go back there alone."

"Okay, but we're doing this as soon as possible. I chickened out once this week, and I'm not giving in to my fears again."

***

Ella continued to mull over what to say to Charlie Meyers during the quiet ride south. Anyone who saw the attractive couple making their way down Interstate 35 would not have imagined they were embarking on a trip to ambush a neglectful father.

"Are you sure you want to do this?" Jordan asked one last time.

"Yes," she said with defiance.

They were parked at Charlie's house, but Ella hadn't made a move to get out yet.

"Do you want me to go and tell him you're here?"

"No. It's my face Dad needs to see when he opens the door."

Ella checked her appearance in the passenger side mirror as if the way she looked might sway the outcome. She took a final deep breath and crossed the street toward her past.

Ella knocked, but it wasn't her dad who answered. It was her father's life partner of more than twenty years.

"Can I help you?" she asked, cocking her head with a questioning look.

Ella already knew the lady's name was Carol. She worked at one of Minnesota's largest law firms and liked collecting antiques. You could find out anything on the internet.

"Is Charlie here?" Ella asked, her voice trembling.

"No, I'm sorry. He's out at his folks. I'm his wife, can I do something for you?"

Ella could tell Carol didn't have a clue who she was.

"I'm Ella."

The blood drained from the woman's face. Ella wondered what a husband might say to his wife to justify never seeing his daughter again. How could this woman have kids with a man who'd abandoned another child without worrying he would do the same to hers?

"I need to talk with my dad. Will he be back soon?"

Carol stared at Ella as if her words didn't make sense.

"Let me give him a call. He's less than half an hour away, and he'd want to see you," she said.

"If it's not too much trouble."

Ella frowned at herself for being more cordial than she'd planned. She wasn't used to putting on a stoic front.

"Why don't you come in? It's getting hot out there," Carol offered.

"No, I'll wait in the car with my husband."

Ella wasn't in the mood to make small talk with her dad's wife.

About fifteen minutes later, Charlie's truck pulled into the driveway. After a brief stop in the house, he came across the street and approached the driver's side window.

Despite his salt and pepper hair, he looked exactly as Ella remembered. She wanted to get out and run into his arms, but the years had made her distrustful of the man she once loved.

"Ella . . . wow, you've grown up." He had tears in his eyes, and his emotion confused Ella. "Come inside. We can visit better where it's cool."

"Let's go in," Jordan encouraged.

"Okay."

Ella's quiet voice carried the yearning of a little girl searching for the truth.

CHAPTER 14

Maggie – Spring 1992

"You take this chair because it's the most comfortable," said Maggie's friend, Pauline.

Maggie had cleared the attic of anything having to do with babies after Mallory's first birthday, and she appreciated Pauline's insistence to host a shower.

"Open this one first," a guest suggested.

Maggie pulled on the bow from around a pink and blue package, and the latest infant gadget appeared from inside. The picture on the outside showed a Diaper Genie, which would be the answer to all her prayers. Apparently, sausage-like garbage bags filled with individual waste nuggets would snake their way to the top of the can in a disgusting parade of sealed surprises.

The women oohed and awed over the incredible invention, like it was the most fantastic discovery since penicillin. Maggie wished she never had to see another diaper, despite how easy they were to get rid of.

"This baby will be so much easier than the others," someone commented.

Maggie imagined every woman in the room thanking God *they* didn't need the contraption as they snacked on cake and pastel butter mints.

She opened at least twenty gifts and participated in a game where everyone took a sniff of melted candy bars inside a diaper. The purpose of the activity was to identify the brand and flavor of the suspicious looking blobs, and even though she hadn't had morning sickness in months, the premise made her stomach churn.

"Thanks again," Maggie said as they loaded the final box into her car.

"Are you okay?" Pauline asked.

"I'm fine. At my age, pregnancy is exhausting, and it's hard to fake it."

"At least Cam's new job allows him to be home during the week."

Now that he didn't travel for work, Maggie and Cam were rebuilding their lives. He seemed to be grieving something, and Maggie wondered why business trips would feel like a loss after giving them up. He was not the same man she'd married, and Maggie didn't know if she could accept who he'd become.

"Life is full of surprises, isn't it?" Maggie asked, hugging her friend.

"You have a beautiful family. This baby will only make things better. Promise me, you'll try to make the best of the rest of this pregnancy. I want you to be content where you are in your life. You don't need to wait until next month, or next year, or the next decade. Do it now."

"I thought there'd be more by my mid-thirties," Maggie pondered aloud.

"Honey, the most you can hope for is happy children and a husband who loves you. You have to *choose* happiness, or you'll never be satisfied."

Maggie waved as she pulled out of the driveway, the backseat of her car overflowing with the generosity of her friends. Pauline's advice and Kimberly's words of wisdom regarding her mental health made Maggie realize she needed to pull it together.

On the way home, Maggie stopped at Dairy Queen and bought a half gallon of soft serve. Then, she swung into the Fareway grocery store and purchased hot fudge, caramel syrup, and colorful sprinkles. It was the kids' favorite dessert and a way for Maggie to get her family excited about having another baby.

*****

The Sanders filled their plates with the pork roast Maggie put in the crock pot before leaving for the shower.

"I have a surprise," she said as they dug into dinner.

Cam looked at her with suspicion. He hadn't been privy to a surprise.

"Are we getting a puppy?" Mallory asked.

Mason waited in anticipation for his parents to answer.

"We are *not* getting a pet," Cam added. "Are we?"

Cam had always wanted a dog, but adding a baby to the mix was all Maggie could handle. And she hadn't been doing a good job of that either.

"It's something better," Maggie said, hoping she was right.

"How can it be better than a puppy?" Mason asked.

"Well," Maggie started. "After we eat, we're all going to K-Mart."

"That doesn't sound fun," Mason whined. "Can I stay here with Dad?"

"No, everyone's going, and we are each buying the baby a present. Then we'll come back and have a party with ice cream sundaes. I already stopped and got everything."

"What a good idea," Cam said, smiling from across the table.

"The baby will be here in a few weeks," Maggie said. "Tomorrow, I'll finish decorating the nursery and washing the clothes from the shower. We need to be prepared in case he or she comes early."

Maggie knew she had the power to impact her family, and a slight change of attitude would have them working toward the common goal of welcoming another Sanders into the fold.

***

When Erin Margaret was born, they were ready for her. The triumphant culmination of their struggles came when Erin let out a cry in the delivery room, letting the world know she'd arrived. Maggie knew she had room in her heart for another little one the moment she held her baby.

After Cam went home to the other kids the first night, Maggie made silent promises to Erin. Committing a lifetime of love and support to her new daughter would provide the only healing capable of taking away Maggie's guilt.

108

Maggie and Erin were welcomed with signs, streamers, and a pink cake after they were released from the hospital. Mason and Mallory did their best to make a party out of the homecoming, and their efforts brought tears to their mother's eyes.

"Wow, look at this," Maggie complimented. "Erin, see how much fun your big brother and sister are going to be?"

"Can I hold her?" Mallory said.

"I'm the oldest, I should get her first," Mason argued.

The kids had come to the hospital to meet Erin, and it touched Maggie's heart that they were excited to get her home.

"I'm the dad, so I get her before either one of you. Make yourselves useful and bring the gift in from the garage."

"A gift? Who's it from?" Maggie asked, getting Erin out of the infant carrier.

"It's from me."

Cam puttered more often since he was around in the evenings. He'd painted Mallory's old dresser and tightened the legs on the rocker before placing both in the baby's room. Maggie noticed he'd been working on a project for a couple of weeks, but she didn't know what it was.

The kids labored to carry the black garbage bag tied with a pink bow into the house. It wasn't the most beautiful presentation, but Maggie only cared about the thought behind it.

Mason and Mallory didn't linger after they completed their task. There was a game of whiffle ball starting in the park, and they didn't want to miss it.

"We're eating in an hour," Maggie hollered as the door slammed, leaving the new parents alone with baby number three.

"You mentioned you needed a side table by the chair in the nursery, so I decided to make this for you," Cam said, pleased with himself.

"Oh, honey . . ."

Cam snuggled Erin while Maggie tore at the sack and silently questioned the durability of homemade furniture.

"I love it," she said, hoping her shock at its beauty didn't offend Cam.

To Maggie's knowledge, he'd never built something like that before, so her suspicions of its sturdiness were warranted.

The table was crafted from stained wood and had a small drawer in the front. Mosaic tiles resembling pastel-colored sea glass adorned the top, and it looked like expensive custom cabinetry when sun from the picture window caught its reflection.

"What do you think?" he asked.

"I already know it will be my favorite piece in the house."

As Maggie gazed at her husband and their new baby from across the room, it occurred to her how surprising life could be. A few months earlier, she'd almost left Cam, and now she felt a deep love for him again.

"This represents so much to me. Our marriage is beautiful again, just like this table," Maggie said.

"I agree. Thank you for giving me the chance to make amends for everything."

Cam began to get emotional.

"I'm sorry for *my* part in the breakdown of our relationship," she apologized.

"You don't need to be sorry."

"No, I do . . ."

"It was one hundred percent me," he interrupted. "Our happiness is the only thing I want to talk about. Would you look at this perfect baby girl?"

Maggie wanted to tell her husband that it really *had* been her fault. Her self-esteem issues and the stress of being alone all the time had exacerbated her feelings of depression. Kimberly was right; Maggie's emotional well-being had taken a toll on her marriage.

They'd survived, so maybe blame didn't matter as much as finding their way back to each other.

***

Erin's first year wasn't as difficult as Maggie expected. Having a baby seemed more enjoyable than she'd remembered. With older kids in school and a maturity she didn't have in her twenties, she carried herself more confidently.

Erin's chubby little fingers dug into the decorated cake during the last refrain of "Happy Birthday."

Cam had erected a tent in the backyard, so everyone could be outside for the party. The entire family made the trip to Spencer to see Erin turn one, including Maggie's parents and Cam's mom, who was still grappling with a split from her third husband.

"I see Hazel's started chain smoking again since Jim moved out," Kimberly whispered, passing Maggie on the way to get another carton of ice cream.

Cam was a good father despite a lack of guidance from his folks. His brother died of a heart condition a few months after birth, and the loss of a child had greatly impacted his mom and dad. They'd often talked of divorce, and Cam made it his life's goal to have a strong and loving family without the threat of implosion. Maggie knew it was one of the reasons why he tried so hard to mend their relationship when things got tough.

Cam's dad passed away before Mason was born, and his mom had taken it as a sign to date most of the eligible bachelors in Northwest Iowa above the age of fifty-five. It embarrassed Cam when Hazel's second and third marriages failed quickly. His mother was never the same after his father's death, and Cam felt cheated when her faltering love life took precedence over everything else.

"Time for presents," Cam announced.

Maggie wiped frosting from Erin's mouth and got her ready to continue with the party.

"Look at all that stuff," Hazel said, leaning against the garage. She took a long drag off a cigarette. "No kid needs that many toys."

Hazel always criticized things, and Maggie assumed the reason came from unhappiness in her own life.

The day of Erin's birth had been one of the best days of Maggie's life. After gratefulness replaced resentment in her heart, she became more patient with the other kids and a better partner to Cam. If it meant a pile of birthday presents to celebrate Erin's life, so be it. Maggie would not allow

Hazel's snide comments to rob her of joy or make her doubt the kind of mother she'd become.

By the end of the night, no signs of a party remained, and an exhausted Maggie collapsed into bed.

"It's been quite a year," Cam said, pulling his wife close.

Maggie knew what he was referring to. Their sweet baby girl had shown them a way back to each other, and without her, who knows where they may have ended up.

"I regret not getting help sooner," Maggie said.

Maggie had taken Kimberly's advice and finally discussed her mental health with the doctor. She chose her first post-partum appointment to address the problem she'd been afraid to acknowledge. After trial and error, Maggie found a medication she could tolerate that helped her immensely.

"I wasn't the husband you deserved."

"I pushed you away, and now we know why. I was dealing with issues impacting my ability to be happy."

"It was easy for me to leave every week and ignore what you were going through, and my selfishness almost cost us everything."

"We wouldn't have let that happen."

"Sometimes it doesn't matter how much you want something. I lived a compartmentalized life. I was one person on the road and another at home. Being gone so often caused me to forget what you and the kids needed. I've done things I'm not proud of, but I'm a different man today."

Cam started sobbing, and Maggie didn't know why.

"What is it?" she asked, touching his cheek to comfort him.

"Nothing," he said. "I only wish I could have protected you better from the loneliness."

Maggie could see that Cam was trying to compose himself.

"I'm not sure you could have. We weren't communicating, and that's on both of us," she reassured.

Her husband's feelings of guilt were unsettling. Did Cam have more on his mind than he felt comfortable sharing? With their lives moving forward in a positive direction, Maggie chose to push the uneasy feeling aside.

CHAPTER 15
Ella

Charlie and Carol Meyers fidgeted nervously, volleying looks of confusion between them. Jordan offered pleasantries from across the kitchen table while urging Ella with his eyes to get on with the reason for their visit.

"Jordan, why don't you join me on the deck so Charlie and Ella can talk?"

Ella appreciated Carol's sensitivity, and it gave her a few more seconds to prepare her offense.

"Is that all right with you, Ella?" Jordan asked.

"Yes. It's fine."

"It's good to see you. How's your mom?" Charlie asked once they were alone.

Ella wasn't confrontational, but she'd come for a purpose, and she didn't feel the need for good manners.

"It's a little late for concern, isn't it?"

"I care about the two of you, regardless of how the relationship with your mom ended," he said.

Dinner simmered in a crock pot on the counter, and the smell of comfort food reminded Ella of the life she never shared with her father.

"Well, here's the abbreviated version. I waited for you to come for me for two and a half decades, and Mom has Alzheimer's disease and lives in a nursing home. A whole lot of other things happened in between, but that pretty much catches you up."

"I'm so sorry. When did your mother's memory issues start?"

Didn't he want to ask what became of his first-born daughter since he last saw her? Ella's father held his composure, and it made her angry.

"Why did you leave me? I've seen your Facebook page. You have other kids—kids I should know. Why didn't my grandparents ever keep in touch? How could all of you walk away and forget me?"

"It wasn't like that, Ella . . . how long has your mother been sick?" he asked again through tears. "I thought she would have discussed this with you."

His reaction continued to puzzle Ella.

"It's been two years since her diagnosis. The Alzheimer's progressed quickly, even with medication."

"I'm sorry. I want to help you, but I'm not comfortable sharing everything without your mother's blessing. You didn't have this talk *before* she got dementia? I feel an obligation to Jillian. Is it possible I could have a little time, and then I'll try to give you the answers you need?"

If he felt any sense of *obligation* to them, they wouldn't be having the conversation.

"No. You are telling me the truth *today*. It can't be worse than what I have experienced or more hurtful than what I've imagined as reasons why you left me."

Charlie took a long pause.

"I loved your mom so much in the early days," he lamented. "I'd always dreamed of having a little girl. You used to follow me around in the yard and call me daddy, and it melted me."

"So, what happened?"

Ella's heart ached with rejection.

"Your mom and I had lots of problems when we decided to split, and one of the issues was custody. I told her I wouldn't sign anything until your visitation schedule was set. It wasn't only about me, your grandma and grandpa Meyers loved you too, and I wanted to make sure they got to see you often."

The word *loved*, in the past tense, destroyed Ella.

"When push came to shove," Charlie continued," your mother kept me from you because—"

"Because why?"

Ella feared what was coming next.

"Because you weren't my child."

Ella hesitated. Had she heard him correctly?

"What do you mean? Of course, I'm your child."

"Honey, it's true. I thought your mom would tell you everything when you grew up. I'd never considered you'd wonder where I was. When I found out you weren't mine, I decided that leaving it all behind and rebuilding my life would be the best option for everyone."

"How did you know for sure? Did you only go by what Mom told you?"

Ella envisioned her mother telling Charlie a lie so he wouldn't fight for custody.

"I loved you and would never have left you if I wasn't sure. I demanded a paternity test, and science gave me the heartbreaking answer.”

“Then who *is* my father?”

Could she trust Charlie’s account? Did she have any choice?

“I have suspicions it was someone your mom worked with. Once the results came back, I didn’t ask for details. Now, I wish I’d pressed her more because the mystery has tortured me.”

“I had no idea.”

Ella saw sorrow in Charlie Meyers’s eyes. The consideration of his feelings had never come into play. She smelled his Brut aftershave—the same kind he’d always worn—and it deluged her softened heart with memories.

Charlie hadn’t abandoned Ella for the reasons she’d construed, but righting her emotional ship would bring consequences. Everything Ella believed about her reality dissolved, leaving a blank page at the beginning of her life story.

“There’s nothing else you can tell me to help me figure this out?” Ella asked through tears.

“If I’d been aware you didn’t know what happened, I’d have found you and told you myself.”

“Mom’s parents are gone. Her sister, Eloise, still lives in Des Moines. Maybe she would have an idea who my father is.”

“Your mom had a neighbor lady friend named Donna Monroe. She lived two houses from us at the little bungalow outside the city. You could try her, because they were tight back then. I heard they packed up for Colorado shortly after we divorced, so I’m not sure if the two stayed close.”

Ella remembered Donna, but after she and her mother moved downtown, they hadn't seen her again. Reconnecting after so many years didn't seem likely.

Carol and Jordan returned to the kitchen, and Ella could tell by the look on Jordan's face that he'd been told about what happened.

"Thank you, Dad—I mean Charlie," Ella said, extending her hand to say goodbye.

Charlie pulled her into a hug.

"You aren't my daughter by blood, but I've never stopped missing you. I'm glad you've turned out well. I can tell your mom did a fantastic job of raising you. Jordan, take care of this special lady."

The truth left Ella hollow, questions flooding the space where the lie had stolen her self-worth. She felt something unfamiliar, maybe grief or longing, but she had no right to either because Charlie wasn't hers to love in the first place.

***

"Are you okay?" Jordan asked as they started for home.

Ella burst into tears.

"My mother lied to me."

"I'm sure the circumstances surrounding your mom's actions would make sense if she could explain them."

Jordan took Ella's hand, and she didn't pull away. She needed his support more than ever.

"That's never going to happen. I've spent all this time assuming my father left me because he didn't love me. I've been blaming the wrong person. It's my mother and the man who fathered me who deserve my anger."

"You shouldn't invent a story without knowing more," Jordan advised. "Your mom may have had a motive for doing what she did. She loves you, and she wouldn't do anything to hurt you."

Ella appreciated her husband's efforts to pacify her, but nothing could alleviate her confusion.

"I can't believe she'd put me through this either, but she did."

"I don't want to be selfish, but if Charlie didn't run out on you, maybe you could find it in your heart to trust me more."

"What do you mean? I trust you completely."

"You've told me before that you worry I'll leave you, but there is no way that would ever happen," he promised.

"Are we talking about a baby again? Because I can't add it to my plate, even if I wanted to."

Ella had a habit of avoiding conflict, and after the conversation with her father, another difficult discussion seemed too daunting to endure.

"I'm not asking you to have a child right now. The part where you say, 'even if I wanted to' is what scares me. I'm afraid your hesitation to have a family stems more from your inability to believe in my commitment to you."

"Now you sound like a shrink. I *do* want a baby. Someday. I just can't worry about it today."

Usually, a woman's biological clock ticked the loudest, but Jordan continued to hit the snooze on his, and Ella didn't know if she could hold him off much longer.

"Let's go home. I'll make dinner, and you can take a hot bath and unwind," Jordan suggested.

"No. I want to stop and see my mother."

CHAPTER 16

Maggie – Summer 2015

Maggie's emotions swelled as she gazed at Mallory and Tom exchanging their wedding vows. The fragrance of her corsage took Maggie back to the day of her mother's funeral when white roses filled out the spray on the top of the casket. Maggie missed her mom and wished she was there to see Mallory get married.

Erin served as the maid of honor for her sister. The pale pink gown she wore was too frilly for her taste, and unease crept up her neck in red splotches.

Mason and Jenny stood at the altar and little Anna was the flower girl. The Sanders' first grandchild was the apple of their eye, but a babysitter had been hired and was waiting near the front in case she got disruptive. It was money well spent because the little girl dressed in all white only lasted about ten minutes. She had a complete meltdown as she was stripped of her petal dropping duties, but once she was gone, the ceremony continued with far less stress for everyone.

The bridal party looked like a treasured scrapbook come to life. The group represented family and friends who'd accompanied Mallory and Tom on their journey to adulthood. Maggie noticed her oldest daughter's resemblance to photos of herself at the same age. Mallory's beauty made Maggie realize she'd been wrong to feel self-conscious about her appearance as a young woman.

Nostalgia swept over her as she recognized how the years had changed and molded those she loved. Where had the time gone, and when had Maggie transformed from an insecure mother of three to a middle-aged woman content with her life?

Kids didn't rush into marriage anymore. Mallory and Tom lived together, and their marriage functioned as a precursor to starting a family. It was a different era, but she and Cam had raised their children well, and Maggie trusted them to know what they wanted out of life.

Maggie felt confident in the union of her oldest daughter who'd just turned thirty-two, despite having tied the knot with Cam at a much younger age. Maybe being older would make it easier for Mallory and Tom.

Maggie and Cam's relationship challenges held no significance on such a special day. They'd made it, and she hoped God would continue to bless them in the following decades of their lives.

"I now pronounce you husband and wife," the minister proclaimed.

Mallory and Tom kissed, and the congregation responded with a round of applause.

As if on cue, their kiss was cut short by the blaring of a fire alarm. The shrill sound echoed off the high ceilings of the sanctuary, ricocheting through the building and prompting guests to cover their ears.

The piercing noise stopped as suddenly as it began. The wedding coordinator rushed to the minister's side, whispered something quickly, then darted from the altar.

"There's no reason for concern," Pastor Bob said with a chuckle. "It looks like the flower girl wanted to have the final say today. Anna pulled the alarm box while the sitter was holding her."

Laughter rippled through the room, and the attention returned to Mallory and Tom.

"You know," the minister said, turning back to the couple. "This ties in nicely with my sermon from a few minutes ago. In the years ahead, your relationship will face its share of unexpected *fire alarms*. But if your foundation is built on mutual respect and unconditional love, you'll be able to put out any flames that come your way and protect the bond between you."

Everyone applauded again, and Maggie wiped a tear from her cheek. It was the perfect ending to a memorable ceremony.

"Okay," the minister said with a grin. "Let's try this again. Tom, you may kiss your bride."

***

The DJ spun tunes, and hotel staff passed appetizers as the reception cranked into high gear. An open bar relaxed the guests as they snacked on crab cakes and spicy meatballs, waiting for dinner to be served.

After they cut the cake, Mallory and Tom took their spot on the dance floor. They swayed to "At Last" by Etta James before Cam gave a moving toast and joined his middle child for a father-daughter waltz. There wasn't a nuptial tradition for the mother to share the same kind of moment with the bride. Still, Maggie experienced it vicariously by soaking in the sight of Cam holding Mallory as if he'd never see her again.

It hadn't been an easy road, but Cam's words rang true. Everything *had* turned out okay.

***

With the newly married couple off on their honeymoon and Mason and his family headed back to Des Moines, Maggie and Cam settled in for wine on the patio. Maggie's feet still hurt from dancing in high heels, and exhaustion had taken over the rest of her body.

Erin was leaving for New Mexico the following day. Her roommate, Tessa, lived in Albuquerque, and her family had connections with a marketing firm. After several interviews, Erin got her dream job and was moving. The prospect of a new career seemed to excite her, and that pleased her parents.

She played soccer in college, but an injury ended her season as a junior. Erin had flourished in athletics, and the loss brought feelings of depression and uncertainty. Lately, Maggie and Cam noticed more happiness in their daughter, and they hoped she'd finally found her way.

They'd finished a second glass of Merlot and were contemplating an early bedtime when Erin joined them outside.

"Can I talk to the two of you?" she asked, plopping into a wicker chair.

"Of course, honey," Cam said, unaware of what was coming.

"I have something to tell you, and I'm not sure how you'll take it."

Maggie's mind raced to all the possible revelations to come. Did Erin reject her employment offer and decide to take a year off and backpack across Europe? Had she maxed out her credit cards again? Did her car need another repair before traveling out west?

Erin was such an easy baby, but as soon as she could talk, she'd challenged Maggie and Cam in ways that put them to the test.

"You can tell us anything," Maggie said, hoping they weren't facing a crisis the day after Mallory's wedding.

"I'm getting married."

"Excuse me?" Cam questioned.

Erin didn't have a man in her life as far as her parents knew.

"Married? To whom?" Maggie prodded.

Did the word *married* have another meaning other than what Maggie understood? Surely, Erin didn't mean making a lifetime commitment to someone they'd never heard of.

"I didn't want to tell you before Mallory's wedding. I'm going to marry Tessa in a few months."

"Tessa?" Cam asked, wild-eyed and confused.

Tessa and Erin had lived together all four years of college, but Maggie and Cam never thought of them as a couple.

"I'm gay," Erin declared. "And I'm thrilled to be engaged to my best friend."

At twenty-three, Maggie didn't think Erin had the maturity to make such a permanent decision, no matter *who* she chose as a partner.

Despite her successes as a star athlete, Maggie and Cam had often looked deep within themselves for the proper way to raise her. Erin had been popular, but she had sometimes drifted toward the wrong crowd. She cut class, smoked pot, and fought to maintain her GPA.

She'd gone out with Tanner Barnett all through high school. They *seemed* like a happy couple in their prom photos and yearbook mentions. Maggie quickly sorted through her memories, wondering what she'd missed. She realized Erin's rebellion might have been about something deeper. Maybe she'd been trying to find herself in a way her parents hadn't understood.

Maggie empathized with her daughter's struggles, but moving directly from telling them she was a lesbian to announcing her engagement was a lot to take in. Especially after a whirlwind of family festivities and the consumption of two glasses of wine.

"How long have you and Tessa been together?" Cam asked, his demeanor calm.

"Since my first week at college."

Maggie was shocked that neither she nor Cam had been aware of the four-year relationship.

"Why marry right now? Why don't you wait until you're more established at your new job? What's the rush?" Cam reasoned.

"Setting the idea of a marriage aside, how do you know you're in love with a woman—with Tessa?" Maggie corrected herself. "You dated Tanner for all those years in high school? The two of you made such a cute couple. . ."

"Tanner Barnett is as gay as I am. We understood each other, and our friendship helped us survive the homophobia of our teenage peers."

Maggie replayed every pivotal moment in Erin's life as she tried to make sense of what her daughter was saying, already missing the Erin she thought she knew.

"I've lived this lie for so long, and I'm done hiding," Erin continued. "Nothing makes a bigger statement than marrying the love of my life. Tessa and I are doing this regardless of timing, support, or rejection from other people."

Maggie liked Tessa, but she'd never appraised her through the eyes of a parent assessing a lifetime partner for their child. It didn't mean she couldn't see her that way in the future, but only time would give those answers. How they handled this conversation would impact everything moving forward with Erin, and Maggie wanted to say the right thing.

"Let's all get some sleep and discuss this again in the morning," Maggie suggested.

"I've kept this hidden for a long time. Choosing honesty, with you and everyone else, hasn't come easily. But I can't take the strain of living in secrecy for another day."

"I love you, Erin. Nothing will ever change that. But your mother and I are just finding this out. We need a little time to process," Cam said.

Erin took turns hugging her parents, and Maggie noticed her daughter held on longer than normal.

"Tessa and I want the two of you to accept our relationship and be an important part of our lives. We already have Mason and Mallory's blessing," she added.

"You've told your siblings?" Maggie asked.

"Yes. I called them over Memorial Day weekend, and they're on board to stand up with us."

Maggie felt blindsided. Why had no one shared this information with her and Cam? It was official; they were no longer in charge of the family.

"I didn't see that one coming," Cam said when they got into bed.

"It isn't Erin being gay that's tying me up in knots. It's going from telling us that she's a lesbian and then jumping right into marriage. Putting her sexual orientation aside, she is way too young. I would feel the same way if she was marrying a man we'd never met."

"I like Tessa. She's always seemed nice."

"Cam, that is not the point. There are many *nice* people in the world, but it doesn't mean I want my child to spend their life with them."

"Do you remember when Mason came to us and said he wanted to marry Jenny? He hadn't proposed yet, but the wedding plans began six months later. Jenny was a stranger too. In fact, we might know Tessa better because at least we've been around her some. We only met Jenny once before she and Mason got engaged."

"This will make having children difficult for our daughter," Maggie sighed, already trying to navigate the roadblocks Erin might face.

"Times are changing. We have to trust Erin to choose what she needs and wants out of life. We've raised our kids to be independent and make good decisions. Everything will be okay. Think of how hard it must have been for our girl to keep this buried. Revealing a secret never comes with a guarantee. She trusted that her openness would be met with understanding, allowing her to go on with life authentically. I wish I possessed the same bravery."

"Why would you need to be brave about something?" Maggie asked.

Cam looked wistful.

"You might be surprised," he said.

***

The alarm clock read 4:30 a.m. when Maggie heard Cam get up and go downstairs. The hallway light slipped beneath the closed door, and she wondered if her husband was all right. She didn't want to leave the warmth of her bed, but she felt compelled to check on him.

Maggie could hear coffee making its way through the Keurig. The familiar aroma of dark roast reminded her that some things never change, and that brought her a welcome comfort.

When she got to the kitchen, Cam wasn't sitting at the island working on a crossword puzzle, which is where she usually found him when he couldn't sleep. Maggie called out softly, not wanting to wake Erin in the first-floor bedroom.

"Cam?"

"I'm in here," he said from an unlit family room.

Maggie joined him on the sofa and saw tears on his face.

"What's going on? Didn't we agree that we'd support Erin no matter what? Why are you crying?"

"Yes, of course," he whispered, his voice catching.

129

Before falling asleep, Maggie and Cam had discussed how Erin's sexual orientation would change their lives. They concluded it made no difference to them who their daughter loved if she was happy. Tessa seemed to provide that happiness, and they chose to embrace the engagement because of it.

"What is it then?"

She moved closer to Cam and took his hand.

"I'm devastated Erin didn't trust us with this sooner. It's triggered me . . . about the importance of truth and transparency."

Cam sounded like a candidate running for city government and not a father discussing his daughter's love life.

"I'm stuck on the fact that I haven't always been the dad or husband you all deserved. Secrets are toxic, and I'm sad Erin thought she needed to keep such a big one from us."

"Where are you going with this?"

"I'm talking about the fallout from keeping things from each other. Humans aren't supposed to hide from the people they love. I'm proud of Erin for deciding that she's stronger than her fear. She couldn't tell us because she didn't know if we'd stand by her," Cam surmised. "Before Erin leaves later today, we have to make sure she understands there is *nothing* she could ever tell us that would change how we feel about her."

"Yes. We'll tell her that we may disagree on marriage at this time, but it has nothing to do with Tessa."

It was too early for Maggie to figure out why Cam was acting so strangely, but she knew something was off.

CHAPTER 17
Ella

"How are you doing?" Jordan asked, taking his mother-in-law's hand.

Jillian didn't answer. She beamed like a young girl with a crush on a neighbor boy when Jordan visited. Typically, Ella saw their relationship as sweet, but nothing was sitting right with her.

Jillian's face flushed. She seemed to question her daughter's attitude, but that would mean she understood the world around her, and Ella didn't think that was possible.

"Say hello to your mother."

"Hi," Ella said, crossing her arms.

Jillian kept looking at Jordan.

"Honey, it doesn't help to take this out on your mom. You'll work through it, but right now, Jillian needs you to love her."

It irritated Ella that her husband always took the high road.

They spent an hour at Hannah's House, but Jordan did most of the talking. Ella didn't feel very generous toward her mother, and trying to draw something out of her took more effort than Ella could muster.

"I've got an idea," Jordan said. "What if we invited your

Aunt Eloise to come up next weekend? You said you'd like more things from your mom's condo for the apartment, and Eloise can bring a load with her."

Jillian's home had been untouched since the day she moved to Minneapolis. Ella hadn't been able to think about selling it, even if she knew her mother would never live there again.

"It would be nice for her to visit Mom. And if I'm asking Eloise about my father, I should do it in person."

***

"How was your trip?" Ella asked.

"The traffic sucked on I-35."

Eloise always spoke her mind, and Ella appreciated it.

"It's wonderful to see you," Jordan said, kissing Eloise on the cheek and offering his chair near Jillian. "I'll empty the car while you ladies catch up."

Before Jillian lost most of her memory, she was a vivacious and active woman. She adored art museums and attending the symphony, and her taste always leaned toward the contemporary.

Eloise brought the abstract artwork from above Jillian's couch and several textured throw pillows for the sofa. The bold colors of her mom's modern style would infuse Jillian's personality into her new living space, even if she no longer remembered what she liked.

"Hello, sis."

"Hi," Jillian said without recognition.

"I'm Eloise—your little sister."

She spoke louder than necessary as if it would nudge Jillian's memory.

"Sister," Jillian said, seesawing the word into two parts.

She looked at Eloise as if she'd never seen her.

"I'll help Jordan and then get us some coffee. Can I ride back to our house with you? I'd like to stay and visit with the two of you."

"Of course. Jillian and I can reconnect while you unload."

Good luck, thought Ella.

***

The smell of Jordan's expertly grilled chicken breasts wafted through the house, and Ella had added vegetable skewers and a salad to complete the meal. They would top off the feast with a strawberry cheesecake, and Ella hoped dinner would be followed by a fruitful conversation.

"What a lovely afternoon. Thanks for inviting me," Eloise said.

"It's our pleasure," Jordan said. "I'm glad you could make it. I have to work in the morning, so I'm calling it a night."

"It's only 8:30," Eloise said.

"This boy needs his beauty sleep."

Ella and Eloise sat on opposite ends of the couch. A cool blast rushed from the air-conditioner register closest to them, so Ella unfurled a throw blanket over their legs, forming a bridge between them.

"Aunt Eloise, there's something I need to discuss with you."

"Of course, dear. What is it?"

"The past couple of years have almost broken me."

"You've done a terrific job handling all of this. I hope if I'm ever faced with a similar situation, my children will do the same for me," Eloise complimented.

"It might sound crazy, but thoughts of my dad have overwhelmed me lately."

"Really? I wonder why?"

Eloise didn't like Charlie Meyers, and Ella knew it.

"Jordan says it's because of Mom's health. Then everything got worse on my thirtieth birthday. My girlfriends and I went to see Felicia Carmichael."

"I never miss her show, even though it's all a bunch of nonsense."

"We saw her at the Norris Center, and I got a psychic reading during the performance. She suggested I'd lost an important male figure in my life whose name started with the letter 'C'."

"Are you saying Charlie died?" Eloise interrupted.

"No, he's alive and well. Jordan and I visited him in Rochester."

"You reconnected with your father? After all these years?"

"Yes. Charlie invited us in, and the conversation revealed more questions than answers for me."

"How is the deadbeat? I'm sorry to speak poorly of your father. He gave you life, but he hasn't done anything else to raise or nurture you. I don't have any time for someone who could run out on their kid."

"He's doing fine, and you won't believe what I found out," Ella said without regard to her aunt's attitude.

"Did he explain why he never paid child support when my sister struggled financially? Did he have a reason for abandoning my niece?"

Ella sighed. From her reaction, Eloise's help seemed unlikely.

"Charlie isn't my biological father."

"What?" Eloise questioned. "Son of a . . . that's what he said to try to get away with his neglect? And I thought I couldn't hate Charlie Meyers more . . ."

"He said he wanted joint custody after the divorce, and Mom wouldn't allow it. She told him I wasn't his child, and he insisted on a paternity test to prove it. It's why he never kept in touch and why none of his family stayed in my life."

Eloise listened while Ella laid it all out, her misunderstanding about Charlie Meyers shifting with each word.

"Well, I'll be damned. Every time I bad-mouthed Charlie, your mother never said anything negative about him. She would say, 'Sometimes things don't work out the way we hope.' Now, I realize she didn't want me to know what happened, but she wouldn't trash the poor guy either. I'd always liked your dad—I mean, Charlie. I couldn't figure out why he would take off."

"Considering all you've said, I can see you can't tell me who my father is."

"Jillian didn't share much with me at that time. I wish I could help you. Did you ask Charlie?"

"He suspects a co-worker might be my father. Do you remember where Mom worked in the early nineties?"

"Hmm. Let me see . . ." Eloise twisted her mouth sideways as she concentrated. "Your parents lived in Des Moines then, and Charlie was at a grocery store chain in the western suburbs. Your mom held a position at Midwest Energy Corporation before you came along. Jillian traveled every week, so she quit after your birth. She took an HR job at Dayton's in Minneapolis, and Charlie accepted an offer at Cub Foods after you all moved to Minnesota. I hated to see you go, but it seemed like a great opportunity."

"She must have met my father when they lived in Iowa. Maybe the move north came from the need to make sure the truth didn't come out," Ella wondered aloud.

"I can't remember who your mom hung out with back then. There's still a chance she told someone else, even if she didn't confide in her own sister."

"Charlie mentioned Donna Monroe, a neighbor at the old house. I already looked her up, and we're not getting anything from her because she died in 2019."

"Oh, Ella. If I only had more answers. I'm flabbergasted your mother would have an affair and then have a child with a man other than her husband. I'm afraid I owe Charlie Meyers an apology for holding so much against him."

It disappointed Ella that her aunt didn't have more useful information, but she enjoyed spending time with a woman who reminded her so much of her mother.

CHAPTER 18

Maggie – Summer 2015

Maggie made a dinner she knew Cam would enjoy, but it did nothing to lift his sullen mood. Despite her efforts to draw him into conversation, he said little while eating and then took his wine to the patio. It was the final straw for Maggie.

Cam claimed to support Erin's life choices, but he hadn't been the same since she left. The time for a serious discussion had come, so Maggie brewed a cup of tea in her favorite red mug and joined her husband outside.

"You need to talk to me if you want my help to work through this," Maggie said. "Didn't we agree that it doesn't matter if Erin wants to marry Tessa, as long as she's the right person for her?"

"I'm proud of Erin. She looked so happy describing her relationship with Tessa, and I'm thrilled she's found someone. I'll accept Tessa as an in-law—just like Tom and Jenny."

"You've been brooding since she left. What's the problem if it isn't our daughter's sexuality upsetting you?"

"Is unconditional love a real thing? Don't we all care for each other based on our expectations for who we want people to be?" Cam asked.

"It's the definition of marriage. It's what we promised when we baptized our children. Where's all this coming from?" Maggie questioned.

"I want to tell you something, and I'm afraid it might change the way you feel about me."

Cam leaned back in his chair and downed the last of his wine. He ran his fingers through his hair and stared into the distance.

"What is it?" Maggie urged.

"I don't want to lose you and the kids, but I can't live any longer with the secret I've carried for almost twenty-five years either. If Erin can embrace honesty and go on with her life—I can too."

"You're not making any sense. We've had our share of difficulties, but I've never doubted your love or commitment."

"Maybe you should have."

Maggie inhaled the night air and waited for her world to come apart.

"You remember the problems we faced before Erin's birth?" Cam continued.

"Of course I do. I'd grown out of those baby days and didn't want to go back. We got Erin out of it, and our marriage improved because my pregnancy helped you decide to get off the road. Then I went on medication for depression, which made things even better."

"I wanted to change jobs for another reason too."

Maggie searched Cam's blank expression for answers,

but nothing could have prepared her for the bombshell he would drop.

"Why else would you have applied for another position?" she asked. "There isn't anything we couldn't face now, and I'm pretty sure we don't have many secrets anyway. So, just tell me."

"Did you know that I'm a cheater? I had an affair with someone for over a year, and when I found out you were pregnant with Erin, I walked away and never saw her again."

Maggie did *not* know that about her husband.

As Cam made his soul-cleansing confession, his words plowed through Maggie's heart.

"You're telling me that you got involved with another women sexually?"

Maggie's anger, immediate and hot, boiled over with nowhere to go but out. She yanked her chair away from Cam, the legs screeching against the concrete. The sudden movement knocked her tea to the ground. The ceramic cup shattered on impact—just like their broken trust. The clatter startled Maggie, and she knelt and began gathering the shards of red stoneware.

"Leave it. I'll get it later," Cam insisted, helping his wife to her feet. "We have to have this conversation, even if it's hard."

"I . . . can't . . . do it," Maggie shouted, covering her face with her hands.

"Maggie, *please*, hear me out. Do you remember Jillian Meyers who worked out of our Des Moines office at Midwest Energy?"

"The one with the short dark hair? Didn't the two of you win an award one year?"

"Yes. At the annual meeting they honored us as top salespeople. We'd often stay in the same location for the week because our territories overlapped. We got close, and unfortunately, it turned into more."

As the memory sharpened, Maggie recalled sitting at a table with Jillian Meyers and her husband at the event. A wave of humiliation washed over her as she realized Cam and Jillian had been sleeping together during that time.

"Why tell me now? Why didn't you keep this to yourself, so I never had to feel this pain?" she sobbed.

Maggie felt like Cam was telling her the plot of a movie and not revealing long-buried marital secrets. Every word broke her further, and she wanted Cam to rewind the conversation by five minutes and take it all back.

"Don't you get it? I've been living a lie, just like Erin. If we're staying together, I want you to know everything."

"*If* we're staying together? You're confusing me," Maggie said, wiping her nose on her shirt sleeve.

"I haven't fully engaged or loved you the way you deserve because of guilt. I can only commit to moving forward with you if you can accept *every* part of me."

"You cheated years ago, but now you are considering leaving *me*?"

Maggie's face was shadowed with uncertainty.

"Only if you don't want the same things as me."

"What are you talking about?"

Maggie's eyes narrowed as her frustration grew. She opened her mouth, but no words could express her shock.

"We're still young, Mags. Hopefully, we have years of life left. I want to decide how to make this time the best we've ever had."

"You've unloaded this secret on me, but it's not something that's easily absorbed. What else have you lied about? Even though this happened three decades ago, it isn't something we can just gloss over."

"I only want your forgiveness and understanding. The relationship with Jillian wasn't supposed to turn into more than a person to talk to, a deep friendship at most. I tried to push the feelings aside, but you kept shutting me out . . ."

"Are you pointing the finger at *me* for your indiscretion?"

Maggie didn't need an accomplice to blame herself. She'd never felt good enough, and Cam's admission of unfaithfulness made her feel inadequate all over again.

"I'm *not* putting this on you," he answered. "I'm at fault, and I'm trying to explain how it all happened. I missed talking to a woman who actually wanted to listen to me, and it got out of hand. I thought I could have an extramarital affair and keep it on the road and then turn into a decent husband and father at home. I got all confused, and I made the biggest mistake of my life."

"You're right. I blamed myself for everything while you were acting like a single man. I don't know how I can ever trust you again. You're the one person I thought I could count on, and now I learn that you're a liar and a cheat. I don't even know who you are."

Cam's shoulders slumped as Maggie unloaded her rage.

"I *chose* you and our children. I ended things when you got pregnant because my conscience wouldn't let me continue the charade. Now Erin's courage has led me to tell you everything. We're strong enough to get through this, and we can live a better life from now on."

"So, you think we can just forget about this and go on as if nothing happened."

"No, of course not," Cam whispered.

Maggie went into the house, ignoring the pieces of her broken mug scattered across the cement. She didn't bother to close the screen door, and after a few seconds, Cam heard a crash from inside.

CHAPTER 19
Ella

Mariachi music played through the restaurant's speakers, and the sizzle of fajitas nearby put Ella in the mood for Mexican food.

"Over here," she waved to Marcy as the host led her friend to their booth.

"Finally," Ella scolded. "Saving a spot on Taco Tuesday isn't easy."

The longtime friends tried to meet once a month. Lately, their plans often took a back seat, and Ella wondered how long the tradition would continue.

"Sorry. I got stuck in traffic. We've got to start meeting in the suburbs. Are Sondra and Lisa coming?"

"They both ditched when I sent them a reminder text today, but I still wanted to get together because I really needed to talk to you."

"I love me some Ella time," Marcy joked. "What's going on, girl?"

"Several things have happened since our night at the Felicia Carmichael show."

"Don't tell me you believe in her psychic powers now?"

"I'm not sure, but I went to visit my dad, and he *didn't* die as Felicia implied."

"Good news for him," Marcy chuckled, dipping a tortilla chip in warm queso.

"I did uncover something else."

"Is he a multi-millionaire and wants to share his winnings with you?"

"No."

"He's had amnesia and couldn't remember you existed?"

"No!"

"Spill it. I can't stand the suspense any longer," Marcy pleaded.

"Charlie Meyers is not my real father. He didn't keep in touch or pay child support because he didn't have to. My mom lied, or at least she omitted an important truth."

"Wow. Now you've got my attention." Marcy motioned for the server and ordered two giant margaritas. "I'm going to need alcohol for this. Do you know who your father *is*?"

"No, and Charlie offered very little. I talked with my mom's sister, and she didn't know anything either, including the part about Charlie not being my dad. So, I have no way to determine his identity."

"That's ridiculous. There's always a way to figure something out."

"I have a feeling she worked with him at Midwest Energy Corporation. My aunt told me she traveled as a regional salesperson in the early nineties. I'm assuming it's how she met the guy."

"Have you looked through your mom's things for any evidence of who he might be?" Marcy asked.

"Ever since Mom moved to Minneapolis, the house has sat empty. I need to clean it out and list it for sale. Mom needs the money for her expenses at Hannah's House, and I have to face reality. She's never going back there."

"You've got a good portion of the summer left, and I could come and help you."

"That's not necessary. I'm sure I can count on Jordan. Mom saved everything, so maybe I might find something stashed away to solve this mystery."

The two friends finished the night with fried ice cream and a promise to get together again the following month. Ella hoped she'd have more answers by then.

CHAPTER 20
Maggie

"The captain has asked us to secure the cabin. Please return to your seats and prepare for landing. We've begun our descent into Harry Reid International Airport and will land in Las Vegas in approximately thirty minutes," the flight attendant announced.

Maggie and Cam had flown to New Mexico for Erin and Tessa's wedding the week before, but the celebration ahead was only for them.

"Are you excited?" Cam asked, taking Maggie's hand.

"Of course. I do wish we'd invited the kids. Don't you think they thought it was strange that we extended our trip when we'd already been gone for eight days."

"We've just attended our first same-sex wedding, and *our* daughter and her partner were the ones tying the knot. If they can follow their hearts, we can too. What we do isn't anyone else's business."

Cam had revealed his affair four months earlier, and six weeks had passed since Maggie agreed to forgive him and move on with their lives.

They'd unofficially separated for almost ninety days. Maggie knew the exact number because she'd marked them on the calendar. They hadn't told a soul about what they were going through, and the stress of all of it had taken a toll. It felt like the early years of their marriage when the miles of Cam's business trips weren't the only way to measure the distance between them.

Cam moved into the guest room, and they met with a marriage counselor weekly. They pulled apart the seams of their relationship and began sewing it back together. What they ended up with only faintly resembled the fabric of their old union. The sessions allowed them to work through long-held resentments against each other, and eventually, understanding replaced anger and reconciliation took the place of accusations.

Maggie decided to forgive Cam rather than live without him. She didn't want to grow old alone. If she'd ventured out to find someone else to love, she'd have spent the rest of her life looking for her first husband's carbon copy. She forgave him because what remained of their bond was worth saving.

Cam responded by dropping to one knee, promising her a new diamond and a trip to Las Vegas to renew their vows. The proposal reminded Maggie of how Cam asked her to marry him in 1979, only this time, she had to help him to his feet while he groaned and cursed getting older.

The years had transformed them in many ways, especially physically, but their desire to stay together hadn't changed.

The one hundred-degree temperatures of Nevada were often described as a dry heat, but that didn't keep Maggie from feeling as if she'd stepped into an oven when she arrived in the Silver State.

Cam tipped the porter as Maggie took in the sights from the twenty-ninth floor of the Bellagio. She'd always imagined staying at the famous hotel, but cheaper lodging won out the last time they came to Vegas.

"This view is amazing," Maggie said, gazing out an expansive window.

"Do you want champagne?" Cam asked.

A room service cart sat in the corner. It held a chilled bottle of Dom Pérignon and a tray of chocolate-covered strawberries.

"Tell me this came with the room, and you didn't have to pay extra?" she begged.

They had plenty of money, but Maggie monitored their spending anyway. She appreciated Cam's efforts, but avoiding bankruptcy before they could enjoy their golden years was all she could think of.

"Let's just say we're not sparing any expense for the weekend."

Maggie wondered what else Cam had in store for her. She envisioned Celine Dion serenading them as she strolled down the aisle of the Little White Church. Maggie would have opted for the wedding drive-thru and a nice dinner, but Cam wanted something more extravagant and had made all the necessary arrangements.

***

Maggie waited at the back of the chapel, her nerves reminiscent of the jitters she experienced at her first wedding to Cam. The small venue's elegance surprised her, with flowers and candles adding a tasteful touch to the ceremony.

Only they knew why a reaffirmation of their commitment was needed when their marriage license still held validity in all fifty states.

Maggie focused on Cam as he stood beside an officiant whose only goal was to collect the fee required for a mock elopement. The moment was make-believe, yet the intimacy of it moved her. This time, they recognized the challenges ahead, and they were still willing to commit.

Memories flooded Maggie's heart as she made her way to Cam's side. She thought of her parents as she walked toward her groom alone. They'd both died years earlier, and she missed them, even their traits that had been difficult to embrace. Everyone had their faults, and forgiveness was the only way to keep love alive.

"Maggie," Cam said, taking her hands. His voice trembled as he began the pledge he'd composed. "I will cherish you every single day of the time we have left and give you more than you ever dreamed possible."

The quiet return of Cam's romantic side touched Maggie, making her feel like the woman he'd fallen in love with years earlier. After all they'd endured, she couldn't fathom her life without him.

Maggie and Cam celebrated their re-marriage at an upscale restaurant, followed by dessert and drinks near the fountains at the Bellagio. Contentment filled Maggie's heart when she looked at the dazzling diamond resting on her finger. Cam had given it to her before they left for New Mexico, and she hadn't waited for their trip to Las Vegas to begin wearing it.

"The kids would be shocked if they saw us right now," Cam chuckled.

"The girls commented on my new ring, and I said that the other one cracked from wear and tear. My explanation didn't stray far from the truth."

"They don't think we have a spontaneous bone in our bodies. I told Mason we'd decided to stop in Las Vegas for a few days, and he didn't say anything—a first for our opinionated son," Cam added.

They both laughed at the thought of their children believing they knew everything about the parents who raised them.

"Let's send them a picture. They'll see we're dressed up, but they won't notice you're wearing a wedding dress," Cam said.

He came behind Maggie's chair and moved in for a selfie.

"Technically, it's just a white lace sheath I found on clearance at Dillard's."

"It's prettier than your first gown, and you look gorgeous in it."

He kissed her on the neck, and Maggie felt a shiver go through her body. Marrying an older and more mature version of Cam Sanders had its benefits, and he'd never made her feel more beautiful and loved.

They snapped several images and huddled as they chose one. Maggie cropped it, added a filter to enhance the colors, and sent it out.

Within minutes, they received return texts.

Viva Las Vegas. Sexy look, Mama! <3Erin

Where are you? A wedding? LOL Mason

Maggie and Cam spent their second wedding night loving each other in a way surprising the older people they'd become. The metamorphosis of their relationship marked the turning point that would shape the rest of their lives.

***

"What do you mean we're looking at real estate today?" Maggie asked Cam as they ate breakfast.

It had only been a week since they'd returned from Las Vegas, and fatigue from the trip still plagued her.

"I can't make it any clearer. When we decided to remarry, I promised to make our years together a dream come true."

"I don't want a different house. We raised our kids here. It would crush them if we moved," she insisted.

"I'm not planning on *selling* anything. We're touring vacation property on Lake Okoboji today."

Maggie almost choked on her English muffin.

"You're kidding, aren't you?"

The two of them had never discussed owning a second home, and the idea seemed preposterous.

It took less than a half hour to get to the lake from Spencer. The Sanders had always made lasting memories in the area, touted for its old-fashioned amusement park and some of the best boating in Iowa.

All three of the kids had worked at the lake's resorts in the summer. They cleaned hotel rooms, rented jet skis, and took visitors on catamaran rides. Many of their closest

151

friendships came from those experiences, and the entire family felt a pull toward Lake Okoboji.

"I'm serious, Maggie. We are considering six places today, and then I'm taking you for a late lunch on the water."

"Do we have the money to buy a vacation home?" she asked.

Maggie handled the day-to-day bills, and Cam took care of the investments. She knew they weren't destitute, but purchasing another residence? She couldn't imagine it.

Cam took her hand from across the table.

"I gave the agent a budget, and you can pick whichever house you think fits us best. You can furnish it however you want, and we'll spend lots of time there. It's a beginning for us, and I want to start over in a place as wonderful as our love."

CHAPTER 21
Ella

The door to Jillian's condo creaked as it swung open, and the stale air reminded Ella of her mother's absence. Eloise checked on things periodically, but a vacant house took on a certain loneliness, and you smelled it the moment you walked in.

"I'll crack a few windows to get some ventilation through here," Jordan said.

Jordan had taken the weekend off, so they had two days to clean everything out. The realtor would arrive later in the day to give them an idea of listing price, and Ella was crossing her fingers that it wouldn't stay on the market long.

"Thank you for helping me with all of this," Ella said, hugging her husband.

"There's no way I would let you do this alone. You try to put on a strong front, but you don't need to do it for me."

Ella had seen her mother handle their lives as a single mom, and relinquishing control and embracing vulnerability didn't come easily for her.

"Let's get this done efficiently. I'll take Mom's room and the other bedroom, and you can have the kitchen and living room. We'll categorize things as either keep, pitch, or donate."

Ella started in the bedrooms because any information concerning her father would likely be found in those rooms. It would make the work more fun if she treated it as a treasure hunt, even if she didn't find anything useful.

Ella could hear pots and pans banging and packing tape being pulled tight as Jordan closed the top of cardboard boxes. The Goodwill pile grew by the hour. It seemed wasteful to get rid of everything, but Ella and Jordan didn't need any of it, and knowing how much the items would help other people gave Ella some solace.

Once she cleared out the closet, Ella moved to her mother's nightstand. The drawer contained cough drops, Kleenexes, and a couple of books with their pages turned down at the corners. The stories had halted in the middle for Jillian, just like her independent life.

"Hey," Jordan said, popping his head through the bedroom door. "How about lunch?"

"I'm almost done in this room, except for the under-bed organizers. You run out and get sandwiches, and then we'll take a break."

"Turkey or ham, my love?"

"Can we share?" Ella suggested.

"Ah, that's why I married you. You're a genius."

"I'd kill for a Diet Coke," she yelled as Jordan made his way to the front door.

Ella continued going through the closet and drawers. Three long storage bins sat beneath the bed frame, and Ella couldn't wait to dig in.

The first box contained tax forms and receipts, which Ella took to the living room to look through later from the comfort of a chair.

The second one overflowed with keepsakes, and a snapshot on top caught Ella's eye. It showed her as a toddler, sitting on a white pony at a carnival. Charlie steadied her so she wouldn't fall off, and Jillian's arm snaked through his as if they belonged together. Ella couldn't help but wonder what had transpired between the seemingly happy occasion and the day Charlie packed his bags and left.

Ella struggled to retrieve what was left from under the bed. She shoved the plastic lid aside and saw it contained stamped tickets from a Destiny's Child concert her mother had taken her to as well as old academic reports and handmade Mother's Day cards.

As she dug deeper, Ella came across a manila envelope marked "Work Stuff." She poured everything across her mother's bedspread, finding an ad from Dayton's department store among the contents. It featured Ella in an Easter dress and bonnet. Her mother had volunteered her as a model for her employer's spring flyer, and Ella got to pose with an adorable live rabbit at the shoot.

Ella pulled a final piece from the packet. It was an article from *The Spencer Daily Reporter* dated May 6, 1991. The headline, *Midwest Energy Corporation Honors Team Members,* ran above a picture showing Jillian and a co-worker. They stood side-by-side with glass trophies, and the cutline read, *Jillian Meyers and Cameron Sanders Honored with Sales Awards.*

Ella gasped, realizing she'd found the name of someone who would have known her mother around the time of her conception.

A smile spread across her face when she heard Jordan coming through the front door with lunch. She couldn't wait to tell him what she'd discovered.

***

"I forgot how exhausting moving can be," Jordan said, joining Ella in bed.

They'd worked at Jillian's condo until Sunday night and then traveled back to Minneapolis in the dark.

"I'm sorry you have to report to the station in the morning. At least I can sleep in," Ella said, acknowledging summer vacation as the best perk of teaching.

"Are you seeing your mom tomorrow?" Jordan asked.

"Yes, I want to take a few more things to her room. I'm also going to try and locate that Cameron Sanders guy online. I want to contact him and find out if he remembers my mom. They were top salespeople, so they surely ran into each other occasionally. It will probably lead to nothing, but it'll give me something to do today."

"Something besides going through all the boxes you brought home from Des Moines? I hate to see the guest room loaded with junk for too long."

"Don't worry. I'll get it done because we need to organize and clean the room for another purpose."

"Babe, I doubt your mom will ever be able to stay with us again."

Jordan nestled close to his wife, putting an arm around her waist.

The visit with Charlie Meyers had lifted the weight of abandonment from Ella and allowed her to soften to the idea of motherhood. Jordan was right, the unanswered questions about her childhood had anchored Ella's hesitation to start a family. The man who fathered her remained a mystery, but Ella no longer clung to the notion that *she* was to blame for his absence.

With those struggles pushed to the background, Ella felt ready to embrace the next chapter of her life. The first page of her fresh start would begin with the words Jordan longed to hear.

"I thought we could turn it into a nursery."

Ella let her statement hang in the air as Jordan processed it.

"A nursery?" he said, raising up on one elbow.

Jordan looked stunned at his wife's sudden change of heart.

"Yes."

"But you said . . ."

"It's not fair to either of us for me to avoid having a baby because I'm scared. I'm not sure what happened all those years ago, but I can finally accept that Charlie didn't desert me. I'm not letting fear stand in the way of our happiness for one more minute."

Jordan pulled Ella close again and kissed her. Although cleaning out Jillian's condo had left them both dog-tired, they didn't let exhaustion keep them from making love with a purpose.

***

Ella opened her computer and entered the name Cameron Sanders into Facebook. She watched while the entries loaded, hoping she'd get a useful hit. She knew he might not have his own account, so she was looking for anything listing his name as a connection. Lots of older men didn't get on social media or shared a profile with their wives, so she was not completely confident that the search would yield any results.

Ella looked through the Cameron Sanders listings. One showed a man in his twenties, and another pictured a woman who went by "Cammie." When Ella combined Cameron Sanders with Spencer, Iowa, she got a hit on a woman named Maggie Sanders. She scrutinized Maggie's Facebook friends for other connections and found Mason Sanders, Jenny Fisher Sanders, Mallory Sanders Martin, and Erin Sanders.

The photos alone told Ella that Maggie fell within the age range of the person she was looking for, so she sent her a private message. What did she have to lose?

CHAPTER 22
Maggie

Maggie wrapped the string around her tea bag and squeezed the excess liquid out before making her way to the porch at the lake house. The sound of Wrigley's toenails clicking on the hardwood sounded like tap shoes as he spun in circles, begging for a bite of her buttery toast.

Maggie loved life at Lake Okoboji. The relaxed vibe that wove through town reminded her there could still be happiness in a world without Cam. It didn't take long to get there from Spencer, but it always felt like a million miles away. The distance was often just what she needed to set her grief aside and catch her breath again.

The week after Cam's funeral, she'd spent several days at the place where she and Cam had planned to spend the rest of their years. It wasn't as lonely there with the boats sailing by and sunshine warming her face as if nothing had changed.

That first day alone, she'd sat in one of the two chairs they'd placed under the overhang of the dock. That had been the spot where they'd often enjoyed the beautiful water view together. The empty space beside her only magnified Cam's absence, and the reality of his death sucked the air from her lungs. Her emptiness screamed so loudly that she half-wondered if the neighbors could hear it.

She recalled the day they'd first seen the house, when Cam had whisked her away to look at properties varying in size and price. He told her to pick whichever one she wanted, and she chose the farmhouse-style ranch overlooking the sweeping lakefront.

The wood beams, which ran the length of the great room, resembled a church sanctuary. The rustic black hardware on the cabinets gave the home a cottage feel, and crisp white molding made the house look clean and new. The tree-filled lot took Maggie back to growing up in rural Iowa and provided the ideal spot for Maggie and Cam to live out their retirement.

Cam bought a pontoon boat and catered to the grandkids by putting in a little beach for swimming. He placed a water trampoline off the end of the dock, and it was everyone's number one activity during visits. The family had clapped and cheered the first time Maggie tried it, and she'd squealed with excitement before budging in line ahead of her grandson to take another turn.

Cam became quite the woodworker, and he designed a custom sign out of a cedar board he'd saved for the perfect project. He painted words on the front, and it read *Maggie and Cam's Happily Ever After.* It hung next to the door in the mudroom where they saw it each time they entered the house. The creation celebrated their new lives, even if they were the only two who knew the full meaning behind it.

After Cam's death, glancing at the wall hanging immediately brought her to tears. She'd taken it down, but even seeing the nail hole where the phrase once lived could sideline Maggie for an entire day.

They'd had a wonderful time at the lake the Friday night before Cam died, sharing a bottle of Cabernet while they grilled filets. Afterward, they watched Cam's favorite television show, *Felicia Feels You*. It led to a deep discussion regarding their religious beliefs, and Maggie later wondered if Cam had sensed something. Perhaps their talk about spirituality unfolded as a premonition of the inevitable.

Later that night, Cam pulled her close and told her how much he loved their life. She would not have left their bed early the next morning to go shopping for flowers if she'd known they didn't have much time.

Likewise, Maggie hadn't wanted to disappoint their son and his wife when they'd received a last-minute request to babysit. It was two weeks before Cam's death, and when he reminded her of his annual physical that Friday, Maggie had insisted he reschedule. She'd regretted it ever since, knowing that the physician would have taken labs, listened to his heart, and asked him how he felt. Seeing the doctor might have uncovered a health problem, and they would have fixed it, shielding the family from the pain of losing such a remarkable man.

Dwelling on the what-ifs served no purpose, but they followed Maggie everywhere. She kept reexamining the choices she'd made, wondering if her husband might still be alive if she'd done something different.

You couldn't take anything for granted, because life knocked you off balance the moment you let your guard down. Cam had persuaded her to believe they were invincible, and when reality shattered that illusion, she wasn't prepared.

***

Maggie sat at the dining room table and began working on the thank you notes from Cam's funeral. In two months, she hadn't put in the effort to write them. She appreciated the flowers, food, and condolences from everyone, but being responsible for writing so many personal messages added an extra burden to an already overwhelming time.

Maybe the cultural norm of thanking funeral-goers came from helping a person stay busy following a loss, and a hundred and twenty notes certainly kept you occupied.

The morning flew by between penning the cards and looking out at the boats. Seeing other families enjoying their summer made Maggie jealous. Why did the Sanders have to face such circumstances when they could be taking pleasure in a day on the water like everyone else?

A phone call from Kimberly came in, and the intrusion startled Maggie.

"Where are you?" her sister asked.

"I'm at the Okoboji house."

"Well, I'm in Spencer, standing at your front door. You can't take off and not let someone know where you're going."

"I have homes less than thirty minutes from each other. I can go between the two without asking permission from anyone."

Maggie rolled her eyes to the benefit of no one.

"I wanted to surprise you. Stay put, I'm on my way."

"Kim, I'm fine. I can take care of myself and don't require a babysitter. Come out for a visit if you want, but it isn't necessary."

"Okay, I believe you," Kimberly conceded. "I need to spend time with my big sister, so set the table because I'm bringing lunch."

With only two years between them, the siblings had always been close. Coming of age in rural Iowa had yielded the backdrop for a wonderful childhood.

Maggie remembered how much their dad loved life in the country with its pink sunsets and cool morning breezes. She could still see him riding his John Deere mower out to the garden, picking a ripe tomato, and sprinkling it with salt from a shaker he kept next to the steering wheel.

Kimberly had always been Maggie's closest friend, so having her as a sister was a bonus. She was grateful to have her nearby again after she and Dave moved back to Minnesota. They lived less than an hour from Okoboji and saw each other often once they all became empty nesters.

Maggie stared at her robe. A coffee stain ran down the front and toast crumbs were attached to the fabric. She stood to the protest of a sleeping Wrigley and headed upstairs to shower. Alarm bells might go off if her sister caught her looking unkempt. Maggie deserved time to grieve in her own way, but that luxury would have to wait.

***

Kimberly arrived with salads from Panera and an overnight bag.

"I thought I'd stay until tomorrow. I need to know where your head is. I'm heartbroken for you, and I'm at a loss for how to help you manage all of this," she said, her hands gesturing in the air at the state of Maggie's existence.

"*All of this* is my new life, Kimberly. I have decisions to make. Should I keep both houses? Will I trade in our cars and get something newer? How will everyone deal with my choices?"

"Screw everyone else."

Kimberly never held back, and Maggie appreciated her support, even if it was unrealistic.

"They're struggling, Kimmie. It isn't as simple as ignoring the kids and doing whatever I want."

In Kimberly's presence, Maggie didn't have to hide anything.

They spent the afternoon sitting on the covered dock. Two wicker chairs and a breeze off the lake made it the best place to sit and share stories and tears about Cam.

Maggie offered to take Kimberly to dinner, so they changed clothes and drove into town.

Cam's favorite restaurant at the lake served fried fish and the best hush puppies around, making it an easy pick as an alternative to cooking. Once seated, the sisters turned to the menu for some comfort food to help them digest the day's conversations.

"How are you ladies this evening?" the owner asked as he stopped by their table.

Frank knew how to work a room, and Maggie and Cam always felt appreciated when they ate at Pat's Hideaway.

"Fine, thank you," Maggie replied.

"Where's Cam tonight?" he asked.

Kimberly shot her sister a sympathetic look.

"I'm sorry to say we lost Cam in May," Maggie murmured.

"Oh no. My deepest sympathies to you and your family. I've enjoyed having Cam as a guest here at the restaurant. Please. . . order whatever you want to eat and drink—on the house."

"No, that isn't necessary," Maggie objected.

"I insist," he said before calling out to his wife. "Pat, bring these ladies two glasses of our best red wine."

Maggie saw no use in trying to argue, so she and Kimberly accepted the gift of a good meal.

***

"Thanks for coming," Maggie said, waving as Kimberly pulled away from the lake house.

Wrigley stood by her side as she blew a kiss toward the car. They went inside, and Maggie unplugged her phone from its charging station and moved to the sofa to check for any notifications. She'd forgotten to take her cell phone to the bedroom the night before and hoped the kids hadn't tried to reach her. Thankfully, none of the children had left a frantic message, wondering why their mother wasn't returning their calls.

She logged into Facebook to acknowledge any birthdays and scan the unlimited number of photos her friends posted of their grandkids. She noticed a message waiting for her and clicked on it to read the contents.

Maggie,

My name is Ella Daley, and I am the daughter of Jillian Meyers, who worked with a Cameron Sanders years ago. From what I see on Facebook, I think he might be your husband, and I'd like to ask him some questions regarding my mother's time with Midwest Energy Corporation. My mom has Alzheimer's disease, and I'm now handling her affairs. The information would be helpful to close a few gaps in her life story.

Thanks,

Ella

Maggie read the message several times before comprehending what it said. Once she allowed herself to breathe again, she threw her phone across the room, and it landed with a thud on the couch. Without giving it much thought, Maggie retrieved her cell and wrote a hasty reply.

Ella,

I am sorry to inform you that my husband died recently, so I can't help you.

Maggie Sanders

CHAPTER 23
Ella

When Ella found the photo of Cameron Sanders with her mother and the year it was taken, she'd felt optimistic. Disappointment soon replaced her hope after discovering the only link to her mom's past belonged to a dead guy. Charlie suspected her biological father had a connection to Midwest Energy, but her dad could be anyone.

When Ella visited Hannah's House, her mom would sometimes ask about Jordan or add something clever to a conversation. Jillian's recall regarding her own childhood or Ella as a little girl came much easier than retaining present-day details, so those interactions didn't happen often. Ella planned to show her mom the old image of Mr. Sanders anyway, hoping it might jog her memory and offer a hint to continue the search.

Ella eased the door open, and Jillian's wide smile instantly told her the visit would be a good one.

"Hi," she said.

"Hi, Mom."

"We had pancakes for breakfast."

Whenever Jillian engaged right away, Ella knew her mother's medicine was working.

"Did you put lots of syrup on them?"

Ella tried to keep any dialogue going with her mother, which could mean a lengthy chat on a mundane topic, like pancakes.

"I guess you aren't hungry for *Fleur's* chocolate croissants."

The French bakery held a special place in Ella's heart. When she was younger, her mother often took her there, and simply entering through the front doors brought back a rush of memories. Jillian had an insatiable sweet tooth and passed the trait on to her daughter. Stopping to get a couple of their favorite pastries to share always brightened Ella's day.

"I want one," Jillian said.

"Shall we have coffee with them?"

Her mother nodded.

While Ella was in the visitor's kitchen filling the two mugs for her and her mom, Nurse Amanda approached her.

"Can I talk with you?"

"Sure. What's up?" Ella asked.

The smell of dark roasted beans always made Hannah's House seem like a home, making Ella feel like she was providing her mother with the very best care.

"It's probably nothing to worry about, but I'm concerned that your mother isn't feeling well. She can't really communicate, but her physical responses make me wonder if she's experiencing pain. I wanted you to be aware so you could mention it to the doctor."

"Thank you for telling me."

"With dementia it isn't uncommon to miss a secondary diagnosis."

Amanda had her finger on the pulse regarding everyone at Hannah's House, and Ella appreciated her insight.

Ella returned to her mother's room to enjoy the croissants and whatever conversation Jillian could offer. The end of their visit seemed like the perfect time to bring up the subject of the mystery man in the picture.

"Mom, I want to show you a photo from a few years ago."

Ella took the clipping from a Ziplock bag and put it in her mother's hands. Jillian raised it to her eyes and squinted for a closer look.

"Do you know those people?" Ella asked.

"No," Jillian said as her face flushed.

"It's you and Cameron Sanders. Do you remember Mr. Sanders from your days at Midwest Energy?"

"Charlie?" Jillian asked.

"No. It's someone named Cameron Sanders. The two of you worked together back in 1991."

"Cam."

"Did you call him Cam?"

Jillian seemed to have some recollection of her old co-worker.

"Cam," repeated Jillian as she became agitated. "He's coming for me today."

Ella didn't want to distress her mother and silently wondered if it had been a good idea to show her the picture. She stuffed it back into her purse and planned to try and find out more the next time she visited.

"I'm heading out. I'll see you tomorrow. I love you," Ella said, trying to diffuse her mother's anxiety by leaving.

"I want to see Cam." Jillian rose from her chair. "We're getting married."

"Mom, Cameron isn't here."

Jillian looked frantic and started toward the exit.

"I need Cam . . ." Jillian said.

"He's not here. Let's get you to your recliner."

Ella made it to the door before her mother and hit the call button.

"What's going on?" an alarmed Amanda asked, charging through the door.

"Mom won't calm down."

Jillian continued to try and push her way to the exit, and the nurse was barely able to hold her back.

"Jillian, it's okay. Let's get some ice cream, and then we'll find a show to watch on television," Amanda suggested, redirecting her patient.

"Is she like this often?"

This side of her mother's illness frightened Ella.

"Sometimes when those with Alzheimer's get upset, they try to flee the situation. Did something happen between the two of you?"

"I showed her a picture of a person she used to work with."

Her mother's reaction shook Ella, but it confirmed that Cameron Sanders held a crucial piece of the puzzle she was trying to put together.

***

"Hi, Aunt Eloise. How are you?"

After the exchange with her mother, Ella needed to talk to her aunt.

"I'm fine. Is everything all right with Jillian?"

"She's doing okay. But I'm not calling about Mom—I have something else to discuss with you concerning my father."

"I'll help in any way I can, but I already told you that your mother didn't confide in me, and I doubt I'll have anything to offer."

"At least hear me out. Do you remember Cameron Sanders?" Ella asked. "He worked with Mom at Midwest Energy Corporation. I found a newspaper article showing the two of them together. They won an award in the early nineties."

"I do recall a dinner at the MEC headquarters in Spencer, but I never saw a news story of any kind."

"It ran in Spencer's local paper. Does this guy, Cameron, ring any bells with you? They surely knew each other if they appeared in a photo for the same company."

"The name does sound familiar."

"I showed it to Mom yesterday, and she got very upset. She called him Cam and said they were getting married."

"Have you Googled him? Maybe he could put you in touch with your mother's friends from back in the day. *They* might know who your father is," Eloise suggested.

"I did Google him, and I tried to contact his wife through Facebook. Her name is Maggie, and she said that she couldn't help me because he died a few weeks ago."

"You contacted his wife?"

Ella heard the concern in her aunt's voice.

"I messaged her last week, but Mom's odd response today motivated me to do more investigation and revisit Maggie's social media account. She posts lots of photos of her kids, and guess who is the spitting image of their daughter?"

"What are you talking about? Can you forward one to me?"

Ella went to her photos and sent a screenshot to Eloise.

"Oh my," her aunt said upon seeing the picture. "She could be your . . ."

"My sister, right?"

Ella looked exactly like Mallory Sanders.

"It's obvious who Cameron Sanders is."

"Tell me what his wife said to you," Eloise implored.

"She doesn't want to tell me anything. Period."

"If this man *is* your dad, she might not have a clue that he fathered a kid outside their marriage."

"Or the timing is bad for her. I swear to you, Maggie Sanders holds the key to everything. I wouldn't have to bother her children if she'd give me something to use for a paternity test."

"Her *children*? Oh, Ella. You're getting way ahead of yourself. Please don't contact this man's kids," Eloise begged.

"Hurting this family is the last thing I want to do. But I've lived with this lie for thirty years, and I deserve to know the truth. Is my happiness less important than theirs?" Ella asked.

"You should leave this alone. At least for a few months.

Let the Sanders wade through their anguish before you try to find out more."

"Do you remember me telling you that we went to the Felicia Carmichael show for my birthday?"

"Of course. I only wish it hadn't spiraled you off into this drama."

"Maybe Felicia's ability to talk to the dead isn't as crazy as it seems. She said I'd recently lost a male figure in my life with the initial 'C' in his name. I thought she meant Charlie Meyers, but what if Cameron Sanders is the man she connected with? What if my father—my *real* father—tried to reach out to me from beyond the grave so I would dig deeper into all of this?"

"Oh, honey. Now the hairs are raised on the back of my neck. Promise me you'll slow down and not go any further with this."

Ella didn't answer.

"Will you at least give me a little bit of time to do my *own* research? Let me see if I can come up with anyone else who might be able to make sense of this," Eloise pleaded.

"You have two weeks, and no longer."

CHAPTER 24
Maggie

Maggie stared at the ceiling, contemplating another day without her soul mate. She hadn't slept well, awakened by a nightmare where she couldn't recall what Cam looked like. Once Maggie calmed down, his face came into focus, but the fear he might slip from her memory panicked her.

The sound of Wrigley's faint snoring let her know at least one of them didn't have any trouble snoozing. The dog's head on Cam's pillow proved he'd finally accepted his duties as man of the house, and Maggie was grateful for his companionship.

In the first days after Cam's death, Wrigley searched everywhere for his best friend. No one else noticed, but Maggie knew her dog, and his canine instincts sensed the loss. Maggie tried to communicate Cam's passing to her pet in soft words and kind touch. When she cried, Wrigley licked the tears on her face as if he could tell she needed him.

Maggie continued to ruminate over the email she'd received from Ella Daley, which only further disrupted her sleep. Why had she been so impulsive, firing off a reply without thinking and regretting it ever since?

The message from Jillian Meyers's daughter left Maggie in turmoil. After finding Ella's Facebook page and clicking on it, Maggie had gasped when she saw the young woman's profile picture. The face staring back at her looked very familiar. Ella was a carbon copy of Mallory, with a hint of Cam's deceased mother coming through her features too.

After checking Ella's personal information, Maggie noted that her birthday fell just weeks after Erin's. She started piecing things together; it didn't take a brain surgeon to figure out what Ella wanted. Maggie closed her eyes, rubbing her temples as the harsh reality sank in.

Every action had its consequences, and now the undeniable truth of Cam's affair had surfaced, and her name was Ella Daley.

Did Cam come clean to Maggie about the relationship with Jillian but keep his daughter with her hidden? Regardless of Cam's culpability, doubting him as he lay in the grave felt disrespectful.

Jillian almost ruined Maggie's life years earlier, and she had no allegiance to this Ella person. She didn't like playing God with the secrets she held. Still, Ella mentioned her mother had Alzheimer's, and her plight pulled at Maggie's heart. If she *was* Cam's child, how could she deny her?

Her thoughts swirled as she weighed the outcomes of getting involved. Torn between opposing sides of her conscience, Maggie didn't know which part of herself to trust.

***

The twins arrived late Friday afternoon. Maggie had volunteered to watch them while Mallory and Tom got away, and it pleased her to know the kids were asking for her help again.

"Are you sure this won't be too much for you?" Mallory questioned, unloading the girls' bags.

"Of course not."

Maggie looked forward to having something else to think of besides loneliness and long-lost daughters of dead husbands.

"Let's plan to go out to dinner on Sunday when we return. We'll treat you," Mallory offered.

"That's nice of you, but not necessary. I'm doing fine."

"How can you be doing fine?"

"I don't really have a choice."

"Are you telling me the truth? Because I'm a mess and miss Dad more than anything, and that's why we want a weekend to ourselves."

"Oh, honey. If only I could take your pain away," Maggie sympathized. "A couple of nights away will be good for both of you."

As Maggie hugged her daughter, she prayed that Tom would have the strength to carry Mallory through such a difficult time.

***

"Can I break the eggs?" Brenna asked.

"The recipe calls for two, so you can crack one, and Callie can do the other," Maggie said, gathering the ingredients for chocolate chip cookies.

"Can Grandpa see us cooking in the kitchen?" Callie wondered aloud.

176

A lump rose in Maggie's throat as her eyes filled. She turned away from her baking partners, wiping her hands on a towel as she regained her composure.

"I'm sure he can," Maggie said. "He loved you both, and he'll always look down on you from heaven."

Losing Cam in such a tragic way had shaken Maggie's faith, leading her to question whether an afterlife existed. Despite her uncertainty, she wanted Callie and Brenna to believe in something to help them cope with their grandpa's loss.

"Mommy told us that Grandpa stays in our room at night and watches over us," Callie said.

"Sometimes she cries because she misses him, and Dad says we have to give her time alone," added Brenna.

The awareness of Mallory's grief hit Maggie hard. Overwhelmed with her own sorrow, she hadn't reached out to the kids as much as she should have. The responsibility of being their only living parent intensified the burden of everything else piled on Maggie's shoulders, and she chastised herself for not doing better.

"Your mommy, Uncle Mason, and Aunt Erin are sad because their daddy isn't here anymore. We have to spend lots of time together and make each other happy again. That's what Grandpa Cam would want."

The girls wrapped their arms around Maggie's waist.

"Our mom says hugs are the best medicine," Brenna said.

"She is a smart one," Maggie whispered to her little loves.

Mallory still made her kindergartners nap on the weekends, and Maggie welcomed the afternoon break.

She'd read a chapter of her book before footsteps on the front porch interrupted the story. Until the bell rang, she thought the UPS man was delivering a new yoga mat ordered from Amazon.

Maggie rushed toward the door, determined to keep Callie and Brenna from waking up. They were light sleepers, and Maggie wanted more time to herself. In her haste, she opened the door without looking through the peep hole and found a middle-aged woman standing on her threshold.

"May I help you?"

She appeared harmless, but Maggie knew living alone meant she needed to be more cautious.

"Are you Maggie Sanders?" the woman asked.

"Yes . . ."

Maggie could see the car in the driveway had a Polk County license plate, and she searched her mental archives to identify the person in front of her.

"I'm Jillian Meyers's sister, Eloise."

The color drained from Maggie's face, and she stepped outside and closed the door.

"I'm sorry to show up uninvited," the lady continued.

"How did you find my address?" Maggie asked, her heart pounding.

"I found it online. My niece recently discovered the man she'd been told was her dad, is not her biological father. She's been researching people in her mother's life from thirty years ago and came up with your husband's name as a possible link. Ella shared with me that you informed her of his death, but I'd like to discuss this with you further," Eloise said.

"Listen, this isn't a good time. My grandchildren are here until tomorrow, and I don't want to get into this with them here."

"Tell me one thing. Did Cameron have a romantic relationship with my sister?"

"I can't do this right now," Maggie reiterated.

"The fact that you didn't say *no* says it all. Can you meet me after your family leaves? If you promise to talk with me, I'll stay the night in Spencer."

Discouraging Eloise seemed unlikely.

"Okay," Maggie said, folding to the pressure. "There's a diner called The Hitching Post on the edge of town. It's quiet and the coffee is hot. Let's say 3:00. I'm sorry it has to be so late in the afternoon, but the kids will be with me most of the day."

"Thank you. You have no idea what this means to me," Eloise replied, her voice full of relief.

Something had lodged in the pit of Maggie's stomach after seeing Ella's picture on social media. She knew the risks of getting sucked into the drama, but Maggie needed to find out more. What would she tell the lady? The stakes were high, and she'd already lost so much.

***

Leaving Spencer and taking the girls to the lake house for a sleepover provided the perfect escape from another possible run-in with Ella's Aunt Eloise.

Maggie waved to her granddaughters when the Tilt-a-Whirl swung them close enough for their faces to light up at the sight of her. Her own children had adored Arnold's Park when they were younger, and the charm of the old-fashioned amusement complex stirred memories of pink cotton candy and summer days filled with laughter.

"Grandma, can we get funnel cakes?" Brenna asked after walking unsteadily from the carnival attraction.

"My tummy doesn't feel good," Callie moaned from behind her sister.

"I can understand that. The attendant allowed you to go several times in a row, but it's time to leave now."

The park wasn't busy, so they'd ridden everything at least once. But Grandma was tired and wanted to get her overnight guests home.

"Let's skip the funnel cakes," Maggie continued. "I promised you a marshmallow roast before bed, and you've already had more than enough sugar for one day."

Maggie led the girls toward an exit as the clanking of the roller coaster hammered at her senses. The train of cars climbed the rickety wooden slats until a dozen thrill seekers released their fear in a chorus of screams. The tangle of tracks with its mounting hills and hairpin turns reminded Maggie of life; just when you started having fun, the ride screeched to a halt.

After baths and bedtime, Maggie reflected on her dilemma. She thought of the challenges she and Cam had overcome, with his lies echoing through her memories. Maggie had made peace with his betrayal earlier in their marriage, but her heart never forgot.

If she chose to ignore Ella's inquiries, she couldn't guarantee that Cam's affair might not come to light in the future. What if Ella came snooping around after Maggie's death, and the kids never had the benefit of understanding what happened from either of their parents' perspectives?

Even though Maggie's religious convictions were on shaky ground, she recalled the words of her wise old Grandpa Anderson, 'When in doubt, look up.' She needed help from a higher power, so she bowed her head and prayed for clarity.

CHAPTER 25
Ella

Ella sat close to her mother while Dr. Reynolds conducted her examination.

"Jillian, how have you been feeling?" the physician inquired as if her patient could judge the status of her health.

"Fine," Jillian answered.

"Have you spoken to Amanda? She thinks Mom is having difficulties she's unable to express."

"Yes, I read in her chart that the nursing staff suspects something is amiss. I've ordered tests, and I'm hopeful we'll have the results back soon."

"Do you have any idea what it might be?" Ella asked.

"Many things can occur with Alzheimer's. Often, a person remains well for a while, but they can fail quickly. It's traumatic for the body when brain changes take place. Patients can have difficulty swallowing, maintaining balance, and controlling their bowel and bladder functions."

Each day, Ella saw her mother struggle. If she'd known how fast the disease would take over, she wouldn't have waited so long to seek the truth about her dad.

"Bloodwork should clarify the issue," the doctor continued.

"Thank you, Dr. Reynolds. I'll look forward to your call so that we can find out what she needs to feel better."

After the exam, Ella stayed for another hour. Jillian did little more than doze in her chair. She hated to wake her up, but Ella had to leave.

"Mom, there's something I want to tell you."

Ella knew her news would not be acknowledged in the way she'd always dreamed of, but she needed the moment with her mother anyway, even before she told Jordan.

"I'm pregnant. I know you can't remember how you always wanted a grandchild, but now you're getting one."

When Jillian turned fifty, Ella enlisted her mother's closest friends to help plan a birthday bash. The women in Jillian's life had formed a family of widows and divorcees, and they never let the opportunity for a party pass them by.

The ladies traveled to various midwestern casinos and scored free nights and other perks, thanks to two in the group who loved to gamble.

Ella's mom didn't like to waste money and never spent much on those girls' trips. But she gladly ate the comped dinners and stayed in the hotel suites her gal pals earned from playing the slots, and the idea of combining a gaming trip with her birthday seemed like a good one.

The festivities for Jillian would take place at the Prairie Meadows casino near Des Moines, and an additional treat was that Ella and Jillian's sister, Eloise, were joining them. When the date rolled around, the two stood outside a private room, secretly listening to everything.

"Jillian, we have another surprise for you," they heard one of the invitees say.

"More surprising than taking me across the Minnesota border to play the one-armed bandits?" Jillian joked.

Ella and Eloise came bouncing through the doors with noise makers and bottles of bubbly.

"Happy birthday, Mom!"

Jillian looked shocked.

"I thought you had tests next week," questioned Jillian.

Ella was a sophomore at UNI, and midterms were coming up in a few days.

"There isn't anything that would keep me from seeing you on your big day."

"And Eloise, you said you had plans this weekend," Jillian said.

Ella had included her aunt in the celebration. Even if she and Jillian weren't close, Eloise couldn't be left out.

"Sis, you've had a great five decades, but they say fifty is the new forty. So, what are you wishing for when you blow out all these candles?" Eloise asked.

"There's only one thing I want that I haven't experienced yet," reflected Jillian. "I'm just waiting to be a grandma."

"Mom, you've been talking about grandchildren since I was in junior high school. I'm only twenty. Can you let me get my bachelor's degree and meet the man of my dreams before you start pestering me to have kids?"

Everyone laughed, and Jillian shut her eyes and blew hot wax across the top of the beautifully decorated dessert.

"I'm giving you five years," Jillian teased.

Ella heard a commotion in the hallway signaling dinner time. It was only 4:30 p.m., but they ate supper early at

Hannah's House. Meals and sleep kept the day moving in a care facility.

"I'll help you to your table on my way out."

Jillian didn't answer, but Ella hugged her shoulders.

"You would have made such a wonderful grandma," she whispered.

***

Ella had a very regular menstrual cycle. A missed period the first month after she and Jordan started trying for a baby roused her excitement. Her annual physical fell during the same week, so she hadn't bothered with an at-home test. Ella didn't want to get Jordan's hopes up for no reason, so she'd kept the possibility to herself.

She had routine bloodwork done before her exam, and when Dr. Brown came into the tiny room to greet her, the grin on his face said everything.

"Well, it looks like I need to congratulate you."

"Really? I thought we'd have more time. My mom isn't well, and . . ." Ella said through happy tears.

"And now you have something exciting to look forward to, along with caring for your mother," he interjected. "Let's get your regular physical out of the way, and then I'll refer you to a good OBGYN."

Jordan had to work on the day of her appointment, so Ella had ample time to assemble a gift she would give the father-to-be. She'd been thinking of a way to share the news for weeks, just in case. On her way home from Hannah's House, Ella stopped to get the items needed to craft an expectant father's survival kit.

185

***

"Ella? It's Dr. Reynolds calling from Hannah's House."

It had been less than twenty-four hours since Jillian's visit with the doctor, and Ella hoped the timely results didn't mean there was a problem.

"Is Mom's bloodwork back already?" she asked.

"We have our own lab, so the findings come in quickly. Jillian's panels show signs of a urinary tract infection. I'll order a prescription, and we'll get her well in no time."

Although not serious, the diagnosis reminded Ella that her mother's health would always be a concern. With the immediate scare set aside, Ella returned her attention to putting Jordan's gift together.

She started with a bucket from the hardware store. She'd printed a label reading "New Daddy" and attached it with adhesive. Ella filled the pail with pink and blue tissue paper. She added a *Best Dad Ever* coffee mug, earplugs, air freshener, baby wipes, a pacifier, ibuprofen, and a bottle of Buffalo Trace. Before long, it looked better than the one she'd copied off Pinterest.

She left it for Jordan on the dining room table and went on with her night.

Jordan's shift ended at 8:00 a.m., and the garage door opened thirty minutes later. Ella heard him putting the extra drinks he'd taken for work into the outside refrigerator. Finally, he entered the house and passed by the surprise without saying a word.

"Good morning, you're up early. How did your day go yesterday?"

"It was pretty uneventful," Ella lied. "I saw the doctor in the afternoon and then went to see Mom."

"How's Jillian doing?"

"The tests showed a UTI, but she'll be fine in a few days. Is that all you have to say?"

She stared at Jordan, willing him to understand.

"What's up? You look like the cat who ate the canary."

"You didn't see anything unusual when you came in?"

"No. What are you talking about?"

Jordan looked confused.

"You need to turn around and go back in there."

Jordan obeyed his wife and returned to the dining room.

"What? Really? You're pregnant?" He hurried back and scooped Ella into a big hug. "Didn't you think it would take longer?"

"You must know what you're doing," Ella joked. "There's a lot going on with Mom, but she could live another ten years. We can't delay our plans to have a family until she's gone. I'll need your help to care for a child *and* an aging parent, but I know we can do it."

"You've got it, babe." Jordan couldn't hide his exuberance. "I think it's a girl, and if it is, I want to name her after our moms."

Ella didn't feel the same way. Hurt and resentment were clouding her attitude toward her mother.

"Rosalind is a lot to go with Jillian," Ella said, giving Jordan another tight hug.

Weeks after Jillian's diagnosis, Jordan's mother passed away suddenly. Losing his mom had been sad, but Ella considered Jordan fortunate to be spared the emotional toll of the long goodbye of Alzheimer's disease.

"Maybe we could call her Rosalind Jill, and she could go by Rosie," Ella suggested.

"Or Elizabeth Rose, since Elizabeth is your given name and your mom's middle name, and Rose for my mother? And if it's a boy, how about William—after my dad?"

Jordan spoke the words just as he realized the sting his comment had for Ella.

"We'd have to come up with something random to honor *my* father."

"Ella, I'm sorry. I didn't mean to bring up your dad again. We'll find the right name when the time comes. Can you believe we got pregnant so fast?" he asked, changing the subject away from Ella's paternity.

"I guess it's meant to be."

Ella placed a hand on her stomach, wondering how long it would be before she started to show.

CHAPTER 26

Maggie

"Girls, we're back!"

Thankfully, Mallory and Tom arrived on time to pick up the girls. Maggie had an important meeting to attend, and she didn't want to be late.

"We baked cookies, and Grandma said we could take them home," Callie told her dad, handing him a plastic container.

Tom opened the tub, gobbling one of the sweets without hesitation.

"Yummy. Grandma Maggie has the best chocolate chip cookie recipe."

"I enjoyed having the girls here," Maggie said. "We had a wonderful time."

"I caught a fish from the dock," Brenna bragged. "And Grandma and Callie didn't catch any."

"You went out to the lake?" Mallory asked.

"I thought the girls might enjoy it."

Maggie didn't give further explanation for why they'd left Spencer in a hurry.

"Do you still want to grab something to eat before we leave?" Tom asked. "I'd love to treat my favorite mother-in-law to a late lunch."

"It isn't necessary. I'm not very hungry, and I'm sure you need to get home."

Maggie had forgotten that they'd made tentative plans on Friday. She hated to rush Mallory and the others off, but she had two hours to prepare for her conversation with Eloise, and her nerves were frazzled.

"I can't bear to think of you eating alone every day."

"I have friends, and Kimberly visits. Believe me, I keep busy."

On any other day, Maggie would have loved spending the afternoon with her oldest daughter and her family.

"Really, Mom? Because I have no idea how to go on without Dad."

Mallory's eyes brimmed with tears.

"Oh, honey," Maggie said, embracing her.

Maggie would provide more support for the kids moving forward, but their well-being would have to wait. Everyone's future hung in the balance, though only Maggie knew it.

"We'll get together soon," Maggie suggested, rushing them out the door.

Tom rolled two Disney Princess suitcases to the car, while Maggie gave hugs.

"Love you," Callie called out.

"I love you too. Goodbye."

"Come to Ankeny next weekend. The twins have a soccer game, and we could go to this new little brunch spot downtown," Mallory begged.

"I'll have to look at the calendar," Maggie said, hoping she remembered to check later.

"Promise me you're doing as well as you appear," she

said.

"I'm fine."

Grief came in waves. Sometimes, it gently washed over her, allowing Maggie to wade through her sorrow without being overwhelmed. At other times, despair crashed into her like a tsunami, knocking her down and dragging her below the surface. Still, she didn't need to burden Mallory with her inner struggles when her daughter couldn't do anything to ease the pain.

Maggie blew kisses toward the car as it pulled out of the driveway. She had time before meeting Eloise, and she wanted to study Ella's Facebook page again. Looking at the photos of that familiar face on social media would give Maggie courage to do the right thing.

***

Maggie arrived at the diner early, hoping to choose a table away from the crowd. Eloise must have had the same thought because she'd already tucked herself into a corner booth before Maggie came through the door.

"Hi," Maggie said, sliding in across from her.

The place smelled like coffee and fried food.

"Hello. I wasn't sure you'd show up."

Maggie sensed Eloise's nervousness, and it made her more anxious.

"Do you want to order something?" the server asked, standing next to the ladies with a note pad at the ready.

"I'll have an iced tea," Maggie answered.

Eloise had a soft drink in front of her, and Maggie wondered how long she'd been there.

"Will the two of you need menus?"

Eating was the last thing on Maggie's mind.

"I'm okay," said Eloise.

"Me too," Maggie agreed, happy she didn't have to share a meal with this stranger.

The women exchanged pleasantries until the waitress returned with Maggie's beverage.

"How can I help you?" Maggie asked, squeezing lemon into her tea and cutting to the chase.

They were not there to forge a friendship, and Maggie wanted to do what had to be done and go home.

"The past couple of years haven't been easy," Eloise began. "My sister started showing signs of dementia, and it progressed quickly after the diagnosis. She lives in a memory unit now."

"I can sympathize with anyone who has to go through the process of taking care of a loved one with that terrible disease," Maggie said, remembering her own mother's battle.

"Hi, Grandma," Mallory said. "I brought you a piece of cake from my birthday party. I'm sixteen now."

She handed her Grandma Anderson a paper plate covered with Saran Wrap, and the elderly woman smiled.

"Thank you. I love chocolate cake with white frosting."

"How are you today?" Maggie asked.

Maggie tried to visit her mom often, but sometimes the kids' activities got in the way of her good intentions.

"We played cards after lunch, and I took a nice nap."

When their mother's memory decline became too serious to manage alone, Maggie and Kimberly moved her into the best nursing home available. The Alzheimer's came twenty-two months after Maggie's father died from lung cancer. They were convinced exposure to farm pesticides had caused their parents' rapid deterioration, but all they could do was take care of them.

"Dad rented a boat, and I got to invite five friends to spend the night. We spent the day at Lake Okoboji and then ordered pizza. We had so much fun, except Erin kept sneaking in—trying to eavesdrop. My little sister is such a pest," Mallory told her grandmother.

Until Erin came along, Mallory had been the only granddaughter to spoil, and she had always been close to her grandma. Before the older kids got into high school, they stayed part of each summer at the farm. Mallory learned how to can tomatoes while Mason fed livestock and baled hay.

Marie Anderson hadn't been the warmest of mothers to Maggie and her sister, but she took delight in the role of a loving grandma.

"Why don't you go to the car, and I'll help Grandma to dinner."

"Don't forget, I've got softball practice," Mallory reminded her.

She bounced out of the room to wait for her mother.

"I wonder what you're having for supper?" Maggie asked as they walked down the corridor.

"It's usually something tasty."

Maggie's mother always had a pleasant demeanor, despite her advancing disease.

"I'll be back soon," Maggie promised.

"Before you go, can you answer a question?"

"Of course," Maggie said.

"The pretty girl that was here . . . I can't remember who she is."

Maggie's heart dropped, and she put her arm around her mother's shoulders.

"She's your granddaughter. Her name is Mallory."

"At this point, there's nothing I can do for Jillian," Eloise continued. "If I could comfort my niece by giving her hope of finding out who her father is, I think it would help her cope with everything better. Did I mention Ella is pregnant too?"

Maggie empathized with the young woman Eloise described.

"Jillian married a man named Charlie Meyers, and Ella was born while they were together. No one suspected he wasn't her biological dad. I'm her sister, and she never mentioned anything to me."

Maggie saw the concern on Eloise's face as she continued the story.

"Jillian and Charlie divorced right around the time Ella turned five. He never paid child support and didn't see Ella again. I grew to hate him for what I *thought* he put my sister through. It turns out I'd been blaming the wrong person. Ella got in touch with Charlie and showed up on his doorstep, demanding answers about why he'd run out on her."

Maggie was engrossed in the suspense.

"Charlie told Ella that during the split, he found out that he was not Ella's real father. After that, he left and never contacted them again, but he assumed my sister would tell Ella the truth when she got old enough. For some reason, Jillian never revealed this to any of us."

"How does this swing around to include my deceased husband?" Maggie asked, squelching the feeling in her gut.

Maggie didn't know Jillian Meyers. She didn't want to pass judgment on her, but Cam may not have been her only indiscretion. Ella's Facebook photo bore a striking similarity to others in the Sanders family, but it could be nothing more than coincidence.

"Ella said that Charlie thought the guy might have worked with her mother. He suggested trying to find an old friend of Jillian's who might know more. I've already told you I didn't have an inkling, and Ella's research on the friend only uncovered the gal's obituary."

"How did Ella come up with Cam's name?"

"When she cleaned out Jillian's house in Des Moines, she came across a newspaper article showing your husband and her mother receiving an award back in the nineties. She wanted to look for Cameron to see if he remembered her mother or anyone in her social circle. She showed it to her mom first, and even in Jillian's state of mind, she had such an emotional reaction to the photo that Ella knew she'd stumbled onto something. I'm sorry to tell you this because it makes Ella sound like a stalker, but she found you on Facebook and noticed how much she resembled your daughter."

The likeness between Mallory and Ella had *not* been Maggie's imagination.

"After you said you wouldn't help her, I took it upon myself to step in and ask you to reconsider. I'm begging you . . . *please* . . . for the sake of my niece. I'm angry that Jillian kept this from us, but I can't hold someone accountable who can't answer my questions, so I'm choosing to replace my anger with action."

Maggie respected Eloise's commitment to Ella, but she'd decided to tread carefully with the information she disclosed.

"I'll admit to you that my husband and Jillian had an affair. It was a painful time, so you'll have to excuse me if I'm reluctant. I wasn't aware of the relationship for a long time, and we shared many good years after that. Our marriage did have its troubles, but I have three grown children, and I want them to remember their father as the man of integrity they admired. The infidelity had nothing to do with our kids. I need your word if I involve myself, and Ella's too, that this will be held in the strictest confidence."

"I'm not here to hurt anyone, but I want Ella to get the answers she needs."

"What does she *need* from me?"

Ella's objectives were still unclear to Maggie.

"She wants a test to determine if Cameron is her father. Could you give us something that might contain his DNA? If you refuse, I'll return and tell Ella to drop this. I don't want her to suffer further, and if you don't want to get involved, I'll encourage her to accept the reality that she'll never know what happened years ago. Ella has no idea that I'm talking to you today, so I can take this in any direction. Level with me, Maggie. Will you help us? Because you and I hold all the cards to what happens next."

It had been three months since Cam's death, and his blue toothbrush with the crushed bristles still sat in a cup on the bathroom vanity. Maggie had almost thrown it away several times, but something stopped her.

If the DNA test proved Cam was *not* Ella's father, Maggie wouldn't have to worry about this intrusion in their lives again. Like Eloise said, you couldn't carry resentment against someone who had no way to answer your questions, and Cam fit that category too.

One thing kept coming to the forefront; she and Ella deserved to know the truth.

"Come back to the house with me. I have something you can use," Maggie said.

CHAPTER 27
Ella

"You're telling me that since we all got together for your thirtieth birthday, you've seen Charlie Meyers, who is not *really* your dad, and you've gotten pregnant by the hunkiest firefighter in the cities. You've also discovered the name of your real father, but he dropped dead before you found him, and your mother's Alzheimer's is getting worse every day?" Sondra recapped.

She always made serious topics seem more humorous than they were, and Ella didn't mind her friend's light-hearted approach to the recent events. The four women hadn't seen each other since the Felicia Carmichael show, and they had a lot to discuss when they got together for dinner at their favorite Mall of America restaurant.

"That's the highlight reel," Ella joked. "I recommend you join us instead of canceling at the last minute—which you've done two months in a row."

"Are you okay?" Marcy asked her bestie.

"You mean pregnancy-wise? Or are you referring to the other calamities in my life?" Ella asked.

"Let's start with the happy stuff. How's that baby doing?"

"We're excited, and I'm feeling good except for being tired and nauseous. I'm not sure if that's because of this little one or everything else."

"Ella. . . all teasing aside, you and Jordan have juggled so much the past couple of years," Lisa observed. "And now all of this with your dad. Wow."

"I'm trying to take things as they come."

"Are you going to contact the guy's wife about the DNA results?" Marcy asked.

When the packet from Family Tree DNA came in the mail, Ella had waited an hour before looking at the contents. When she ripped open the manilla envelope, and discovered there was a 99.9% probability that Cameron was her father, she felt like she'd finally found the missing piece of herself.

"Maggie Sanders needs to be told, but I have no idea what comes after that."

***

As summer drew to a close, Ella and Jordan took a day to do something fun. With the fall semester just days away, and most of her break consumed by the strain of everything she'd been dealing with, there hadn't been much time to relax.

They woke up early, and Jordan packed sunscreen and a cooler while Ella made sandwiches. She planned to put any stressful thoughts out of her mind and allow herself a carefree day on the water.

Jordan kept the rented pontoon ambling through the wake of a passing speed boat while Ella settled in under the vessel's

Bimini top. The sun reflected off the watercraft's stainless-steel railing, causing her to squint, even behind the tint of her sunglasses.

Ella's stomach was still flat above her black bikini bottoms. When she imagined the baby blossoming inside of her, a maternal instinct began to take root where doubts had lingered. Ella's own strength grew too, born out of the pain from her past and a willingness to open her heart to the future. She had a feeling her relationship with Maggie Sanders would be part of that metamorphosis, and she was ready for it.

"You're pretty quiet over there," Jordan said, keeping his eyes fixed on the water ahead.

"Yeah. I'm thinking about Maggie. This is *not* her fault, and I hate to dump all of this on her when she's still grieving."

"No time is a good time to discover your husband had a child with another woman."

"True, but finding out right after his death would be devastating. What bothers me most is not knowing what I want from all of this. If my dad were alive, I'd ask him questions about his family—*my* family. But . . ."

"Maggie and her children aren't dead. They could tell you a lot."

"If they're willing. I'm afraid they'll all reject me, and then what will I do?"

"Maggie gave you the toothbrush, and she didn't have to. She cares for you, and when she finds out you *are* Cameron's daughter, I have a feeling she'll give you answers."

"Do you think so?"

"They'll love you as much as I do. Well, maybe not *that* much, but they'll adore you."

"I can barely remember you and me before mom got sick and we didn't have so many worries."

"That's who we used to be. No one stays the same, but we can survive anything if we lean on each other when times get tough."

The couple spent the rest of the day on the sun-kissed lake, but Ella couldn't allow herself to fully unwind. Uncertainty churned in her belly, and it wasn't the pregnancy giving her such an unsettled feeling.

Ella and Jordan returned home with pink cheeks and wet towels after being on the water all day.

"I'll meet you in bed after I shower," Jordan said.

"I'm going to send Maggie a quick email, and then I'll come upstairs."

The day's outing had given Ella time to think. She'd been drafting a message to Maggie in her head all afternoon, and if she waited until morning to send it, she knew she wouldn't be able to sleep.

***

The beginning of an academic year always brought excitement. As the students filed in looking scared, Ella tried to ease their fears by calling them each by name and warmly welcoming them to her classroom.

She tired easily because of the pregnancy, and the first day of school started to drain her by lunchtime. She called

Hannah's House over her break to check on her mother and planned to drop by after work. The thought of spending all day teaching and then going to see her mom each day made Ella want to put her head on the desk and take a long nap. Things would intensify if Jillian's condition worsened and a new baby needed her attention as well. Hopefully, it wouldn't be too much for her and Jordan to manage.

As Ella lowered the lights so the class could watch a movie about bird migration, her thoughts wandered to the email hanging out in cyberspace. It had been several days, and Maggie still hadn't responded. What if Ella never heard back from her father's widow?

***

Dr. Reynolds visited residents each week, and Ella hoped she hadn't missed the stop in her mother's room. When the physician came to Jillian's bedside, Ella felt relieved that she was there to get an update on her mom's health.

"It looks like the UTI has cleared up, so that's good. Cases like your mother's are why I decided to become a geriatrician. It's rewarding to treat older people, especially those in facilities like this one."

"Now that I'm back to teaching, it's good to know you're here often, and the wonderful staff watches over her the rest of the time. I'm pregnant, and I'm running a little ragged right now," Ella said.

"Congratulations, what an exciting time. Getting back to your mother, I appreciate you alerting me to the issues she was having so we could get the infection cleared up quickly.

An involved family member can make such a difference in a patient's quality of life."

"That's why I try to come every day. I want to make sure she's okay."

"You need to take care of yourself too. Jillian is fine here, and if you missed a day once in a while, it wouldn't be the end of the world."

"My husband says the same thing."

"Jillian's lucky to have such a caring daughter. Many seniors are abandoned by their children because of life-long conflicts. It's quite common, and I'm glad the two of you have a good relationship."

"She raised me as a single mother, and I owe her everything."

Ella genuinely felt that way toward her mother, despite the secrets between them.

CHAPTER 28
Maggie

Maggie hadn't been to yoga all summer. Taking an exercise class struck her as frivolous, like returning to daily activities would disrespect Cam's memory. She couldn't delay forever, and the day had come to reclaim a small piece of her old life.

Maggie and Cam's church attendance had been sporadic since the kids left home. Covid hadn't helped, and when quarantine restrictions lifted, sleeping late and grabbing an extra cup of coffee on Sunday mornings had become the norm. Yoga became Maggie's spiritual outlet, and she'd missed the feeling of movement and time to center her soul.

She finally had enough composure to handle the condolences her friends would shower upon her. But that readiness did not eliminate Maggie's dread about getting through the first session.

The group had endured several significant losses in the lives of its participants, including the death of one of their instructors from breast cancer. Maggie knew the routine when someone had been gone for a while. Everyone offered hugs and kind words, and then the ladies found their spots in the room to prepare for class. After that initial ten minutes, no one spoke of whatever tragedy had befallen the member again, as if lying on the ground and turning your palms over made it all disappear.

When Maggie walked into the room, they welcomed her with compassion as their leader looked up from queuing music and smiled.

"Good to see you, Maggie," Lanora said.

The attractive, dark-skinned yoga teacher had a toned physique, probably due to genes as much as her strenuous workout habits. Some women were born beautiful, and Lanora fit that description. She could fold her legs into a pretzel and had fun doing it. Maggie envied her flexibility and the life she shared with her anesthesiologist husband. He was still young and alive; Lanora had it all.

Maggie unrolled her new mat and lay flat on the linoleum. The chilly floor brought goosebumps to her arms as meditative music began to fill the room. Pine-Sol tickled her nostrils while the events of the past weeks came to the forefront of her thoughts.

"Let's close our eyes and prepare for practice . . ." Lanora started, her tone even and grounded.

Maggie's body followed the instructions and moved with muscle memory. She'd taken a spot in the back of the room on purpose, and as she went into downward dog, her tears fell onto the mat.

***

Mason and his family came for the weekend. Maggie wasn't up for company, although getting the house ready and preparing food provided a timely diversion.

"Mom, are you keeping the Okoboji house?" Mason asked as they sat on the patio after dinner.

Maggie enjoyed splitting her time between her two homes. If loneliness in one place got to her, she'd stay at the other for a few days until she felt stronger.

"I'm not selling either. Why do you ask?"

"The market is exploding right now, and you'd make a killing on the cottage."

Mason ran a mortgage lending company, and Jenny worked as a realtor. Maggie sensed her son moving into the unnecessary role of financial advisor, appointing himself by virtue of being the eldest.

"Honestly, if I need to sell, I'd lean toward staying at the lake house and living *there* full-time."

"I don't think that's a good idea. What if Jenny and I bought it? Then you wouldn't have the hassle or expense of two properties, and you could stay there whenever you wanted."

Mason's sudden concern for his mother's ability to handle two residences seemed a little self-serving. It felt more like an opportunity for him and Jenny to gain the inside track on waterfront property, and it made Maggie uncomfortable.

"I have no intention of leaving the lake," she said. "I'm sixty-six years old and can afford to take my time with any decisions. They say not to make any major life changes for twelve months following the death of a spouse."

She still adored their home and the town of Spencer, where their family roots ran deep. The kids couldn't begin to understand their mother's draw to some place she'd only owned for a short time, but she could never let it go.

"Who's going to pull the dock out this fall and oversee things during cold weather when you aren't out there?" he asked.

"Mason, we've hired the dock work ever since we've been there. Surely, you didn't think your dad and I hauled that thing out of the lake every year. I want to spend lots of time there this winter. It brings me joy to see the water when it's frozen as much as in the summer."

"Well, I talked with the girls . . . we're worried. Will you have enough money now that Dad's gone?"

"We did our estate planning long ago, and I'm financially secure."

Mason had no idea that instead of being concerned about his mother's bank account, he should be worried about enduring secrets from his parents' marriage. Secrets that could destroy the people he loved.

***

Mason's family left on Sunday afternoon, leaving Maggie alone again. She was looking forward to watching television and going to sleep early, but she was wide awake at bedtime.

She tried to divert her thoughts away from Cam by organizing the pantry. She'd just turned all the labels on the canned goods to the front when she heard a notification on her phone. It worried Maggie to get a message after 9:00 p.m., and she hoped there wasn't an emergency.

When Maggie saw the communication from Ella, she didn't open it immediately. She knew the DNA results were probably back and how the findings could change her life. Waiting would not make any difference to the outcome, so

207

she finished with the kitchen staples and made herself a cup of chamomile tea. The effects of the brew usually helped her fall asleep, but Maggie doubted anything would do the trick once she read Ella's email.

Maggie,

Thank you for meeting with my Aunt Eloise. I am very sorry for any pain this situation has caused you. I'm grateful she talked with you and explained the importance of this to me.

The DNA test came back a few days ago, proving Cameron is my father. I need to decide where to go from here. I'd love to have you fill in some blanks for me, but I understand if you'd rather not.

Please let me know how to proceed. I promise not to contact you again unless I hear back from you.

Ella

Maggie wasn't shocked by the news, even if a part of her hoped the young woman's paternity belonged to another man. Regardless, Ella Daley's existence was as real as Cam's death.

Maggie didn't want Ella to see her father as a philanderer who abandoned her. She owed it to Cam to make sure his daughter understood the wonderful man he was, even though flaws and indiscretions were overshadowing his memory.

Maggie felt protective of the man she'd loved her entire life. She would not allow his frailties to tarnish his posthumous reputation. Now, she'd have the unenviable task of revealing the secrets, doling out the facts for everyone involved.

Maggie needed to get back in touch with Ella. This time, she didn't want to regret shooting off a thoughtless reply. She would confide in someone who could help her resolve the most challenging predicament she'd ever faced and then decide what to say in her response.

***

"What are you doing?" Maggie asked after her sister answered the phone.

"I'm taking an apple pie out of the oven and scrutinizing Dr. Phil's advice to some lady who left her kids alone for the weekend. The bald guy says he's calling CPS."

"I'm sorry I asked . . ." Maggie chirped back. "Any chance you could meet me at the lake for the night? I want to talk to you about something, and I'd like to do it in person."

"Is everything all right? You don't sound good."

"I don't want to discuss it over the phone. Can Dave fend for himself tonight?"

"Give me an hour, and I'll be on the road. Before I head your way, I need to know if you're okay?"

"I'm fine. I'll explain when we see each other."

Maggie packed an overnight bag and pulled a loaf of pumpkin bread out of the freezer. She wasn't sure how many groceries remained after her last visit to the lake, but a full wine rack and plenty of coffee would sustain them.

***

"You're telling me that Cam cheated on you, and it resulted in the birth of a child you knew nothing about. Now, you're considering letting this kid come into your life to get to know your deceased husband through your eyes?" Kimberly asked, draining her Chardonnay and pouring another.

"Well, when you put it that way, it does sound crazy. The kids don't know, and I'm begging you to keep this from Dave and the boys too. I can't do this without at least one other person knowing, and I've chosen you."

"Yes. You definitely need a family member who can identify your body when it washes up on the riverbank and Dateline NBC shows up to do a documentary."

Her younger sister tended to be dramatic, but Maggie understood the concern.

"Pardon my shock here," Kimberly continued, "I'm having difficulty catching up. Why do you seem so calm when this might blow your life apart? What if this girl wants money, or she's a drug addict, and when she gets to your house, she robs you blind or takes you hostage?"

"She teaches third grade and is pregnant with Cam's grandchild. She's none of the things you're implying."

"Well, her mother is a . . ."

"Stop! This is not Ella's fault."

"How can you be this understanding? If this were Dave, I'd already have severed his man parts."

"I'm over the shock and the hurt," Maggie interrupted. "When Cam came to me with this six years ago, it devastated me. I went inside the house and started breaking things. I lost all control of myself. You know how I love that mosaic table Cam built for me when I had Erin?"

"The one sitting next to your reading chair?"

"Yes. It's the most beautiful gift Cam ever gave me. That night, when I realized he'd made it not long after splitting up with his mistress, I threw it against the wall. It smashed into several pieces and made a huge dent in the plaster. I didn't know I had that much strength, and my anger scared me."

The feeling of anguish came rushing back as Maggie remembered.

"Well, you don't seem angry now. How did you put all those emotions aside and not toss Cam to the curb?"

"We had to go through it *alone* because we didn't want anyone else to know. A few weeks into counseling, Cam took me to the garage to show me that he'd rebuilt my cherished table. He reinforced the legs and glued the colorful tiles back in place. The night Cam told me about the affair, I was drinking a cup of tea as we talked on the patio. When he finished telling me about all of this, I got up and knocked my favorite red mug to the ground and shattered it. He'd saved the ceramic fragments and added them to the top of the table in the shape of a heart. It looked perfect again—even better than before. He assured me we could do the same with our relationship, and eventually, I believed him."

"Oh, Maggie. I wish you'd told me. I could have helped you through it."

"Relationships evolve. Spouses who get divorced often fall in love with someone else and remarry, and sometimes that doesn't work out either. I decided if I took another shot at having the marriage I'd always wanted, I'd have the best chance of success if I did it with Cam. At least I knew what I was getting with him."

"You simply started over?"

Kimberly seemed to have difficulty wrapping her head around the story.

"You're just finding this out, but I've had years to process it. I've moved past the betrayal, and you need to do the same. Knowing about Ella is something different. Cam didn't mention a child. I'm choosing to believe he was clueless, because otherwise, it means there were more lies that Cam never admitted to."

"And this *woman* never shared the truth with anyone in her family, including the daughter she conceived with your husband?"

Kimberly kept going over the details as if she thought repeating them would make it easier to accept.

"Help me decide what to do. Should I get together with Ella in a public place and let her ask me questions? Or invite her to the house where I can feel Cam leading me in what to say?"

"Meet this gal at a rest area on I-35, give her the necessary answers, and change your name and phone number. Don't bring this stranger into your home," Kimberly warned.

Maggie sighed, knowing what she had to do.

CHAPTER 29
Ella

Ella opened Maggie's email with trepidation. Although grateful to have something back from her father's wife, fear for what the contents might reveal twisted in her stomach. Five days had passed since she'd told Maggie that the test proved Cameron Sanders *was* her father. Every day that she didn't hear back made her feel more insecure about what was going to happen.

Ella,

Thanks for allowing me time to collect my thoughts. You are right, this has been difficult. I did know about Cameron and your mother but was unaware you were born from that relationship. My heart tells me that my husband would have been in your life had he known about you. It's hard to accept those we love as imperfect human beings, but we don't have a choice.

I'd like to invite you to spend an afternoon at my lake house. I'll show you pictures of your father's side of the family and answer any questions you might have.

Maggie

She closed the message by adding her complete contact information so the two women could begin communicating outside the internet. It gave Ella hope that she'd finally get some resolution.

***

The biting October air demanded a coat, despite full sunshine and a cloudless sky. The irony of the weather reminded Ella that things weren't always what they seemed, and uncertainty kept her excitement at bay. Ella doubted this woman she'd never met posed any threat to her, still, uneasiness lingered. Maggie held the key to unlocking the mystery of who Ella's father was, so she had no choice but to put her hesitations aside to uncover those truths.

Ella sat in front of the lake house for a minute, aware that her life would change once she crossed the home's threshold. She was caught off guard when Maggie opened the door and waved her in before she'd had a chance to get out of the car.

"Hi, I'm Ella," she said when Maggie greeted her.

A shaggy pooch appeared from another part of the house, standing on his hind legs and resting his paws on her growing middle.

"This is Wrigley," Maggie said. "I guess he's the welcoming committee."

A sweet aroma came from inside, and knowing Maggie had baked something for them to share began to ease Ella's apprehensions.

"Hey, good boy," Ella said, scratching behind Wrigley's ears as he sniffed her and wagged his tail.

"Do you like animals?" Maggie asked.

The introduction felt awkward, and talking about Wrigley seemed like the safest starting point between two people who didn't know each other.

"Of course."

"Cam adored dogs and loved the Chicago Cubs, so the name Wrigley fit."

Ella wondered if she'd inherited some of her interests from the genes of her biological father, even though she was a Minnesota Twins fan.

"Let me take your jacket, and we'll sit down. I made a lemon bundt cake and it's fresh from the oven. Would you like coffee or iced tea to go with it?" Maggie asked as the women entered the house.

"I'd take some water."

Ella followed Maggie as she led her into the dining room. Memories of a father Ella would never fully know covered the table.

"I brought photo albums," Maggie said, presenting the pile of pictures like a precious gift. "You must have lots of questions, and I'll do my best to answer them. Go ahead and look, and I'll get the refreshments."

Before Ella finished flipping through the first album, Maggie returned with dessert.

"You knew about my mom and your husband?"

There was no easy place to start this conversation, so she jumped right in.

"Yes, however, I didn't know while it was going on. Something unrelated happened several years ago, and it opened the lines of communication between Cam and me. That's when he told me he'd had an affair with your mother."

"What a confession to make."

"I'm afraid we wouldn't be sitting here today if we hadn't worked hard to fight our way through the heartache. I chose to stay with Cam, but trusting him again didn't come easily."

"How did you forgive him?"

Ella needed all the forgiveness advice she could get.

"Well, when you're a mother, there's no limit to what you will do to protect your family. I couldn't walk away when our children and grandchildren were depending on us. Before I had Erin, I dealt with undiagnosed depression and anxiety. I'm not saying those issues gave my husband the right to have an affair, but at the time, they did contribute to our problems. Nothing is ever black and white, and blame is plentiful, even if it isn't equally distributed."

"I'm pregnant with our first child and already feel responsible for the happiness of this little one. It changes everything, doesn't it?"

"It certainly does. Congratulations, your first pregnancy is so exciting."

"My husband, Jordan, will be a wonderful dad. That brings me to why I'm here. I want to know all there is to know about my father."

"I'm afraid I won't be able to do Cam's persona justice. He has a mark against him since you know about the cheating. I realize it's a significant blemish on an otherwise spotless life record, and we can't brush it aside."

Ella respected *and* questioned Maggie's devotion to a husband who betrayed her.

"It's so odd to see a resemblance to strangers, because it doesn't feel like I fit in this family. I've never had a sibling, but I thought sharing genes with people would give me a sense of belonging.”

“The two of *us* aren’t related, but I’m drawn to you since you’re a part of someone I love. I don’t think personal connections are ever a given. You have to work at relationships, and they’re always a two-way street.”

“These baby pictures are similar to ones my mother saved of me.”

“You and Mallory look the most alike, but here . . . I want you to see a photo of Cam’s mom. You have her profile.”

Maggie pulled a tattered picture from under a yellowed plastic cover and handed it to Ella.

“I can see it. Is that Cam’s dad standing by her?”

“Yes. We named Mason after him, and Hazel was Cam’s mother. She had several husbands, and the only thing that stopped her from getting married again was a heart attack,” Maggie joked, hoping Ella didn’t think her too flippant.

“Isn’t it strange? Both my father and his mother died without warning.”

“I guess you kids will have to let your doctors know of the history,” Maggie warned.

For the next few hours, Maggie shared stories about Cam and their family and showed Ella pictures spanning seven decades. She also told Ella about her three half-siblings.

“I can’t believe I have sisters and a brother,” Ella affirmed as if the reality of her father’s identity had finally sunk in.

“Yes, we had two girls and a boy. Mason is the oldest,

followed by Mallory and then Erin.”

“There’s quite a gap between the older kids and Erin. She looks like she’s about my age. How hard was it to have children at such different stages in life?”

“Erin was a complete surprise. We had a troubled marriage before my pregnancy with her, and I struggled to accept having a child we hadn’t planned for. Around that time, Cam and your mother were together. Something seemed off, but I missed all the signs. He waited twenty-five years to tell me about this, and that’s what made me the angriest. I spent a lot of years blaming myself for our problems, when I wasn’t the only one at fault.”

“When is Erin’s birthday?” Ella asked, changing the subject when Maggie began sharing a little too much.

“Ella, I saw your birthdate on Facebook. You and Erin were both born in the spring of 1992. It’s obvious your mother became pregnant around the same time as me. That makes the story more salacious, but those are the facts.”

“I can’t understand why Mom kept this from me. She let me live my entire life thinking my dad—I mean Charlie—abandoned me. She never told me the truth and always made excuses for him.”

“We’ve both seen how a secret can have long-lasting effects. I’m trying to help you process this while I’m working through it myself,” Maggie said. “With the death of Cam and your mother’s health issues, it’s impossible for us to know how and why things happened. The DNA test has proven you *are* his daughter. We have nothing else to go on but biology, and we need to move forward without anger and resentment.”

"My mom loved me, so why would she hide such an important detail about my life?"

"Ella, I don't know her, and I can't speculate on her intent. When you become a mom, you'll learn that parents usually try to do what's right for their children, even if they get it wrong."

"I don't want to be angry at my mom or Cameron. It's gnawing at my insides, and that's not good for me," Ella admitted.

"I feel that way too."

Ella had no idea where her relationship with Maggie would lead, but she liked her and felt close to the woman who cared enough not to turn her away.

***

The call from Hannah's House came before lunch. Ella had a break during the noon hour, so she allowed it to go to voicemail. Her heart dropped when she listened to the ten-second message.

"Ella? It's Amanda Bartels. Please get back to me as soon as possible. There's an emergency with your mother."

Ella pushed her midday meal aside and dialed the care center.

"Hello, this is Jillian Meyers's daughter. May I speak with Amanda?"

"Let me see if I can find her," the nurse who answered said.

Surely, Amanda would not be on an extended break during a crisis, forcing Ella to be in a panic state longer than necessary.

"Ella?" Amanda answered. "Oh, honey. Are you in a place where you can talk privately?"

***

It had been a month since Ella and Maggie had met, although they'd talked on the phone whenever Ella thought of another question, and the women had formed a stronger bond with each communication.

After the news about her mother's death sank in, Ella dialed Maggie's number.

"What happened?"

"They found her dead in her bed," Ella began. "She went to breakfast and then took a morning nap. When they tried to wake her for lunch, she was gone. This is devastating, but I couldn't wish for a better passing for Mom than to go in her sleep. At least I have that to comfort me."

Ella knew complications from her mother's Alzheimer's disease were a possibility, and she thought she'd prepared herself for the inevitable. She hadn't foreseen the feelings of shock, and the weight of her grief surprised her.

"What can I do for you?" Maggie asked.

Ella's mother left her body long before her last breath, and her father was a stranger who died without knowing her. Ella felt a pull toward Maggie as a surrogate parent.

"I just wanted you to know. The funeral will take place in Des Moines where Mom's family is buried. It won't be a large gathering. I doubt if any of my friends will be able to make the trip from Minneapolis."

"Would you like *me* to come?" Maggie asked.

The women had formed an unlikely friendship in the weeks since their first meeting. Maggie's support let Ella know that their relationship existed separately from Jillian and Cameron.

"If you're sure it wouldn't be too much of an imposition," Ella replied. "It would mean the world to me."

CHAPTER 30
Maggie

Maggie stared at Cam's former lover lying in her open casket. When Cam confessed his affair, she'd pictured her nemesis as a gorgeous woman with everything to offer a man. Maggie had always felt too plain, too short, or too something, and her husband's willingness to seek companionship outside of their marriage left her questioning herself again. She realized in that moment that Jillian had grown older with the shadow of a lifetime of mistakes too, and the time for comparisons had passed.

After taking a seat at the back of the chapel, Maggie began skimming the funeral program. Like Cam's obituary, some of the darker moments in Jillian's life weren't included. Getting pregnant by another woman's husband and nearly wrecking the lives of two families hadn't made the cut.

Ella and Jordan were seated in the front row, and Maggie noticed Ella's resemblance to Mallory again. She wasn't related by blood to Ella, but her sense of familiarity connected Maggie to her. She was already part of the Sanders family, and her looks proved it.

***

Wrigley lay at Maggie's feet as she finished the last few chapters of a book she hadn't enjoyed. The storyline grabbed her attention for sure. She loved Liane Moriarty as an author, but a novel called *The Husband's Secret* was hitting a little too close to home.

As host of the next month's book club gathering, finishing it wasn't an option. They chose titles months in advance, and Maggie had never heard of Ella Daley when she made the selection. The only criteria to consider was its availability at the Spencer Public Library for those ladies who didn't like purchasing books. The group hardly ever read a new release because of this unwritten rule, and Maggie kicked herself for not going rogue and picking *Lessons in Chemistry* by Bonnie Garmus.

The phone rang, and it gave Maggie a reason to put her mind on something else.

"Mom? Where are you?" Mason asked.

"I'm just sitting here with Wrigley."

"Were you in Des Moines today?"

Maggie hesitated, scrambling for a response. Des Moines was a three-hour drive away, and she'd spent most of the day getting back and forth. Coming to Des Moines for a funeral would have brought an interrogation she wasn't ready for, so she hadn't told any of her kids about her plans.

"Why do you ask?"

"Jenny was on her way to show a house, and she saw you at the Casey's convenience store on 14th Street. She was running late, or she would have stopped to check on you."

A person couldn't be inconspicuous with a vanity license plate reading "TGIF10," which stood for This Grandma Is Fabulous and the year Anna was born. Mason and Jenny gave Maggie the plates as a Christmas gift in 2009, and it's how she and Cam discovered that they were going to be grandparents.

"I did make a quick trip down," Maggie confessed.

"I know, because after talking to Jenny, I tried to call you. When you didn't pick up, I checked your location, and it showed your car on the interstate downtown."

Maggie knew she'd regret letting her children track her phone on Life360 as a safety precaution. She'd stopped to get gas on her way home, never suspecting a family member would see her.

"Well, you don't need to keep tabs on me. I didn't want to bother you during the week when I would only be in town for a few hours. I didn't even exit off I-35 in Ankeny to visit Mallory."

Silence echoed from both ends.

"Mom, are you seeing someone?" Mason asked.

"You mean like a man?"

Maggie laughed at the thought.

"Well, I would *assume* a man . . ."

"What makes you ask that question?"

"We've all talked. Something is up with you, and we'd like to know what it is."

"Are you the family spokesperson now?" she asked.

The accusation that Maggie might be dating was ludicrous.

"I guess I am. We'd all like an answer," Mason demanded.

"I was there for the funeral of a friend's mother. I don't have a boyfriend—either in Spencer or Des Moines. And that's all I have to say."

Maggie *was* seeing someone behind her children's backs, but they had no idea it was their half-sister.

***

A week had passed since Jillian's funeral. Maggie flipped through a pile of mail after checking the cooking time left on the appetizer she would serve at book club. Below the Visa bill, Maggie found a small envelope with Ella's return address in the corner.

Maggie,

I wanted to thank you for coming to Mom's funeral. I appreciate it more than you will ever know.

I remember you told me that it's hard to accept our loved ones as imperfect human beings, and that has stuck with me. I've struggled with anger toward my mother, and your example of understanding where my father is concerned has helped me to believe I can forgive my mom in the same way.

Ella

Maggie glanced at the clock and saw that she had an hour before the ladies would begin arriving. She'd have to get back to Ella later.

225

***

"All I'm saying is that we never know the people in our lives the way we think we do," Maggie asserted to her book club.

After Cam's death, it didn't seem as if Maggie had much in common with her friends anymore. They still had living husbands and children who all knew who their siblings were.

Maggie contested one woman's statement, who made it clear she'd kick her spouse out immediately if he'd kept a life-long secret from her. Book club could get heated at times, but Maggie usually enjoyed it. Invariably, bragging about grandkids or town gossip sidelined their discussion on literature. If they decided to open more wine, they could continue talking for hours.

"Why did we pick this story from 2013?" Lori asked.

As the club's unofficial leader, she liked to select a fresh bestseller when it was her turn to choose. She didn't care what the rest of them thought about spending money on a book, and Maggie admired her tenacity.

"I hate to *buy* a book when I could borrow it, and newer titles are so hard to reserve," admitted Kathy. She was a trustee on the Spencer Library Board, and her life's work was to promote its value to the community.

"Yes, we *know*. I'll send you an Amazon gift card for your birthday," Kendra said, rolling her eyes.

"I'm only asking you to consider what it would be like to find out that your spouse had kept a secret through many years of marriage. Would it alter your love for them if they'd done everything possible to make it up to you?"

Maggie continued to try to get the focus back on the plot, and the women became uncomfortable with her inability to move on.

"Let's revisit how Bev can get Roger to stop clipping his toenails in the kitchen," Kendra suggested to laughter from the group.

"If we can put the jokes aside for a minute, I'd like to talk about commitment and standing by your life partner. The wife in this story knew her husband's heart and couldn't turn him in and risk losing what they'd worked so hard to achieve," Maggie harped.

"If George killed a girl, I'd gladly rat him out and take the king-sized bed for myself," Kathy teased.

The friends laughed again as their banter started to go in other directions.

"One bad action doesn't define the sum of a person's life," Maggie muttered, though no one was listening.

She had to accept that the conversation about long-held secrets was over.

"It looks like we've hit a nerve for you, Maggie. Let's move on from the book and see if anyone else has something to share," Lori whispered, attempting to reclaim the night.

By the end of the evening, only one friend remained.

"Do you want to grab lunch next week?" Kendra asked. "It might do you good to get out."

"I'm fine . . . *really*. It's easy to presume how you'd react to an indiscretion until you face it. That's the only point I was trying to make."

"You succeeded in getting that across," she said with compassion. "Take care of yourself."

Maggie went to sleep that night hoping her inability to let go of the debate about *The Husband's Secret* hadn't raised any suspicions. Even if it seemed odd, she doubted her friends could conceive of the reality she was facing after Cam's death.

***

The peak of an Iowa autumn had passed, but the air still felt warm on some days. A dusting of snow had fallen earlier in the week, but the balmy temperatures melted it as soon as the flakes hit the ground. Maggie took what was needed for Thanksgiving dinner out to the lake and got busy with preparations for her family. She wanted Erin and Tessa to arrive on Wednesday to the smells of pumpkin pie and sauteed onions, greeting them at the door like a welcome home.

"I'm so happy to be here," Erin said, hugging her mother after their arrival.

"How was your flight?" Maggie asked. "I could have come to Des Moines to pick you up. You didn't have to rent a car."

"It's easier this way," Tessa said. "It's a long drive for you."

"Well, I appreciate it. It allowed me to start cooking and make all the beds. Now we can have fun without any worries tonight."

All of Maggie's children would be together for the holiday weekend. It would be the first time since their father's death, and Maggie was looking forward to it.

"When will everyone else get here?" Erin asked.

"Tomorrow morning. They're staying until Sunday, so this evening it's the three of us."

"That works out great," Tessa said. "We're going to take you out to dinner."

Although Maggie usually protested when the kids wanted to treat her, she didn't put up a fight.

***

The crowded parking lot of Ted's Pizza was proof that no one cooked the night before Thanksgiving. Maggie and the girls were lucky to snag a table, and Erin started the conversation while they waited for drinks.

"Mom, Tessa and I would like to discuss something with you."

Maggie's pulse stalled at the possibility of more life-altering news.

"We've signed with an adoption attorney. We want to raise a child, and we aren't getting any younger," Erin said, taking Tessa's hand.

"The last time we talked, you'd decided Erin would carry a baby via a sperm donor. What's changed?"

Maggie had nothing against any means of forming a family unit. But it seemed less complicated for Erin to get pregnant, removing the worry of birth parents coming back later. Maggie had learned about the complex issues of ancestry the hard way.

"You're right, Maggie," Tessa interjected. "But with no biological ties, Erin and I can *both* feel like we're equal parents to our babies."

229

"Mom, we don't believe bloodline has to have anything to do with family. We know the universe will send us the children we're supposed to have. We wouldn't care more for a child because one of us gave birth to the baby. We could even adopt a toddler."

Maggie wondered if Erin and Tessa could be as accepting of Ella Daley.

"I'll support you in any way I can. I'll love whoever God brings into our family."

Maggie truly felt that way, even though it had taken time for her to get there.

***

Everyone bowed their heads at the first Thanksgiving without Cam. They'd never had a holiday at any place other than their home in Spencer. Cam's absence wasn't as prominent in a less familiar setting, which had been Maggie's intent all along.

Maggie made the turkey early and cut it off the carcass. She'd put it into a roaster with the poultry juices, sparing her family the stark reminder that Cam was no longer there to carve the bird. Things were changing, and the sooner Maggie helped her family accept it, the better.

After the meal, they watched football and took naps. When their food comas wore off, they all gathered at the dining room table. The younger kids were running around, enjoying time with their cousins, and Maggie introduced something for the adults to do. The outcome of the activity would direct her to keep to herself or share the important secret she held.

"I've got a fun and easy game with no time limit, and we can play it as long as we want to. There are no winners or losers."

Maggie wasn't sure if she should use manipulation to get the answer she needed, but that inner conflict didn't stop her.

"What? How can it be *fun* if it doesn't have a winner?" Mason asked.

"My brother, the competitive one," Mallory quipped, with a good-humored jab to his arm.

"Ouch. Mom, Mallory hit me!" he sing-songed.

The play fighting took Maggie back to when the kids were younger. They'd always enjoyed games, and Maggie taught them never to cheat or gain an unfair advantage to get the outcome they desired. She was giving herself a pass to expose her children's true feelings about a chapter of family history that carried a plot twist they weren't prepared for.

"It sounds fun. Explain the rules to us, Mom. Pay no attention to Mason," Erin said.

"I have a conversation generator pulled up on my phone. I'll pose a random question, and each of you will respond. Then, we can discuss it further if we want to."

"Is this one of those things where everyone goes to bed mad because the answers bring on arguing and bitterness from being part of a dysfunctional family?" Mallory asked.

"We are *not* a dysfunctional family," Maggie insisted.

"That's what all mothers of dysfunctional families say," Mason scoffed.

His siblings rewarded his remark with laughter, and he raised his can of beer to them in mock victory.

Maggie liked seeing her family happy again. They all missed Cam, but getting some normalcy back in their lives felt good. It was almost enough for her to abandon the plan to tell the kids about Ella, regardless of what they had to say.

"The first question is: what if you could teleport yourself to any location, but when you reached your destination, you'd be naked. Where would you go?" Maggie asked.

The group laughed at the ridiculous scenario.

"The Playboy Mansion," Tom joked.

"Church," Mason added. "I'd love to see all those old ladies when they got a glimpse of this body."

"I'd like to see Pastor Bob tie that into his sermon," Erin mused.

"Let's try another one," Mallory suggested, snatching Maggie's phone. "I want to choose."

Maggie hadn't expected one of the kids to take over. She had the questions loaded in a particular order and had not planned on Mallory messing it up.

"The next one is, what if you woke up as an eighteen-year-old with all the knowledge you have right now? What would you do?"

"Jackie Dillon, I'm coming for you, baby!"

Mason couldn't resist referencing his high school crush, even if Jenny looked less than amused.

"I'll answer," Maggie said. "If I could wake up with what I know today, I'd tell myself that I was beautiful, smart, and capable. I'd drop those business classes and switch my major to journalism so I could become a news anchor. I'd cut my hair short, go to the lake every day, and spend more time with my grandparents."

Maggie's eyes glistened, and the mood became somber. "Buzzkill, Mom."

Mason's attempt at humor did not entertain his mother.

"I didn't know you wanted to be a journalist," Erin said.

"Well, there you have it. You don't know everything about me."

A hush fell over them until Maggie continued.

"The one thing I wouldn't change is marrying your dad and having all of you."

The Sanders matriarch excused herself to grab snacks while she pulled her emotions together. Erin must have taken the phone from her sister because her voice presented the next question. Unaware of the gravity of the topic she raised, Erin asked for the answers Maggie needed.

"What if you had a long-lost sibling? Would you want to meet them?"

Maggie hadn't planned to be in the kitchen when her children tackled the subject she had painstakingly inserted for later. She stopped pouring chips into a bowl so that she could hear their responses.

"Definitely," Mallory said.

"I agree with Mal. First, I'd want to know who Mom or Dad was screwing before they met. Remember all those scary sex talks we had to listen to?" Erin kidded, never imagining a situation where one of her parents might have been unfaithful *during* their marriage.

"I'd say yes," Mason agreed. "Unless they want to steal a quarter of Mom and Dad's estate."

Tom and Tessa added replies as well, but Maggie wasn't listening to them. She emptied a jar of salsa into a dish and rejoined the family.

The question had been asked, and each of her children had given an answer. What else did she need to know?

CHAPTER 31
Ella

"That's all the dishes," Ella said, handing Eloise the last serving bowl.

"I loved your pecan pie," her aunt complimented.

"It's Grandma's recipe, via Mom."

"I thought Jillian always made it better than your grandmother. I never told either of them because I didn't want my mother to be mad or my sister to have the satisfaction."

Ella had survived the first Thanksgiving without her mom. It helped that she and Jordan did something different and joined Eloise and her family for the holiday. Ella hadn't spent time with them in years, and she enjoyed reconnecting with her cousins.

"Now that it's just me and you," Eloise started, "how are you *really* doing?"

"I miss Mom, but I'm still angry with her. Finding out the truth and learning why Charlie didn't ever see me again has my emotions all stirred up. I wish I'd asked more questions when Jordan and I visited him. I had an entire speech ready to go, and when I realized I'd been wrong about him, I couldn't think of what to say."

"You need to let this go. Maybe you could write a letter to your mom or visit her grave and tell her how you feel."

"She's dead. I don't see the point."

"It would give you the opportunity to get some things off your chest, and it might do you good."

"We're stopping at the cemetery before we head back to Minneapolis today. Do you think it would be beneficial to share my feelings with her while I'm there?"

"Your mom would want you to do whatever is necessary to overcome this. You're going to have a baby soon, and you need to enter motherhood without this heaviness in your heart."

"Maybe you're right."

"Did meeting Maggie help at all?" Eloise asked.

"It gave me answers, but that's about all. Charlie is the man I've always regarded as my father, and I don't feel that way toward Cameron Sanders. I wanted to know if I have traits or interests like his, but beyond that, what does knowing the truth do for me now? Bonding with my half-siblings after so many years isn't likely. I'm not even sure I want to."

"Sweetheart, don't forget that you are in charge of your life. You don't have to decide how any of these relationships will progress right now. Time has a way of sorting things out."

***

Oakwood Cemetery sat squarely in the middle of metropolitan Des Moines. Yet once you turned onto the gravel road leading to the grounds, the sounds of the city slipped away as if you'd entered another dimension. Light snow covered Jillian's grave, the mound of earth already settled in the weeks since her funeral. The monument company had not finished the work on Jillian's headstone, but a small name plate and a familiar live oak tree helped Ella locate her mother's final place of rest.

"Hi, Mom," Ella whispered, her breath swirling in the late November air.

A rabbit darted from a nearby bush, startling Ella before she got back to the reason she'd come.

"Now that you're in heaven, I know you don't have Alzheimer's anymore, and I have a few things I need to discuss with you."

Ella missed her mother, and the quiet around her only made that longing more profound. Beneath her ache, a smoldering bitterness over what they'd never resolved fought against that yearning.

As she thought of the child inside her, Ella pictured a younger Jillian facing single motherhood and the loss of her marriage. In that moment, she knew that letting go of her need for the truth was the only way forward.

"I've decided to forgive you, even if I'll never understand. I'm choosing to trust that you had my best interest at heart in keeping this secret from me, because I can't continue holding on to this resentment. I don't want it to affect my relationship with Jordan and my child. So, rest easy, Mom. I love you, no matter *what* happened."

Ella hadn't planned for her words to be so brief, but in the face of her mother's silence, grace was all she could summon.

"Oh, and guess what? We're having a girl."

Ella looked back at the SUV where Jordan waited for her. After their daughter came, visits to the cemetery wouldn't happen often.

"I wish I could talk to you when I have questions about how to raise my baby. It isn't fair you should have to miss this. I'd give anything to have one more day with you. But I promise I'll be a good mother—that's the best way I can honor you."

Ella started to walk back to the car. Jordan leaned on the passenger door, waiting for her. He was so handsome, and Ella's heart overflowed with tenderness for the man who'd finally made her feel lovable. Her daughter would have the father Ella always wanted.

***

Jordan stood back and admired his handiwork. He'd hung the floating shelves Ella had ordered from Amazon, and the white wood popped against the fresh paint.

"Those look amazing," Ella complimented.

"What will you put on them?" he asked.

It had taken an entire weekend to clean out the guest room. Painting and putting the crib and changing table together monopolized several more days. Ella mostly watched Jordan do the work from the comfort of the expensive glider rocker the couple picked out at a chic baby boutique. Deciding how to decorate the nursery offered a diversion from the other things going on in Ella's life.

"I'm going to place family photos, all framed in white, on each shelf. I'll add small potted plants to pull out the green from the color on the walls to finish the look."

238

Ella had started an inspiration board on Pinterest and combined the ideas she'd saved into the design for the baby's room.

"Family pictures, huh? Sounds complicated," Jordan said, chuckling.

"What's so funny?"

"After the year we've had, I think highlighting the family tree for our little girl might be daunting."

"Well, there's us, your parents, and my mom. We could include your brother too."

"I didn't mean to get into this again," Jordan apologized. "I'm hungry. Let's order a pizza."

"Sure, but I want to discuss something with you first."

"Shoot," Jordan said, taking a seat on the floor.

"Charlie Meyers didn't abandon me, and my biological dad may not have known of my existence. I can't blame either of those men when my mother is the one responsible."

"Yes, we've gone over that a hundred times. Where are you going with this?"

"I was ready to lambaste Charlie as the loser I thought he was when we went to see him. When I found out the truth, I couldn't say much of anything. Now, I wish we'd had a more positive interaction. He wasn't my real dad, but at one time, I'd loved him as if he were."

"Is there any reason you couldn't see him again?"

"I don't know. Charlie has already given me more than he needed to. Is it reasonable to ask for more effort and emotion from him now?"

"Love and biology are not the same thing."

"If I contacted Charlie and asked if he wanted to get together again, do you think he'd agree?"

"Without a doubt. In fact, I've got his phone number in my top drawer," Jordan revealed. "He slipped it to me when we said goodbye at his house, just in case."

"Why didn't you tell me?"

"I didn't think the timing was right."

"I need that number," Ella said.

CHAPTER 32

Maggie

Everyone left around noon on the Sunday after Thanksgiving, but Maggie hadn't found a way to bring up the important issue never far from her thoughts. Cam would have known what to say to his kids to cushion the blow of his betrayal, but Maggie was at a loss.

It wasn't fair that she had to disclose something that should have come from their father, as if she'd been pulled into a cruel game of postmortem telephone. She didn't want to tell her kids about Ella without having a plan for them to meet, and that would take more consideration.

Maggie scratched behind Wrigley's ears as they snuggled under a blanket. Orange flames flickered beneath the mantle. Maggie had always loved the crackle of a real fire. It took her back to Sunday afternoons on the farm when the smell of roast beef and vegetables simmering in the oven made her feel safe and cared for.

Nostalgia aside, why had she put the brakes on plans to convert the wood-burning fireplace to gas when they first bought the house? Maggie hadn't anticipated it ever being her job to keep the embers going, and every time she tended the blaze, she imagined Cam whispering, *I told you so.*

Commitments during the busy holiday season used to overflow the squares on the December calendar. Now, only a few obligations marked the cold and blustery month. Maggie had lots of time to decorate, fill the space below the Christmas tree with gifts, and sort out how to tell her adult children they had another sister.

She'd hang the embroidered stockings with their names stitched across the top, except for Cam's. His would remain in the Christmas bin from now on, alongside the broken ornaments that Maggie didn't have the heart to throw away.

The Sanders family didn't usually celebrate both Christmas and New Year's together. This year, the kids had abandoned their in-laws and friends to ensure their mother wasn't alone for the first set of holidays without Cam. That meant they would share back-to-back weekends at the end of the month.

Erin and Tessa would be back for Christmas and stay through the first of the year. Everyone else would travel back and forth, with a party at the lake house on New Year's Eve serving as the finale to 2022. A new year always promised renewal, and the symbolism of a fresh start played a big part in Maggie's plans for how things would unfold.

***

"Hi, Maggie. Did you have a nice Thanksgiving?" Ella asked after she answered the phone.

"Yes. Did you?"

"I missed Mom, but Aunt Eloise put on a spread of food. Jordan was off this year, so we enjoyed time in Des Moines.

Mom's house sold, so we had to sign papers and close it up too."

"I'm glad the condo is not a worry for you anymore. Anyway, I have something important to talk to you about. What would you think about meeting the kids?"

There was a beat of silence before Ella continued.

"Nothing would make me happier, but that's up to you. I'm grateful for what you've shared with me about my father, and I don't want to jeopardize Cameron's memory over this."

Maggie appreciated Ella's understanding of the situation's sensitivity. But Mason, Mallory, and Erin had spoken, and she didn't want to lose her nerve.

"I think it's time. Would New Year's Day work? You and Jordan could come for brunch and spend the afternoon with everyone."

Ella was silent.

"Ella?"

For a moment, Maggie thought the call had dropped.

"Yes. I'm just touched that you'd do this for me."

The baby wasn't due for a while, so Ella could still travel. Maggie wanted to host the introduction at the lake house. She'd begun to feel like that place held her future, and Maggie hoped Ella would be a part of it.

CHAPTER 33
Ella

Ella's anxiety spiked the morning she dialed Charlie's cell. She wanted to see the man she'd hated for years again, but the possibility of rejection constricted her chest.

Carol had answered, telling Ella that Charlie was at the store. She promised to have him return the call when he got back. The hour Ella had to endure until hearing his voice seemed like an unfair punishment. When he agreed to meet her the following Saturday, she exhaled a breath she'd held for twenty-five years.

Ella chose a table as far away as possible from the weekend mob. She loved the Starbucks atmosphere, with its aroma of coffee beans blending with the hiss of frothing milk. It made her pine for a post-pregnancy espresso. For now, she'd have to settle for a hot chocolate and the knowledge that she was taking care of her unborn baby by limiting her caffeine.

It wasn't long until Charlie came through the door and headed toward her as if he knew right where she'd be.

"Hey, Ella. Nice to see you again."

Ella stood, and the two hugged awkwardly before Charlie took his place in line to get a coffee for himself. The delay gave Ella a chance to center herself and clench her hands to stop them from trembling.

"You look good," Charlie said after joining her at the table again. "Now, when is this baby due? If I remember, you don't have much time left."

Charlie appeared as nervous as Ella, and their common reaction helped to calm her.

"Early March. I'm feeling okay, so I can manage my last trimester of pregnancy."

An uncomfortable pause lingered between them as they concentrated on their hot beverages, wondering how to begin. After a moment, they started speaking at the same time.

"No, you go ahead," Charlie said when they both halted to give the other the lead.

"I just wanted to thank you for offering to drive all the way to Minneapolis. I'd have met you someplace closer to Rochester," Ella said.

"I would've driven to California to see you again."

The affection in Charlie's reply poked a hole in Ella's strong façade. She didn't want to cry, but when she let her guard down, her fragile emotions spilled over.

Ella took a napkin from Charlie to dry her tears, and he grabbed her hand and squeezed it.

"I'm sorry. I should have checked in on you. I thought I was doing the right thing by staying out of your life."

Neither cared that they were drawing the attention of other customers. Their reunion had been years in the making, and curious stares over a man talking with a crying woman would not deter their need for closure.

Charlie continued, "I drove by your school a couple of

times that first year and saw you playing during recess. Fear kept me from going over to the fence, but I wanted to."

"Really?"

Ella could hear desperation in Charlie's words.

"Losing you shattered me. After Carol and I got together, she helped me get some perspective on the situation. Once we got married and had our own girls, things improved, but I never forgot about you."

"I've never stopped thinking of you either. Although I wasn't your biggest fan until you told me the truth, and I spent years hating you."

"That's understandable. Did your mom ever mention *anything* about me? I never knew her to be vindictive, and I can't believe she'd let you think I walked out on you."

"Mom agonized over me not having a father in my life, but whenever she brought it up, I'd try to change the subject as quickly as possible. I didn't want her to feel guilty, so maybe I made it harder for her to tell me because I acted like it didn't matter."

"Your mom is a good woman. I'm sure she didn't intend to be malicious. How's she doing these days?"

Ella forgot that Charlie hadn't been told of Jillian's death.

"She died a few weeks ago."

"Oh, honey."

"Honestly, I'm relieved she doesn't have to live for years locked in her own world due to that terrible disease. I've heard of people who have spent over a decade in memory care. I'm glad she maintained her dignity until the very end."

"You've had a lot going on," Charlie sympathized.

"How can I make this right?"

"Things are already better because of you coming here today. You aren't my dad, but I've missed you as if you were. I'm not expecting to reconnect as father and daughter. I only wanted to express my gratitude. I remember how well you treated me, even though I was only a little girl when you moved out. That's why I couldn't trust myself in relationships as I grew up. Without knowing the reason you weren't in my life, I worried that I couldn't read people correctly. It's caused me to pull away from every man I've ever been with, including Jordan."

"You were wrong about the reasons I left, but you read my feelings exactly as they were. You felt like I loved you, no matter how confusing it was, because I *did* love you."

The two talked for hours and watched the morning Starbucks rush turn into the beginning of the lunch crowd. As the minutes passed, their conversation got easier, and Ella's heavy heart began to lighten.

"I guess we should get out of here," Ella said.

She didn't want to end her time with Charlie, but the barista kept eyeing them as if she wondered how long they'd monopolize the table.

"Can I ask you one more thing?"

"Of course," Ella said.

She wanted Charlie to take what he needed from their time together too.

"What made you look for me?"

"I turned thirty this year, and my friends took me to see Felicia Carmichael at the Norris Center."

"You did turn thirty, didn't you? Wow, I can't believe how twenty-five years have slipped away."

"Out of all the people in the room, Felicia came to our section of the theatre and did a reading on me. I assumed Jordan had arranged it as a birthday surprise, but neither he nor my girlfriends had anything to do with it."

Charlie seemed enthralled as Ella continued.

"I know that psychics are all for show, but I allowed myself to get caught up in the moment. Felicia said she saw a woman with the letter 'J' in her name, which ended up being a hook pulling the lady back. Then she started talking about how she could sense that I'd lost a father figure, and it brought me back to you."

"I'm flattered . . . I guess," Charlie said with a smile.

"That's when I did my investigative work to try and locate you."

"You thought I'd died?"

"I didn't believe much of what she said."

"And yet here we are," Charlie mused.

"Here we are. And once you told me you weren't my dad, I looked through Mom's stuff to find a clue about who my father might be. And I came across a name . . ."

"Do you suppose Jillian could have had a hand in this, trying to make it right with you? I mean, that 'J' *can't* be a coincidence."

Thinking about Felicia Carmichael spurred memories from the night of the birthday surprise. Ella had an impeccable memory, and when she replayed what happened at the Norris Center in her head, she kept coming back to one thing.

At the beginning of the performance, Felicia said, "The dead have a way of making things right in the afterlife.

Whether you are open to helping them find the peace they deserve is up to you."

Could Charlie be on to something? The 'J' might stand for Jillian, and the 'C' could represent both Charlie and Cameron. What if her mother, in her own way, had given Ella all the fragments of truth she needed?

"Mom wasn't dead when I saw Felicia Carmichael, but maybe the world of Alzheimer's is closer to heaven than we realize."

"The universe is an incredible mystery. Is it a coincidence that the reading had so much validity to it, or did it all happen the way it was supposed to? It seems to me that fate aligned things perfectly, and now you have answers—except for why your mother kept this from you."

"And I'll never be able to figure that one out," she said.

"You mentioned that you came up with a man's name. What was it?"

"My father is Cameron Sanders."

"Cameron Sanders?" Charlie asked with a look of surprise.

"Yes, but when I reached out to him, I found out he'd recently died."

"I know who that is," Charlie said, looking as if things finally made sense.

"You knew him?"

"He worked with your mom at Midwest Energy Corporation. She won a sales award one year, and we went to a dinner at the headquarters in Spencer where they were honored. We sat at a table with Cameron and his spouse. Your mom spoke very highly of him."

"Obviously," Ella said as they both laughed.

"He's your father?"

Ella could see that Charlie was having a difficult time accepting the facts.

"Yes. Cameron's wife gave me his old toothbrush for a DNA test, and she's invited me to meet my half-siblings over the holidays."

Many years had passed since Charlie Meyers had discovered his little girl was fathered by another man. He'd moved on with his life, but Ella saw that finding out who Jillian once had an affair with still hurt him deeply.

"I'm sorry you had to go through that," Ella said. "It wasn't fair to either of us. Mom is gone now, and I have to stop blaming her. Can you do the same?"

"Ella, I'm a Christian man. I believe that everything happens for a reason. Your mom and I didn't have half the marriage I share with Carol. And seeing you again—well, that's a wonderful gift I hadn't expected."

Ella knew she'd done something good by giving Charlie the resolution he needed. Ella's forgiveness would allow her mother the eternal rest she deserved too.

"I couldn't agree more," Ella added, wiping another tear away.

CHAPTER 34

Maggie

Maggie looked down the length of the pew at her children and grandchildren; they barely fit in one row now. Each person held a lit candle as the melody of "The First Noel" filled the sanctuary, and the shadows on the faces of those she loved brought back cherished memories. She smiled at her grandsons. They ignored the formality of church and pushed one another when their space was invaded, until their father raised his brow with a silent scolding.

The fragrance of fresh pine and the sight of everyone looking casually elegant for the occasion only deepened Maggie's ache for her husband. Christmas had always been Cam's favorite holiday. After the kids were in bed, he used to go outside and shake sleigh bells next to their windows, disturbing the snow near the fireplace so they'd think Santa had stopped at the house. Maggie was never sure if he did it to make Christmas more magical for himself or his children.

It warmed Maggie's heart to know that Mason, Mallory, and Erin would sleep in their childhood bedrooms on Christmas Eve. With all the decorations stored in the attic in Spencer, it was foolish to haul everything out to the lake to avoid Cam's absence again. Thanksgiving in Okoboji had insulated them from the first big celebration without him, but after surviving it, Maggie wanted her family to move on and be comfortable in both of her homes.

As the meeting with Ella loomed, it seemed to Maggie like part of Cam would be with them for the holidays. She doubted her children would see it the same way.

The adults gathered at the dining room table while the grandkids watched a Christmas movie. The Sanders family hadn't shared Christmas Eve in ages. They didn't usually get together until the next day, and to fill the void, Maggie and Cam had started their own traditions years earlier. They'd go to the midnight church service, then drive around Spencer to see the lights while they sipped on hot chocolate from a stainless-steel thermos.

"I'm glad you're all here this year, and to know we'll see each other again next weekend for New Year's makes me very happy. These firsts without your dad are only bearable because I can lean on all of you."

"We wouldn't have it any other way, Mom," Mason said.

"You've all been wonderful the past few months."

"We're proud of you for handling all of this with such dignity and poise," Mallory added.

She had no idea of all the things her mother had *handled*.

"I appreciate that, honey. . . I do need to discuss something with all of you, and this seems like the appropriate time to do it."

"What is it?" Erin asked.

Maggie saw her kids exchanging uneasy glances with each other.

"Mason said you're all worried that I'm hiding something," Maggie began.

"Mom, you aren't sick, are you?" Mason asked.

"No, no, and I am *not* dating anyone. That's not even on my radar."

The Sanders children looked relieved to find out they weren't gaining a stepfather anytime soon, even if they were still unsure of what their mother was getting at.

"Mom, you're scaring me," Mallory begged.

"I don't know where to start. I've contemplated this for weeks and still don't know how to tell you."

"Just say it, and we'll go from there. We love you, and you can tell us anything," Erin said.

Maggie remembered saying something similar when Erin told her and Cam about Tessa.

"Okay, here goes. After your dad died, I got a message from the daughter of one of his former coworkers. She was looking for information concerning her mom because her mother now has Alzheimer's disease. This young woman, Ella Daley, believed *your* father might have been *her* father too."

"What? No way. I thought you and Dad had been together since college?" Mason shot back.

"I can explain everything, but I don't want any interruptions. I invited Ella to visit me at the lake house after the results came back from the DNA test."

Maggie wanted to tell the story in perfect succession, but it was hard not to jump ahead. She wished there were some way to soften the impact of what needed to be revealed, but no amount of wordsmithing could make the proof of Cam's betrayal easier to accept.

"A DNA test?" Erin questioned.

"There is no way Dad has another kid," Mallory insisted.

"You spent time with her at the lake? Alone?" Mason asked in shock, slipping into the role of protector.

"Well, it didn't seem right to invite her to come here. This is your home, and it felt wrong for Ella to be here before I talked with all of you."

"How did she get a sample for a DNA test?" Erin asked, skipping ahead in the story.

"I gave it to her," Maggie admitted.

The room exploded with more questions.

"Is this lady scamming you, Mom? This sounds like a 20/20 episode where someone tries to get money from an old person," Mallory added.

"We need to do a background check on her," Mason asserted.

"Why don't you all let your mother speak? She's trying to tell us something important," Tessa said, coming to Maggie's defense.

"I know this isn't easy, and I wish I could spare you the hurt and confusion. Your father and I had difficulties around the time I got pregnant with Erin. I found out later that your dad had an affair during that time, but he didn't mention anything about a child. We worked through all the fallout from the extra-marital relationship years ago. If he'd known about Ella, I don't think he would have deserted her . . ."

Although Maggie could not be sure of Cam's intentions, the narrative she wanted her kids to embrace didn't leave room for another interpretation.

"How old is she?" Erin asked.

"Honey, she's thirty. She was born around the same time as you," Maggie said as she saw the light go out of Erin's eyes. "Ella's not dangerous. She's a third-grade teacher in Minneapolis."

"At least that's what she's told you, *Mother*." Mason's tone took an accusatory turn.

"And she's pregnant with a baby girl," Maggie added.

"I'm looking her up on Facebook," Mallory said, taking her phone out.

"What do you know for sure about this woman?" Mason pressed.

"She looks just like me!" Mallory exclaimed, moving right past her brother's doubts.

"Let me see," Erin ordered.

"She does look like you, Mallory, and the strong resemblance convinced me I needed to believe Ella's story." Maggie let her words hang in the air before continuing. "I've invited Ella and her husband to join us for New Year's Day brunch, at the lake house, so all of you can meet her."

This declaration ended Maggie's discussion on the matter.

In the late hours of December twenty-fourth, Maggie's stunned children stared at their mother in disbelief. The holidays always brought surprises, and what they learned that night was one of the biggest they'd ever received.

****

Christmas Day didn't feel very celebratory, but the family went through the motions for the sake of the grandchildren. Their melancholy moods were not only about missing Cam; apprehension about New Year's Day also put a kibosh on their spirits.

"We need to hire an investigator to check this woman out. All I could think of last night when I went to bed was this lady showing up, trying to con us. What if she was watching the obituaries for a widow to take advantage of, and she chose you, Mom?" Mason asked.

"I agree. There is a ton of private information in those things. Anyone with half a brain could figure out where someone lived," Mallory added.

"Do you think I'm a complete idiot? I'm not a pushover who has no idea what I'm doing," Maggie protested.

"Mason, I'm only an in-law, but listen to what you're saying," Tom interjected. "Your mother already knew of Cam's affair and what the mistress's name was. Would a random stranger know any of that?"

"This isn't your dad and mom we're discussing. I suggest you keep your opinions to yourself," Mason argued.

"Don't talk to Tom like that," Mallory snapped.

Things were getting heated, and Maggie didn't want the situation to spiral on Christmas.

"I'm sorry, but it's the truth. What else can we do but meet your half-sister and take it from there?" Tom asked, pushing back against Mason's efforts to bully him.

"Thank you, Tom," Maggie said before Erin cut her off.

"She *would* be our half-sister." Erin took Tessa's hand. "It seems different when you look at it that way. How can we ignore her?"

"I can't believe Dad cheated on you, Mom," Mallory said, bursting into tears. "Did we even know our own father?"

"Are you talking about a one-night stand, or did he do this all the time?" Mason asked. "And how do we explain this to the kids?"

"I hadn't thought of that. Dear God," Jenny groaned.

Maggie's thoughts went to her grandchildren. How could they possibly make sense of their grandfather's mistakes? She hadn't really considered that angle.

"We've got a few days before *this woman* and her husband show up. We should consider the impact of this on Dad's memory for the entire family," Mallory warned.

"We need to plan for how New Year's Day will go," Mason said, taking control.

"Their names are Ella and Jordan. We'll welcome them into our home with hospitality, and the conversation will unfold however it happens. I know this is shocking, but so are many things in life. We have no choice but to handle this with tact. If I can accept Ella, you all can too."

Maggie demanded the last word, and her children gave her that respect.

****

The days between Christmas and New Year's allowed everyone to take a break from each other. Erin and Tessa stayed at Maggie's, and after they put away one holiday and grocery-shopped for the next, they headed to the lake house to prepare for the weekend.

"I love it here," Tessa said to Maggie as they sat in front of a mid-afternoon fire. "You're lucky to have such a peaceful getaway."

Tessa and Maggie were not very close, but a nap for Erin had given the two women a chance to visit alone. Tessa was not who Maggie had envisioned as a spouse for her youngest, but she was the person Erin needed. Maggie had never seen her daughter happier.

"These surroundings have served as my quiet refuge. It's different at the lake, and whenever I'm overcome with grief, I come out here to soothe the ache."

"It's almost as if Cam knew you would need this place after he was gone," Tessa said.

"By the way, thanks for your support last night. I appreciated how you listened to me and didn't conclude I'd fallen prey to a con from someone claiming to be my deceased husband's illegitimate child. I wouldn't allow a stranger to come into our lives without confidence in the facts."

"Your kids are just being protective. They all feel an extra responsibility toward you since Cam's death. That's why I'm looking forward to adopting a child with Erin. We want the assurance that, if something happens to one of us, the other will have family to care for them."

"It will happen. Have they indicated how long it might take?" Maggie asked, squeezing Tessa's hand.

"Adoption can be a roller coaster. We have a lead on a mother who's interested in us. I hesitate to say too much until we know more, but we hope to become parents next year. I see this thing with Cam's daughter differently than everyone else. How will your kids accept our future children if they don't have room for Ella to join the family? At least Ella has a biological connection to them."

"Honey, we'll all love your little ones the same as the other grandkids," Maggie promised.

She had to admit that Tessa brought up a good point.

***

Maggie sat with her adult children and their spouses, waiting to ring in the new year.

They'd held a more festive celebration at 9:00 p.m. when the grandkids wore silly hats and blew noisemakers before they grew too tired to keep celebrating.

"It's the end of an era tonight," Mason lamented.

"Come on," Jenny said. "That's a little dramatic. Ella sounds very nice, and I'm looking forward to having another sister-in-law."

"What? We aren't good enough?" Mallory asked, faking offense.

"It depends on the day," Jenny joked.

"I'm happy it's almost 2023," Erin said through tears. "This year has been the worst."

Tessa moved closer to her wife, putting an arm around her.

"Every year brings challenges," Maggie offered, trying to bring her loved ones together. "But we're all fortunate to have each other. I've never faced anything more difficult than losing your father. I had him in my life for more than

259

forty years. It's not easy to weather the twists and turns of life, but we don't have any choice."

The Sanders were bracing for change. Maggie couldn't shield them from reality any longer, and they would have to navigate meeting their father's other child on their own terms.

"I can't believe *our* mom is handling her husband's love child as if it's no big deal," Mason spouted off as his tone turned aggressive. "None of us asked for this, and you're shoving it down our throats like you always do when we disagree. So, here's a toast to who we used to be."

"Who we *used* to be? How dare you speak to me like that. I'd rather drink to who we're becoming, at least that's something we can control. This situation has forced itself upon me. If the rest of you agree with Mason that I'm somehow brushing it off, well, then I'm afraid you don't know me very well."

"Mom," Mallory started. "It's just hard to see you embracing Ella, despite what we think about it."

"Life is about making the best out of what you're given. Tackling this is almost as challenging as facing your father's death, but what else can I do? I'm not listening to another word from any of you. I can't protect everyone and honor your dad too. Not to mention, I'm looking after a young woman who shares your blood—*but not mine*. It's more than I can take tonight, and I'm going to bed."

"Mom, it's ten minutes until midnight. Stay and have champagne with us," Mason backpedaled. "I'm sorry."

"Let's not get mad at each other. Mason is just being a jerk," Erin said.

"I don't want to celebrate with any of you. Come on, Wrigley."

Maggie left the room without saying goodnight.

By the time she brushed her teeth, the alarm clock read 11:59 p.m., and Wrigley had already claimed his spot on the bed. He sighed when she pulled the comforter from beneath him. He looked at Maggie with his soft brown eyes, as if to let her know he was on her side.

"I know, boy. They didn't mean it, but it still hurt my feelings."

As the digital numbers flipped to 12:00 a.m., Maggie heard cars honking and fireworks exploding in the night sky, drawing her attention away from her troubles. Wrigley whimpered in fear, but not a sound came from the six adults she'd left sitting in the family room.

Maggie ran a hand over her dog's curly coat to comfort him, grateful that she wasn't alone.

Maggie tossed and turned all night. She hated it when distance came between her and the kids. Teenage conflicts surrounding curfews, homework, or what friends they should hang out with were much easier to settle. Adult issues were more complicated, and Maggie couldn't escape her uncertainty this time.

Before Cam died, things seemed easier. Whenever Maggie doubted herself or her parenting, Cam would support her stance and reassure her that she was a good mother. She missed him and wished he could be at the lake house with his family, preparing to meet his daughter.

Maggie knew Cam would agree with her; he'd want his children to embrace Ella. It was no more her fault than theirs, and she deserved acceptance.

***

When Maggie came into kitchen, Mason was tending to the coffee.

"Morning."

"Hi."

Mason grabbed a mug from the cupboard and filled it with hot brew.

"Here," he said, handing the cup to his mother.

"Thanks."

Maggie added sugar without saying anything more.

"I'm sorry, Mom. I wish I hadn't ruined New Year's Eve for everyone."

"You need to understand that this isn't just about you and your siblings. I know it's difficult to accept. It's hard for me too. Your father and I resolved this years ago. A child coming out of the relationship doesn't change things for me."

"You're right. I'm mad at Dad for doing something selfish and so unlike him, and I'm taking it out on you—and Ella too."

"And that's not fair," Maggie agreed.

"No, it's not."

"What's important is that we forgive each other. It's a part of loving someone, and I love you very much."

Mason hugged his mother.

262

"How can we go on without Dad?" he asked, holding on tightly.

"We'll take all our love for him and share it between us. Maybe we could offer some of it to Ella too," Maggie said, feeling as if she'd finally found the right words.

***

Ella and Jordan would be there at noon, and Maggie had made an egg casserole and various breakfast items for brunch. She set out a tray of pastries to hold her family's hunger until later, and the adults sipped their morning beverage of choice in silence.

Maggie avoided setting out their traditional holiday mimosas and Bloody Marys. Ella couldn't partake, and with emotions running high, alcohol wasn't a good idea.

Erin and Tessa smiled and seemed happier than the rest of the group, who looked like they were mentally preparing for a root canal. The grandkids were running around the house, playing hide and seek, oblivious to their parents' sour dispositions.

"Why are the two of you so giddy?" Mallory asked as she fixed a bagel for the twins.

Erin stood next to the island, and Tessa came to her side.

"When we went to bed last night, Tessa checked her email, and we got a message from the law firm working on our search for a baby."

"And?"

Maggie hoped for some good news to help improve everyone's mood.

"And a birth mother has chosen us to adopt her baby!" Erin exclaimed.

The room filled with excited chatter as the expectant moms beamed with hopefulness.

"It's a girl, and she's due in April," Tessa shared.

Maggie hugged Erin before moving on to Tessa to do the same.

"I'm so happy for the two of you," she said. "What did I tell you all last night? We're only ten hours into the new year and already have something to look forward to."

CHAPTER 35
Ella

The trip to Maggie's lake house seemed to take forever, with excitement and fearfulness fighting for control over the mood in the car.

"This is a cute resort town," Jordan noted as they drove around Okoboji, killing time before their scheduled arrival.

"What if they're hostile toward us? I would understand if they were apprehensive about meeting the result of their father's infidelity," Ella said, ignoring Jordan's effort to get her mind off her worries.

"Maggie knows her kids well enough to be sure she isn't putting you in an uncomfortable position. She invited us to join them. Let's take it as it comes, and if it doesn't feel right, we'll leave."

Jordan always knew what to say.

When the time came for them to park behind the fleet of cars already in Maggie's driveway, Ella was ready for whatever might happen.

"Wow, this place is impressive," Jordan said.

Tall pine trees encircled the property, and the frozen lake sprawled out in back of the house, reflecting the sun like a mirror. A large wreath with a red velvet bow hung on the door, and Ella hoped her welcome felt as warm as the view in front of them.

Jordan put his hand on Ella's leg. She smiled, pondering the journey she'd taken to find her father and his family.

"Thank you," she said.

Her simple words carried a depth of gratitude she could never fully express.

"I'm Ella, and this is Jordan."

Sets of eyes looked at them from every direction.

"Oh my gosh. You *do* look like me!" Mallory exclaimed.

"This is Mallory," Tom said as his wife stared at the woman who could have been her identical twin. "And I'm her husband, Tom."

Maggie and Wrigley appeared in the tight entryway, and the dog ran straight to Ella. His tail and bottom waggled with excitement as if to tell the rest of the family that she was one of them.

"Hi, Wrigley," Ella said. "How've you been, buddy?"

"I guess you've met Wrigley," Mason said. "Hi, I'm Mason, your handsome big brother."

He offered his hand, and after a moment of hesitation, he pulled Ella in for a hug.

They all took turns introducing themselves, and a lump formed in Ella's throat as she greeted Maggie again.

It didn't take long for the atmosphere to change from tentative to welcoming. Ella and Jordan joined everyone as they gathered in the kitchen and prepared to share brunch.

The grandchildren had eaten earlier and were off playing, so the adults had uninterrupted time together.

"You'll love Mom's egg soufflé," Mallory said. "She won't tell us the secret ingredient, but I know it's heavy whipping cream."

"It's not cream, I promise you," Maggie bantered back.

"We shouldn't let Ella see us argue," Erin joked. "Mom and Mallory are constantly giving each other a hard time."

"We are not," Maggie said. "Mallory's just afraid she'll never be as good a cook as me."

"Thanks for proving my point," Erin kidded.

They filled their plates with mounds of eggs and bacon, along with a raspberry coffee cake and sliced fruit. Ella was a stranger to them, but the Sanders kids included her as if she'd always been one of them.

"When are you due?" Erin asked when there was a lull in the conversation.

"March," Ella said, cupping her stomach. "We're having a girl, and we couldn't be happier. It's been a difficult year, and we're thrilled to have this little sweetie to look forward to."

"We're also hoping for a baby soon," Tessa said, looking at Erin for reassurance.

"We found out we've been chosen to adopt a child," Erin said.

"That's fantastic," said Jordan. "Do you have names picked out?"

"We've only known for a few hours, so we haven't gotten that far," Tessa answered.

"Maggie tells us you're a teacher," Jenny said. "You sure have your hands full these days. Tom and I have twins who are kindergartners, and handling two can be a challenge. I have to give you credit for dealing with an entire classroom. I wouldn't be able to do it."

"I must admit, pregnancy has made it much harder to get through the day. I love kids, and my career is very rewarding, so that keeps me going."

"Ella was named teacher of the year at her elementary school. She's an amazing educator," Jordan bragged.

"Tell us how you figured out our dad was your father too?"

Ella saw a look of disapproval cross Maggie's face.

"Mason, Ella might not want to share such information when you've only just met her."

"No, it's understandable you'd all be curious, and I'm happy to explain," Ella said.

She began with the night of her thirtieth birthday outing and then gave a synopsis of what had transpired over the past months. She ended by telling them about her mother's death and her recent conversations with Charlie Meyers.

The afternoon went quickly, and by 4:00 p.m., Ella and Jordan were ready to leave.

"This has been fun. Looking around the table and seeing my resemblance in your faces is so special."

"Dad must have had some strong genes," Mason observed as the group laughed.

Ella had worked hard to discover the truth, even if the result of finding her family seemed less life-changing than she thought it would.

***

Meeting her half-siblings had gone better than Ella could have imagined. Everyone smiled and exchanged hugs when they left the lake house, and plans for a reunion after the baby came were already taking shape. Her fears had been for nothing, and Ella felt like she was stepping into the new year with a mended heart.

As Ella and Jordan traveled north to Minnesota, the early darkness of a midwestern winter swallowed the landscape around them. The roads were clear, and the car heater warmed them after being outside too long during their goodbyes.

"How do you think it went?" Ella asked.

"They're very nice people. I didn't know what to expect, and their openness surprised me."

"It's Maggie who deserves the most praise. She's allowed me into her family, which must be hard for her. I'm shocked at how kind she's been to me. I don't think I'd react in the same way."

"The relationship between your mom and her husband was over years ago, and you *are* Cameron's daughter. Considering his recent death, I can see how she couldn't turn you away. You represent a piece of him, and maybe in her grief, you're a way to hold on to him."

"That's a little deep for me right now. I'm exhausted, and the rich egg dish is not sitting well. Do you mind if I close my eyes for a bit?"

"Of course not. Sleep will pass the time for you, and we'll be home and in bed in no time," Jordan assured her.

Ella had been sleeping for about twenty minutes when something jolted her awake.

"Where are we?" she asked.

"We just passed over the Minnesota border. You haven't been asleep for long. Are you okay?"

"No," Ella said.

"What's the matter? Is your stomach still upset?"

As a firefighter, Jordan worked with EMTs and paramedics. When he offered unsolicited medical advice, Ella often brushed his concerns away. But she had an odd feeling, and it worried her.

"I'm nauseous and am having abdominal pains. Let's pull off at the next exit."

"You'll be fine. Why don't you lie back and relax?"

"You're right. I'm probably overwhelmed by all that happened today."

Ella leaned back and tried not to dwell on her discomfort. Jordan touched his wife's leg and raised the cruise control's speed.

They took an off-ramp, and after pulling into the gas station lot, Ella noticed the lights weren't on inside. A sign on the front door indicated that they were closed for New Year's Day.

"I've never heard of interstate businesses closing for a holiday. How are you doing now?" Jordan asked.

"Not good. It's getting worse. I think I'm going to throw up," Ella said, searching for a plastic bag in the glove compartment.

"There's a truck stop across the way, and it looks like it's open. Let's get you some fresh air too."

Jordan sat for a moment and tried to formulate a plan. He cracked the windows, hoping the frigid temperatures would help Ella feel better. Suddenly, he heard a gushing sound and wondered if the radiator hose on the car had snapped.

"Jordan?" Ella said in a small voice. "I think my water just broke."

CHAPTER 36
Maggie

When the call came early the following day, it concerned Maggie to hear Jordan on the other end of Ella's cell.

"What's going on?" she asked.

Jordan had never phoned Maggie, and it gave her an uneasy feeling about why he would, especially when they'd been together the day before.

"I'm afraid we had a little excitement after leaving your house yesterday, and we're in Sioux Falls, South Dakota."

"Sioux Falls?"

It was an hour and a half from Lake Okoboji in the opposite direction from Ella and Jordan's home in Minneapolis.

"Are you okay?" Maggie asked.

"Ella is fine, but our little one entered the world at 5:00 a.m. this morning, and she's in the neonatal intensive care unit."

"What?"

Maggie couldn't imagine what might have happened after they left the house. Now, sixteen hours later, Ella had given birth in a strange hospital far from their home. Was the stress of meeting the Sanders too much for Ella to handle?

"We drove north, and just over the state line, Ella's water broke. We stopped because she wasn't feeling well. We were trying to find the closest emergency room when Ella started getting lightheaded, and she passed out. I called 911, and the ambulance took her to Spirit Lake. They made the decision to life flight her to Sioux Falls not long after that."

"What about the baby? How is she?"

"We'll be here for a while because she only weighed four pounds. Ella had a panic attack after her water broke, and that's why she fainted. She's going to be okay, and with time in the NICU, our baby girl will be too."

"I'm heading your way," Maggie said.

"You don't need to come. I've got things under control, and Eloise will be here tomorrow."

Maggie didn't know Jordan well enough to take him at his word, but she wanted to see how Ella and the baby were doing for herself.

Erin and Tessa were leaving later that morning and would drive their rental car to the airport, so Maggie said her goodbyes and left for Sioux Falls. She could always come home if she determined Jordan didn't want her there.

Maggie called Mallory from the road to let her daughter know what was going on.

"Jordan can handle this, Mom," Mallory said after taking her mother's call. "I'm worried you're getting too involved with these people, given the circumstances."

Maggie heard a tinge of jealousy in her daughter's voice, and she was aware that even though things had gone well, the kids were not thrilled to find out they had another sibling.

"I need to check on them. The baby would have been born in Minneapolis if they hadn't made the effort to come to Iowa to visit us. Now they could have to spend weeks at a hospital in a city they aren't familiar with."

"I get it, but you're overstepping your bounds. Plus, there's bad weather moving in later tonight."

"I promise I'm only checking on them and then heading back home."

Maggie didn't mention she'd packed an overnight bag, just in case.

"You left Erin and Tessa at your house to spend their last day alone?"

Mallory wasn't letting up.

"They planned to leave shortly after me, so it wasn't an issue."

Mallory went quiet, and her silence said more than anything she could have expressed verbally.

"Mom, we're all worried that you're getting a little carried away with all of this. I'm not a psychologist, but is there a chance you're substituting Ella for Dad?"

The kids had been using "we" more in conversations, and their criticisms hurt Maggie.

"Ella is a part of your dad," Maggie said, suggesting she had no choice.

"So are we," Mallory reminded her.

"What's her name?" Maggie asked Jordan as they looked at the tiny baby through the glass window.

An incubator with lights kept the little one warm, and machines monitored her vital signs.

"Rosalind Jill after our mothers," Jordan said, gazing at his new daughter. "And we're going to call her Rosie."

"That's lovely."

Maggie liked Rosie, but it had crossed her mind that they might name her Cameron. Even if it honored a grandfather whose sole contribution was his DNA, the name would have been a beautiful choice for the baby girl.

Maybe the kids were right. She *was* going off the rails a bit.

"Have you held her yet?" Maggie asked.

"Only for a few minutes. If Rosie does well, she can graduate from these machines and spend more time in the room with us. The doctors say she's healthy, but she's small, and it will be a while before we can take her home."

"That's such good news. I can't believe this happened last night. Did you consider turning around and coming back?"

"I couldn't think of anything else but getting Ella some help. We were out in the middle of nowhere, and when she fainted, I knew she needed medical attention," Jordan recounted.

The two made their way to Ella's room, where Maggie gave her flowers she'd picked up from a gas station. It wasn't the most attractive arrangement, but Maggie could not depend on the hospital gift shop being open on a holiday.

"Thanks for making the trip over here, Maggie. Things certainly didn't go as planned after we left your house yesterday," Ella said, retelling the story of their harrowing experience. "And I never dreamt I'd have the first baby of the new year."

Maggie couldn't help but see Rosie's birth as a symbol of a fresh start.

"I'm glad you're both doing well."

Maggie's cell phone rang, and she excused herself to take a call from Mason.

"How's it going?" Mason asked.

Maggie slipped into a visitor's lounge and leaned beside a window overlooking the parking lot. She tried to find her car among the snow-covered vehicles below as she filled Mason in on Ella and the baby.

"How long are you staying?" he asked.

"Well, I . . ."

"I want to make sure you're okay. You said that Ella and the baby are doing well. Jordan can take care of this . . ."

"I feel an obligation to them since they were with us yesterday."

"Go home, Mom. They're fine. You need to get back to your own life."

Maggie put her hand on the cold glass, and her breath made a faint impression across the pane.

"You've been talking to Mallory, haven't you?"

"Yes, Mom. We all liked Ella, but she isn't a replacement for Dad. I'm sorry, but this is getting out of hand."

"Maybe you're right," Maggie conceded.

*****

Maggie returned to Spencer before dark, avoiding the four-inch snowfall Mallory had predicted. Wrigley curled against her leg and whined when she tried to move him over to give herself more room on the sofa.

The kids had pulled out home videos earlier in the week, and Maggie popped one into the VCR. Watching the old footage over the holidays had become a tradition when Cam was alive, and the comfort of the past drew her in. The flap over Ella took precedence over the family's enjoyment of the reels this year, but Maggie didn't want to put them away without viewing a few.

She smiled as a young Mason showed his sisters how to go down a slip-and-slide Cam made from an old tarp, dishwashing liquid, and the garden hose. Hearing Cam's narration of the video startled Maggie, and she rewound the tape several times to listen to him.

His voice was so clear and familiar that it seemed as if he were only in the next room.

Her children's innocent laughter took her back to the day Cam insisted they make their own fun instead of going to the public pool. Maggie remembered feeling perturbed at Cam's inability to understand how much easier it would have been for *her* if he'd taken them across town to the aquatic center, giving her a couple of hours alone.

As little Erin ran toward the camera, Maggie caught a glimpse of her youngest's dimpled knuckles, still baby-like at three years old. She looked at her own hands, dotted with age spots. They resembled her mother's, and a longing tugged at her.

"Mommy, can we have an ice cream cone?" her toddler asked a younger Maggie behind the lens.

"That's up to your father," she heard herself say with more than a hint of attitude. "He's in charge of this afternoon's entertainment."

Tears came to Maggie's eyes, realizing everything she'd missed while wishing the early days of her life away.

She spent several hours reliving their lives in two-minute clips, and the longer she watched, the more she dissected the years. She couldn't help but see the footage in a different light, knowing how naive she'd been to what was happening behind the scenes. Each frame now seemed like another piece of a picture she'd never fully seen. The signs of Cam's betrayal had been there, but she'd been too unsure of her own worth to imagine she wasn't the one at fault.

CHAPTER 37
Ella

Ella held Rosie close as she gave her a bottle. The garage door opened, and Jordan came in from his work shift and joined his family on the sofa.

"Happy thirty-first birthday. Look what I brought you."

"You stopped at *Fleur's*?" Ella asked.

"Of course. I called ahead and asked them to reserve two chocolate croissants, so you weren't stuck with the pistachio ones."

"Birthday complete," Ella said, making a check mark in the air as Rosie made grunting sounds.

"Oh, no," Jordan said with dread. "Did she save a dirty diaper for me?"

"I guess I'm not the only one getting a gift this morning."

Four and a half months had passed since Ella's meeting with the Sanders. Discovering her father's identity didn't provide the perspective on life that she thought it would, but Jordan had been by her side, helping her wade through all of it.

"Have you been inundated with birthday calls and texts?"

"I got a few. I also received an email from my long-term

sub asking how to close out the semester."

Ella had taken a leave of absence from her teaching job after Rosie's premature birth, and she'd decided not to go back until classes resumed in the fall. She hadn't intended to have so much time off, but everything had shifted for Ella when motherhood changed her priorities.

"What do the girls have planned for you this year?" Jordan asked.

When Marcy, Sondra, and Lisa had whisked Ella off to the Felicia Carmichael Show a year earlier, she could never have imagined what would transpire in the twelve months following her psychic reading.

"We're going out on Friday night. Remember, you have Rosie duty? I told them all I wanted was a quiet dinner."

"Thank goodness. I can't take another year like the one we just survived."

"Me either. An uneventful trip around the sun would be perfect," Ella said, showing Jordan her crossed fingers.

***

Ciao was busy, even for a Friday night. White linens and bottles of wine in an enormous rack along the back wall gave the space a touch of elegance. The trendy Italian eatery was one of Ella's favorites, but she hadn't enjoyed their shrimp linguine and homemade garlic knots in months.

Marcy waved Ella over to their table where Sondra and Lisa were already seated.

"Sorry I'm late. I had the cutest top on, and then I held Rosie for a second while Jordan got her bottle ready, and she spit up all over me."

Marcy and Sondra laughed, but Lisa stared at Ella and then headed for the restroom without saying a word.

"What's her deal?" Ella asked.

"I don't know. Lisa wasn't sure she could make it tonight, and when I pressed her, she acted as if it was a huge imposition for her to leave the house. It looks like she forgot to do her makeup too. Lisa never has a hair out of place, and she isn't even wearing lip gloss. Do you think she and Seth are fighting?" Sondra wondered.

Lisa and Seth had just celebrated their first anniversary, and the thought of marital troubles worried Ella.

"Tell us what's going on with the birthday girl," Marcy urged.

"Everything is great," Ella began. "Rosie is a good baby, and Jordan couldn't be a better dad—when he's there. It's difficult to have her alone for a full twenty-four hours when he's at work. I guess I'm still trying to figure it out."

"Have you heard more from your *new* family?" Sondra asked.

Ella had filled them in on what happened on New Year's Day at her first post-baby outing with them.

"We haven't seen each other since then, but I've been busy with Rosie."

"I mean, are they like a *real* family to you? Will you spend holidays with them and get yourself added to the will?" Sondra asked, her humor shining through.

"I don't know. It's weird. We're related by blood, or at least I'm linked to the kids in that way, but I'm closest to Maggie. They're all great, but we live hours apart, and I'm not sure where it will go from here."

"Is knowing the truth enough?" Marcy asked.

"Maybe . . ."

Lisa returned from the bathroom, looking pale and sweaty. She sat down and put her head in her hands.

"What's the matter?" Sondra asked. "You look terrible."

Lisa took a drink of water and sighed.

"I didn't want to say anything yet, but I guess now I don't have a choice. I'm pregnant, and I'm so sick, I can barely function."

They all congratulated Lisa and began firing questions about due dates, how she told Seth, and if the couple were moving from their one-bedroom loft in the city.

Lisa started to respond to their interrogation but had to make another abrupt trip to the restroom before she could answer.

"Oh. My. God," Sondra said, shocked at Lisa's news. "Every time we get together, one of you makes a major announcement. Unfortunately, I haven't landed a new job or hooked up with Channing Tatum . . ."

"I hate to give you the satisfaction of being right," Marcy said. "But I have something to tell all of you too."

She pulled her hand from underneath the table, and a sparkling diamond sat on her left ring finger.

"I'm engaged!"

Ella looked at her best friends and thought of the celebrations and heartaches they'd shared. For better or worse, change was the one thing they could always count on.

CHAPTER 38

Maggie

The drive from Spencer to Des Moines gave Maggie time to reflect on the past twelve months. It was hard to believe it had been a year since she opened the garage door to find Cam dead on the cement floor. The hours after her discovery had felt like walking through quicksand, and now she'd endured three hundred and sixty-five days without Cameron Sanders. Maggie had faced her firsts as a widow with unshakable resilience, and she was proud of herself.

Rows of similar houses lined the subdivision where Mason lived, their irrigated lawns protected by white vinyl fencing. The neighborhood was designed for checking off the boxes of a successful life, and it reminded Maggie that her grown children were still trying to figure it all out.

She knew it wouldn't always be easy for them, but Maggie hoped she'd served as a guiding influence on how to face life's challenges with grace. When they needed strength, she'd be there for them, just as they had been for her.

When she pulled into the driveway at Mason and Jenny's house, her grandsons greeted her.

"We were watching for you, Grandma," Henry said.

He and his brother were throwing a baseball in the front yard, and Maggie made note of how quickly they were growing up.

"Mom says we're celebrating Grandpa Cam tonight," Daniel added.

"That will be lovely. Where's your sister?"

"Anna has gymnastics until five," he answered. "Do you want us to help you carry your bags inside?"

"Thank you, boys. I might even have a surprise for you."

Maggie never came for a visit without treats for her grandkids, even if it meant cookies or their favorite candy from the Dollar Tree.

Mallory and her family arrived before dinner, and they all seemed in a good mood despite the occasion. Erin and Tessa wouldn't be joining them since they lived in New Mexico. They were still adjusting to parenthood after adopting Isabelle, and they didn't feel comfortable traveling across the country yet.

Their little girl's arrival had proven that love doesn't require a biological connection. Izzy had snuggled her way into Maggie's heart, her birth bringing the happiness everyone craved following Cam's death.

Maggie had flown out to meet her granddaughter in April, but the trip felt bittersweet without Cam. Special occasions were when the absence of the Sanders family patriarch weighed heaviest. Maggie tried to lavish her children and grandchildren with extra attention to make up for the affection they missed from Cam, but it was never enough to make them forget.

"Who's ready for some chow?" Mason asked.

He handed a tray of grilled hamburgers to Jenny, who placed them on the kitchen island along with the rest of the food.

"Before we eat dinner, I have something to say," Maggie announced.

"Sure, Mom. Boys, quit arguing. Grandma has the floor," Mason chided.

He moved next to his wife and put his arm around her, and Mallory and Tom stood on either side of their twins. Anna joined them, wearing her sweaty leotard, much to Jenny's chagrin, who'd asked her to shower as soon as she got home.

They were all talking at once and volleying for positions as they prepared to listen to what Maggie had to say.

The scene reminded her of the imperfect beauty of her family. They loved and supported each other, even if the previous year had brought harsh words and power struggles as they worked to redefine their roles.

"First, thank you for all you've done for me this year. Checking in with me, sending flowers on my first wedding anniversary alone, and spending weekends with me when I know your schedules are so full."

The faces of her family softened with emotion.

"And sweet Anna," Maggie continued, her voice catching, "when you made that playlist of Grandpa's favorite songs and shared it to my Spotify—well, I don't think anyone has ever done something so thoughtful for me."

Anna blushed at her grandmother's praise, and Maggie immediately regretted drawing attention to the meaningful gesture her granddaughter would have probably preferred to keep between them.

"There have certainly been plenty of changes in our lives," Mason acknowledged.

"I know, honey, but change is a lot like the sunrise. You can count on it each morning, even if you don't know what the hours ahead will bring. Some days have calm winds and blue skies, but a storm can blow in from nowhere, forcing you to adjust your plans. That's how I feel about this past year. None of us asked for any of the challenges we faced, but we got through them. And if we can be stronger after all of this, I know we can handle whatever comes next. Your father would be so proud of the family we've become."

"Mom, Dad would be proud of *you*," Mallory complimented.

"I hope so. There is one more bit of news . . ."

"Oh, God. Dad doesn't have another kid, does he?" Mason joked.

Maggie looked at her son and wanted to express her displeasure, but she only smiled.

"Too soon?" Mason asked, his attempt at humor receiving groans.

"Ignore him, Maggie. Tell us what's on your mind," Tom urged.

"I've decided to sell the Spencer house and move to the lake full-time."

CHAPTER 39
Cam – Fall 1991

On the Monday after Thanksgiving, Cam pecked Maggie on the cheek before he left for Toledo, Ohio. He wanted to take her into his arms and tell her everything would be okay, but she'd turned away, making it clear that she didn't want his affection. He deserved it and would spend the rest of his life trying to make it up to her, but he had to get through the few days ahead of him first.

When the kids were little, Cam would fill his coffee mug and take off for his weekly work assignment. He would act like he didn't want to leave, but when Maggie said goodbye, and Mason and Mallory needed bottles or breakfast, Cam couldn't wait to retreat to the sanctuary of his company car.

He usually flew out of the Des Moines airport each week. The three-hour drive gave him time to take in the day's top news stories on the radio or listen to a book on tape. The trip lost its luster in lousy weather, which occurred often in Northwest Iowa, but he'd grown used to it.

Over time, Cam began detaching from Maggie and the kids, though he tried hard to control it. He loved his family, but escaping the chaos of a home with young children seemed like self-preservation. Putting them out of his mind during the week was much easier than it should have been.

Cam spent a decade traveling for work. His weekends included soccer games and little league practices, and he and Maggie kept busy with church activities and social events. Despite the monotony of their routine and responsibilities, they had a good life.

When they met at Iowa State in the seventies, Cam could never have imagined his feelings for Maggie would change. He still loved her; he would always love her, even if their passion had fizzled. Many men he knew complained about a disconnect in their marriages, and he'd considered it an unavoidable progression that wouldn't last forever.

When Cam encountered Jillian Meyers, her striking looks and laid-back personality captivated him. Although she was married, she didn't have any children. Carefree and fun, Jillian reminded him of how life used to be, and he took every opportunity to be around her.

Jillian laughed at Cam's jokes and made him feel handsome and charming. She was interesting and loved to visit museums and take in art exhibits. He thought he could refrain from doing anything immoral, even if the time spent alone with a woman who wasn't Maggie felt like holding a lit match next to a marriage made of straw.

Cam's guilt didn't outweigh his desire, and his friendship with Jillian turned into a full-blown affair that had gone on for more than a year. He hated to admit it, but being with her was exciting, and he didn't want it to end.

He'd agonized over the future after finding out about Maggie's pregnancy. He needed to go in one direction or the other, and he knew which way would lead to happiness for his family. He only hoped the chance to make things right hadn't slipped away.

Midwest Energy Corporation's monthly newsletter listed all the open positions available at the company. Cam saw a management posting, and he held the credentials required. His boss had encouraged him to try for several career advancements previously, but he'd never followed through on them.

If he landed the job, Cam would transfer to the central office in Spencer and get off the road before it ruined his life. It would be hard. He thrived on sales and was good at it. It had also led him down a dark path that he couldn't leave behind without a clean break. A leadership role at MEC headquarters meant he'd be at home every night. He wouldn't likely run into Jillian very often either.

"I'll have a Coke," Cam said to the bartender in the lounge of the Renaissance Hotel, one of Toledo's ritziest places to stay.

He usually knocked back a scotch once he reached his destination for the week, but Cam needed a clear head, and what he had to say to Jillian couldn't be made easier by alcohol.

"Are you here on business?"

Cam wasn't in the mood for idle chatter with the guy behind the bar, but he didn't want to be rude.

"Yeah. I work for MEC. I'm here a few times a year as we have a satellite office in the suburbs."

Another businessman sat nearby, scanning a menu. He gave Cam a nod of recognition, a silent acknowledgment of their common lifestyle. In the corner, a hotel employee wrapped silverware, the clink of metal pulling Cam from his thoughts—just as Jillian had pulled him from his marriage.

Cam took a glass with ice and his can of soda to a booth.

He wanted to find the most private space available, so he chose a spot at the back of the bar. His stomach felt queasy. He knew he couldn't keep making excuses for his actions, but living without Jillian seemed unbearable.

Cam wouldn't have believed it if someone had told him years earlier that he'd be involved with a woman other than Maggie. His relationship with Jillian was supposed to be harmless fun, but it had evolved into more, although he couldn't remember how or when.

The ding of an elevator drew Cam's attention, and he saw Jillian walking toward him. She looked beautiful, dressed in black pants and a cream-colored sweater. Seeing her almost made him change his mind.

They both knew this couldn't go on forever and Cam planned to end things immediately, even if Jillian didn't know it yet.

He stood and smiled as she leaned in to kiss him.

"Hi. I've missed you," she said.

A trace of Jillian's perfume wafted in his direction, and the knowledge that he was about to break her heart nearly leveled him.

"What's wrong? You look terrible," she said.

Concern settled on Jillian's face as the server stopped by and asked for her drink order.

"I'll have a club soda with lime," she said.

Cam and Jillian always met as soon as they arrived in the same town. They'd have drinks and a quiet dinner close to the hotel. Then, one would abandon their room, and they'd spend the night together.

They tried to be discreet, even though they sometimes booked adjoining rooms. It would not look good if people found out they were a couple, and neither wanted to risk their reputation.

Cam knew dabbling in something so reckless had been stupid. He was a better man than he'd become. Even at home, Jillian slipped into his head at the kids' school events, while watching TV, and mowing the grass. She even lingered in his thoughts when he crawled into bed with Maggie.

His only choice was to eradicate her from his life.

"Did you have a good flight?" he asked Jillian.

Cam had come to end it, but a foreplay of polite conversation rumbled between them like the storm about to break.

"Kind of bumpy, and I wasn't feeling the best."

Cam noticed Jillian seemed nervous too. Unsure whether he was projecting his own state of mind onto her, he pushed through his dread to begin.

"Listen, we need to talk," he started.

"I agree. You go first."

She placed her hand on top of Cam's, and her touch brought him to tears.

"Maggie's pregnant," he said, taking no time to temper the news.

"What?"

The statement spoke for itself, and Cam didn't want to repeat it.

"We both knew this wouldn't last, and it's over today."

He didn't want to be cruel, but the words didn't exist to soften the blow. What Cam shared with Jillian was different than how he loved Maggie. In some ways, his feelings were deeper for his mistress. If he allowed his inappropriate longing to grow, it might strangle his desire to do the right thing.

"When is she due?" Jillian asked.

"Does it matter?"

"It does to me. You told me the two of you weren't sleeping together . . ."

"She's my wife. The strain in our relationship doesn't mean it's dead. Regardless, what's happening between you and me has to stop. My parents were always threatening divorce, and I can't put that on my kids. I'm re-committing my life to Maggie, and you should do the same with Charlie. We made a mistake getting involved with each other."

"I'm a *mistake* to you?"

Jillian's body slumped, the pain stealing her strength.

"I care about you, but it doesn't matter anymore. I have to prioritize my marriage and family. I need to focus on Maggie and try to make up for what I've done," he explained. "You're very special to me. Please don't think this has anything to do with me not thinking you are beautiful or deserving of love. I just can't be the one to give it to you."

Jillian burst into tears. Cam wanted to take her in his arms to comfort her, but he stayed frozen in his seat.

"Goodbye, Cameron."

Jillian got up from the table and left.

Toledo held the estranged lovers captive all week. Seeing Jillian during the day at meetings was exciting when Cam knew they'd be together later. After their breakup, sitting across from her and acting professional demanded more strength than he'd anticipated.

Cam tried to concentrate on work and ordered room service instead of eating alone at a restaurant in the evening. He wasn't hungry anyway; regrets had killed his appetite. He'd never intended to fall for another woman, and the selfishness of his actions overwhelmed him with shame.

He couldn't be concerned about Jillian anymore. He had enough to manage, trying to reclaim his life. She would have to deal with her sadness on her own.

***

"Hi. How's it going?"

Cam called his family each night from the road, and despite what he was dealing with, he didn't change his routine.

"I took Mallory to the doctor. She's got pink eye. Other than that, nothing has changed since yesterday when you left."

Maggie was wrong. Things had changed, and Cam could barely hold his emotions together.

"How are *you* doing?" he asked.

Considering the self-induced stress of his week, Cam couldn't offer adequate support to his wife.

"Fine."

Maggie didn't seem like she wanted to talk, and Cam didn't feel like faking it. Their nightly phone exchanges never lasted long, and they were often more obligatory than an attempt to close the distance separating them. That corrosive pattern had spilled into their marriage, poisoning their bond from the inside out.

***

Cam got home before 5:00 p.m. and stopped to empty the mailbox. It contained advertisements and junk, but you had to go through it all, or you might miss the bills and cards that periodically showed up.

Cam noticed a pizza delivery car in front of the house when he pulled into the driveway. He planned to take the family out to dinner, but, like always, Maggie hadn't asked for his input. He pushed his annoyance aside, promising himself he would make the offer the next night.

"Pizza tonight?"

Cam stated the obvious as he walked into the house. He continued looking at the mail he'd collected on his way in, without greeting Maggie.

A suitcase sat by the back door, and he wondered if Mason or Mallory were going to a sleepover.

"I thought it would be easier for you," Maggie answered without further explanation.

Cam took his place at the table as the kids ran in from the family room to pile cheesy pizza onto paper plates.

"Mom, can we have pop?" Mallory asked.

"Sure," she said.

"What's the bag doing by the door?" Cam asked, continuing to separate the mail.

"I'm leaving for a couple of days."

"Leaving? Where are you going?" he asked.

When Maggie didn't answer, Cam looked at his wife fully for the first time since he'd walked through the door.

"I'm taking the weekend off. Call the Harvest Inn if there's an emergency."

Maggie kissed the children, and Cam surmised that she'd already told them *something* about the situation. She collected her belongings to leave as Cam stood beside the refrigerator, looking puzzled.

"Maggie, what's wrong?" Cam asked.

"Everything," she said.

***

Maggie's plans took Cam by surprise. He had to admit that he'd been nervous about coming home. His feelings were raw after ending the affair with Jillian, and being alone would give him time to collect his thoughts.

Maggie had left instructions for what Cam might need during her absence, and the detailed notes reminded Cam of what a good wife and mother she was. He'd taken her for granted for too long, and he vowed never to do it again. She deserved better, and he wanted to give it to her.

"Hi," Cam said.

"What's wrong?"

Cam didn't know what Maggie needed from him, so he'd made the phone call as an attempt at a peace offering.

"Please come home," he begged.

He couldn't come up with anything else to say.

"This pregnancy has thrown me for a loop, but more than that, I've realized I'm not happy."

"You aren't happy with us? Or do you mean you don't like being a stay-at-home mom anymore?"

"I'm not sure. You don't love me in the same way you used to, and I don't know how to get *us* back. Now I'm having a baby I don't want. Can you believe that? What's wrong with me?"

"I know we've grown apart, but it doesn't have to continue this way. You talk to any couple at our stage in life, and I guarantee you; they're going through a difficult time too."

"We can't go on like this. At least, I can't. I need this time, and I'll be back on Sunday afternoon and we can figure things out."

"Don't give up on us, Maggie."

Cam had been the one to give up months earlier, and he hoped it wasn't too late for Maggie to offer him another chance. He planned to demonstrate to his wife that he still loved her if she would allow it.

***

"Alecia?" Cam asked when their neighbor from across the street answered the phone.

"Hi, Cam. What's up?"

Cam knew Alecia Maxwell would wonder why he'd be calling her. The couples spent time together, but Cam never reached out to her. She and Maggie were the ones who organized outings for the four of them.

"Are you and Mike around tonight?" he asked.

Cam didn't know what he'd do if the Maxwells refused his request.

"It's the one Saturday this month that we have free. Why?"

"Could Mason and Mallory spend the night with you? Maggie and I need a last-minute evening away. We can return the favor for the two of you if you want . . ."

"Well, that's not necessary. We'd love to host them, and our kids will be thrilled."

"You have no idea how much I appreciate this," Cam said.

He took a shower and put Maggie's favorite aftershave on. Cam hadn't romanced his wife in a long time and had almost forgotten what she liked.

He chastised himself again for ignoring the needs of his family.

On the way to see Maggie, he bought flowers and stopped at the *Wok and Roll* to pick up food. It didn't begin to compensate for his actions, but he had to start somewhere.

The Harvest Inn was an old drive-up motel, where guests parked right outside their accommodations. Cam knew Maggie's room number because her car sat in a numbered spot. It took Maggie a minute to come to the door, and for an instant, the thought crossed his mind that she could be there with another man. He doubted Maggie's infidelity and recognized that his suspicions could be a manifestation of a guilty conscience.

Maggie unlocked the deadbolt and faced him, looking displeased that he'd shown up to bother her.

"What are you doing here?" she asked. "Where are the kids?"

"They're spending the night with the Maxwells. Can I come in? This chicken lo mein is getting heavy."

Maggie opened the door to let hm in, and Cam put the food on a table near the window and handed her the bouquet.

"I should have brought you roses more often. I'm sorry. I love you and can't make it without you."

Maggie laid the stems aside before Cam took her in his arms, and they both began to cry.

"Is there any way we can find our way back to each other?" Maggie asked.

"I didn't know you felt as disconnected as I did. We could have saved ourselves a lot of distress if we'd talked about all of this sooner."

"It seems like being on the road all week would be a dream, but it must be hard to live out of a suitcase and sleep in a strange bed," Maggie acknowledged.

Cam's moral compass pointed toward self-reproach when Maggie mentioned sleeping in a bed that wasn't theirs.

"You really don't want this baby?" he asked.

"I *really* don't want this baby. A mother shouldn't say such a thing, even if it's true. I was looking forward to having more time to myself now that Mason and Mallory are older. I'm more than a wife and mom, and I've lost so much of what makes me happy, and I don't know if I can do it again."

"Are you considering an abortion?"

Cam couldn't believe he was even asking the question.

"Should I?"

"No. We need to make our marriage and family a priority again. It's no different than when we found out about

Mason. We hadn't planned for him either, but remember how ecstatic we were?"

"I have no idea how to get back there."

"What if we started over and tried to rebuild our lives, making it better than it's ever been? I've made so many mistakes, and I'll do whatever it takes to make up for it."

"Do you still love me?" Maggie asked.

"I love you more than the first day I met you at Iowa State, even if I haven't been showing it. I take the blame for not giving you what you need lately. I've been selfish and insensitive, and I promise to make it up to you if you'll give me the chance."

Cam exaggerated his current marital affection, but if they were going to move forward, he knew that Maggie needed to feel loved.

"Let's go home," she said.

"What? Why would we leave? I brought your favorite dinner, and Mason and Mallory are taken care of. We can't waste a night at one of Spencer's classiest motels," Cam teased.

When they went to bed later, Cam caressed Maggie's back and reluctantly kissed her neck without taking it further. He wanted his wife to know that their reunion didn't depend on a revival of their missing sex life, or mostly missing, considering Maggie's pregnancy. And if he was being honest with himself, Cam wasn't ready for that kind of intimacy either. They weren't who they used to be, and they'd become familiar strangers,

Only Cam knew how far the threads holding them together had unraveled and how much work it would take to mend their relationship. If their marriage survived, it would be his burden to repair the damage caused by allowing another woman into his heart.

Before they drifted off to sleep, Cam whispered life-changing words to Maggie.

"I'm applying for a different job with the company. I'm done traveling. With three kids in the house, you're going to need my help. There is no reason to take a baby out in the cold when I can provide chauffeur duty after school."

"We'll both have plenty of responsibilities. I don't want you to act like a weekend visitor in our lives anymore. I could get excited to have a family of five if you're serious about all of this," Maggie admitted.

"Everything will be okay, because I'm never letting you down again."

Cam had never made a more sincere promise in his life, and he hoped he could keep it.

CHAPTER 40

Jillian – Fall 2017

Jillian sat in her car, trying to gather the courage to enter Dr. Rachel Mathis's office for her first therapy session. Although it felt good to take steps to fulfill her only 2017 New Year's resolution, trepidation threatened her intentions. With less than three months left in the year, she still hadn't found a way to tell Ella who her dad *really* was.

Ella had turned twenty-five in May, the age Jillian always thought would be the right time to reveal the name of her daughter's father. The future disclosure seemed far away when Ella was little, but the time had arrived to face the gauntlet she'd laid down for herself.

A fine sleet drizzled across the windshield. It blurred Jillian's vision of the front door, where the warmth of the doctor's office waited to coax her into sharing her private torment. A few feet stood between Jillian and the building's threshold, but the journey that led her to that moment felt long and unforgiving.

"What brings you here to see me today?" Dr. Mathis asked, using a leather binder to take notes.

"I need help revealing a secret I've hidden for years," Jillian began as her voice cracked. "Sorry, I'm a little nervous. I've kept this to myself for so long, and bringing it to the surface causes me incredible anxiety."

"What's making you anxious?" the doctor asked.

"I could lose my only child over this. My fear is enough to consider not exposing the truth to her and living with the consequences."

"And what would those *consequences* be?"

"That's the problem. The negative outcome might ruin my life, and I'm not sure if telling her the truth serves any purpose now."

"Keeping something buried can cause devastating effects. I won't tell you what to do or agree or disagree with your decisions. My job is to guide you to do what's best for *you*. Your daughter is not my patient, so it's your well-being that I'm most concerned with."

"I was hoping you could lead me in the appropriate direction with your professional experience in dealing with sensitive issues."

"Why don't you start at the beginning? Then we'll go from there," Dr. Mathis suggested.

The therapist's office overlooked downtown Des Moines, and from her seat, Jillian could see the gold dome of the state capital on the horizon. Somewhere behind her, a clock ticked, deliberately out of sight so clients wouldn't be reminded that they were paying for advice by the hour.

Jillian leaned back and let her mind return to the fall of 1991.

"I was employed by a company out of Spencer called Midwest Energy Corporation. We assisted businesses in making decisions on products to help them reduce their power consumption. The cutting-edge technology drew me in, and I thrived in a setting where we had an important goal."

"Were you happy then?"

"In some aspects of my life, but my marriage to a man named Charlie Meyers floundered. We'd eloped after a quick courtship, and he was a nice guy. But I never loved him the way I should have."

"Why did you marry him?"

"I don't know. That's where the problems came from. He adored me, and the more he tried to get close to me, the more I pulled away. It made things worse when my career took me on the road each week."

"Worse in what way?" Dr. Mathis prodded.

"I had an affair with a man I worked with. I knew being with him would cause me heartache the first time we kissed, but the few nights a month we spent together were heaven. He was attractive, funny, and thoughtful . . ."

"And married?"

"Yes. And married."

"Let's return to Charlie for a minute," the doctor suggested. "Tell me again why you decided to marry someone you didn't love."

"Charlie seemed to have enough love for both of us. It sounds crazy, but I knew he'd provide a good life for me, and I hoped my feelings would become stronger. And then meeting Cameron Sanders changed everything."

"What *changes* took place?"

"Cam and I lived in unfulfilling marriages, and as we became friends, we shared those struggles. We'd grab dinner or a drink after our day of meetings, and before long, it turned into something else."

"What did it turn into?"

"A passionate affair. He was the love of my life, but his commitment to his wife showed me that he didn't feel the same way about me."

"That must have been devastating for you," the doctor sympathized.

"I knew Cam probably wouldn't leave his family for me, but he wasn't beyond doing the wrong thing. It's hard to explain, but we lived in an alternate universe on the road. We were lonely and needed each other, but we didn't mean to hurt anyone."

"In a way, the two of you played make-believe, didn't you?"

"Yes, and deep down, I had to accept that it wouldn't last."

"Let's jump ahead to how it ended."

"When I got pregnant with my daughter, Ella, I knew Cam was her father. We had a conference in Toledo, Ohio, the week after Thanksgiving, and I intended to tell Cam the news then. It complicated things for sure, but with a baby coming, I hoped he'd want to make a life with me. He had two children already, and I could have raised those stepkids as my own and loved them with all my heart. Despite how we'd come together, Ella deserved to have siblings and an amazing father. The unplanned pregnancy made me feel like the universe was rooting for us, and I would have done whatever it took to make it work."

"How did Cameron react to the news?"

Jillian's demeanor changed. Reliving that day had always been heart-wrenching for her, and she fought back tears telling the psychologist what transpired.

"I got to the hotel and met up with Cam. I knew right away that something was wrong. He insisted that we meet in the lounge, and we normally reunited in one of our rooms."

Jillian took a drink from a water bottle the receptionist had given her, taking a moment to collect herself.

"Before I could speak, Cam announced that we were done. He shocked me by saying they'd just found out that *Maggie* was pregnant, and he planned to apply for another job so he could quit traveling for work and help with his kids more. The promotion meant he wouldn't run into me either."

"That must have shattered you."

"It did. Cam said our relationship had been a mistake. I accepted his decision because I loved him and wanted the best for him. I never told him about *my* pregnancy. Considering his wife's condition, I realized their marriage was more intact than he led me to believe."

"I'm sure you felt betrayed."

"I didn't have a right to feel betrayed."

"You have a right to *feel* any way you want," Dr. Mathis said. "Let's get back to Charlie. How did you explain the situation to him?"

"I went home and convinced him that we should have a baby. Miraculously, within a few weeks, I was pregnant. I fibbed a little on my due date, and he never questioned whether he fathered Ella when she came earlier than expected."

"And after Ella was born?"

"She looked exactly like Cam. I cried every time I looked at her, but I had our futures to think of. I did something terrible by allowing Charlie to believe Ella belonged to him. We stayed together for five more years before divorcing."

"And your husband never knew?"

"Not until we split. Charlie wanted fifty-fifty custody, and I couldn't let that happen. I had no choice but to tell him he wasn't her biological father. After I told him, he never asked about the details of my affair, and I didn't offer them."

"It must have been difficult for him to lose a child he'd raised since birth?"

"He adored Ella, and I have lived with the guilt of taking her from him for a very long time. He demanded a DNA test, thinking I might be lying. It destroyed him when the results came back. He was a good man, despite the failure of our union. I wish I'd loved him. It would have been much easier for us."

"For you and Charlie?"

"No, for me and Ella. I couldn't provide for my daughter as well after the divorce."

"Did you ever see Cam again?" the doctor asked.

"If he was at a meeting or conference for MEC, I did everything possible to avoid him. The few times we were in the same place, we didn't make eye contact or speak. I worked so hard to get over him, and I couldn't ignite that flame again."

"Did you ever consider contacting Cameron for financial help?"

"No. I've made many mistakes but leaving Cam out of this wasn't one of them. His family didn't need to have this forced upon them. Cam would never have abandoned Ella, and that devotion would have caused him to lose everything. I didn't want to be the reason Cam lost what mattered most to him. I knew if he left Maggie for me, he'd grow to resent the pain I'd brought into his life, so I've kept this to myself for all these years."

"It's interesting that you feel as if you can judge what's best for those around you. What makes you think you have that kind of power? Cameron willingly participated in your relationship, yet you didn't require much of him after he told you that he and his wife were staying together. He got off pretty easy, don't you think?"

"When you love someone, you'll do anything to protect them. I knew I had to let Cam go," Jillian professed.

"And did you accomplish that goal? Did you protect those you love?"

Dr. Mathis didn't shy away from the tough questions.

"I hope so," Jillian whispered.

"If you do decide to tell Ella, how would you share this information?"

"I've thought about writing her a letter. That way, I could explain what happened without leaving anything out. But I know it would be better to tell her in person, even if I'm scared to do it."

"Are you still considering keeping this to yourself?"

"I'm not sure. If I tell Ella eventually, does it matter when?"

"You're the one determining what you can live with. I will say, in my experience, the truth has a more positive outcome. That's all the time we have for today. Do you want to schedule another appointment?"

"No. Thanks for your help. After going over all of this with you, I know what I need to do."

***

"Mom? I'm here!"

Jillian came from the bedroom and greeted Ella with a hug and kiss.

"How was the traffic from Minneapolis?"

Jillian had invited her daughter for the weekend, and she planned to reveal what she'd held for so long during the visit.

"It wasn't too bad, although it got busy around Ames. The Cyclones must have a game today with the number of cars sporting Iowa State bumper stickers heading south."

After lunch, Jillian and Ella found themselves on the screened porch, ready to enjoy a beautiful autumn afternoon.

"Honey, I need to discuss something important with you."

Jillian's heart pounded, and she wondered if Ella could see the palpitations under her shirt.

"Before you get into it, I have something to tell *you*," Ella gushed.

"You do?"

"I've met someone," Ella said with a wide grin. "His name is Jordan Daley, and he's a firefighter. We've only been seeing each other for a short time, but I'm already falling for him."

Jillian hadn't been prepared for Ella to have news of her own, and the turn of events threw her off course. She hesitated to redirect their discussion so drastically when Ella was giddy with happiness.

"What did you want to talk about?" Ella said, still beaming.

"Oh . . . well, I've been reflecting on how things might have been easier if you'd had a father around over the years, and . . ."

"Mom, you raised me perfectly. We didn't need a man to show us the way. You taught me how to make it on my own. A fabulous single mom is better than adding ten dads to the equation."

Ella's validation made Jillian feel even more ashamed. Her daughter seemed well-adjusted, and everyone had moved on. Was it too late to bring the truth to light? What if that truth made Ella angry and their relationship changed forever? If she decided to search for Cameron, who knows what might happen.

"Thank you for that, Ella. Life is full of challenges, and to know you believe you have had the best one possible makes me happy."

Jillian knew it wasn't the time to divulge her life-altering secret. Maybe she'd wait until her daughter turned thirty. What difference would another five years make?

"I love you, Mom. Now, I want to tell you about spending last weekend in Chicago with Jordan."

EPILOGUE
May 2024

"How have you been, Ella?" Maggie asked.

The two hadn't talked in a while, and the sound of Rosie playing in the background made Maggie smile.

"We're doing well. I planned to call you later today because Jordan made it to the final round of interviews for his promotion."

"And?"

"He got it. Jordan is now Captain Daley! It won't make much difference for Rosie and me. He'll still work a twenty-four-hour shift, but it's more money, and he's excited to move up in the ranks."

"Give him my congratulations."

"I will. I'm sorry I haven't gotten back to you, but we can't make it for Memorial Day," Ella said.

Ella had waffled on plans for the holiday weekend at Lake Okoboji from the moment Maggie invited them. Since their first meeting sixteen months earlier, Ella had only seen the Sanders kids one other time. They'd met at a state park for a picnic, and it had gone well, even if it felt like a group of strangers trying to connect because of obligation.

Ella knew the relationships were not progressing beyond a surface level, and it didn't seem likely they ever would. Biological connections didn't make them a family.

How could they make up for what they'd already missed?

Uncovering the truth about her father and half-siblings allowed Ella to realize that she hadn't been looking for herself as much as she'd been searching for where she belonged. Ella had come to understand that the place she'd been seeking was with Jordan and their growing family.

When Rosie came along, Ella's perspective had sharpened. Maggie and her kids were lovely people, but they lived more than three hours away, and their lives never crossed without effort. Ella had chosen to step back from her new relatives and felt at peace with her decision.

"Of course," Maggie said. "I only wanted to extend the invitation so we could all see each other again."

Maggie could feel Ella establishing boundaries now that she had a child of her own, and she knew those parameters meant moving away from spending time with the Sanders. Maggie's children had resisted the idea of including Ella in the Memorial Day festivities to begin with. The kids liked their half-sister, but they didn't *need* her to feel complete. Maggie hoped she'd helped Ella achieve that same contentment.

"Can I call you in a few days? I have to go—*Rosie*, don't touch that!"

Ella had planned to tell Maggie that she was pregnant again, but she decided to keep the secret a little longer. Maggie wasn't her mother, and Ella knew she shouldn't allow her to take on that role.

"You'd better go before Rosie gets into trouble," Maggie said, bringing their call to an end.

The conversation with Ella carried a sense of finality. A lump rose in Maggie's throat, but she knew she'd done what she could to honor Cam, and that tempered her sadness.

For so long, Maggie had searched for purpose and self-worth, trying to earn her place in the world. In guiding Ella toward the truth and forgiving Cam for the pain he left behind, Maggie had finally begun to heal.

She'd moved from Spencer to Lake Okoboji the previous fall. The season's rich colors had faded by the time she began spending all her time there. Leaving the home where she'd raised her children hadn't been easy, but Mason was right—she didn't need the responsibility of two residences.

Sorting through her belongings had taken an unexpected physical and emotional toll as Maggie chose what to carry with her into the next season of her life. She treated her memories the same way, holding the good ones close and letting the rest slip away.

Wrigley was thriving at the lake too. He relished lying in the sun and chasing squirrels and the occasional stray cat from the property. He and Maggie spent hours looking out at the boats, and when their wakes gently rocked the dock, Wrigley would get up and go to the window. Two years after Cam's death, the hopeful pup still longed for his owner to return with a stringer of fish. Maggie's heart ached every time, and she'd call him over for a belly rub to console him.

All of Maggie's things found a new spot after her move, and the only item that hadn't survived intact was the table Cam built for Maggie years earlier. The movers had accidentally pushed the couch against it, and it collapsed to the ground like a stack of Jenga blocks.

Maggie shrieked when it toppled, and the crew of men stared at her as she knelt to collect the colorful tiles scattered across the floor. The guy in charge promised they'd pay for the damage, but each fragment held a memory she couldn't bear to lose, and he had no idea how priceless the treasure was.

Maggie had been able to glue the base together again, but half of the glass pieces had cracked, and the red ceramic shards—once forming a heart on top—were shattered. It may have looked ready for the curb, but to Maggie it endured as a symbol of love's fragility and the power of forgiveness.

The 'Maggie and Cam's Happily Ever After' sign had come down the week after Cam's funeral, but Maggie dug it out and re-hung it after moving to the lake house permanently. She chose to focus on the 'happily' more than the 'ever after,' and that decision brought her comfort.

Although Cam wasn't there to enjoy it, she could still be content in the place they'd created for their fresh start. Happiness had become a state of being for Maggie— something she drew from within, regardless of what else was happening around her.

Summer had arrived as if it had only stepped away for a moment, and the Sanders would not let the occasion slip by without a celebration. It disappointed Maggie that Ella, Jordan, and Rosie wouldn't be able to join them. Finding Ella didn't mean an automatic bond formed between the siblings, and Maggie knew she had to give up on trying to make a family out of people who didn't want to be one.

The second year after Cam's death brought even more changes to the Sanders family. Erin and Tessa moved back to Northwest Iowa with their daughter, Isabelle, and Mason and Jenny purchased their own cottage on Lake Okoboji. The resort town had become the family's stomping grounds again. Cam's efforts to make Maggie's dreams come true provided the perfect setting for everyone to reclaim their lives after his death. It was a final gift from a man who never stopped trying to prove his love.

Mallory and Tom found out over Easter weekend that they were expecting another baby, proving you never knew what was coming next. They weren't prepared for the news after having undergone two rounds of IVF to conceive their twins. The doctors called it a miracle, especially since Mallory was in her forties.

Maggie had done her best to support her daughter through the ups and downs of a pregnancy when the timing and circumstances weren't ideal. She'd lived through the experience and assured Mallory that she would have more than enough room in her heart for another child.

It saddened Maggie to know that Cam didn't get to meet all of his grandchildren, including little Rosie. It didn't seem fair, and if she was having a bad day, the reality angered her.

Maggie still doubted herself at times, but she never questioned Cam's love for her. She'd think about him while sitting on the deck in the morning and sometimes had conversations with him. If God could hear her prayers, she was sure that Cam would listen to her other ramblings.

Cam's death had marked a turning point for their family, placing Maggie at the helm. She trusted that her example would guide her loved ones in the right direction, because she'd always carried on, even when she didn't want to.

The one-of-a-kind table Cam built and rebuilt over the years emulated life itself. It still stood in the corner of the den. Its imperfections, etched by the passage of time, made it all the more treasured for Maggie. The heirloom served as a quiet reminder that even when things seem broken, there is always beauty in what remains.

Finished the book?

Scan below for the discussion guide.

Acknowledgments

Things usually happen for a reason, and with that in mind, I must admit this book was initially scheduled for release a year ago. Life has thrown me a few curveballs lately, including a broken arm that put me months behind schedule. However, the extra time provided me with opportunities I hadn't expected—such as collaborating with a coach and discovering writing tools that significantly improved my editing process. I genuinely believe the delay made this manuscript stronger and enriched the journey of bringing it into the world.

This is my third novel, and with each new creation, I gain more people to acknowledge. I am thankful to those who willingly read early versions, advise on storyline revisions, and patiently listen as I drone on about plot ideas. Your excitement for my dream of being an author is something I will always treasure.

Thank you to my ever-faithful ABC Book Club in Waterloo, Iowa. They have been with me from the beginning, and though we've dwindled over the years, Kathy Bailey, Lori Johnson, and Kendra Richman remain constants in my life. Other beta readers include Lisa Boyer, Criss Edgar, Bobbi Eskey, Kay Harrison, Tracy Kahl, Lauren

Nelson, Morgan Nelson, Emily Rollins, Suzzanne Shelton, and Teri Sporer. Bobbi and Kay not only provided feedback but also invited me to a celebrity medium's performance, giving me the chance to research one of this story's recurring themes.

When I asked for volunteers to join my launch team, I was hoping for ten willing souls. I was shocked when nearly ninety of you signed up and promoted my last book with such heart. There are too many of you to name here, but that doesn't lessen my appreciation for your efforts. You sure know how to make a girl feel loved.

I had the privilege of working with a book coach through the Women's Fiction Writers Association certification program. Colleen Scott was instrumental in sorting through issues and offering advice for improvement. Likewise, Ginger Calum gave insight into shaping the footprint of my next novel, which ultimately strengthened this one as well.

I'm humbled by the support given to me by other writers in my home state of Iowa. I'd especially like to thank New York Times bestselling author Heather Gudenkauf for her continued encouragement. Additionally, author Kali White VanBaale selected *Everything Will Be Okay* as a project for her master's in creative writing class at Lindenwood University, and their suggestions were very helpful. Another of my favorite Midwestern storytellers, Nicole Baart, shared her knowledge early in the process, guiding me to put my best foot forward with my query package.

Every time I try to find the words to pay tribute to those closest to me, I'm reminded of how the seasons of life keep changing us. We've added a name to our family roster with each book I've published, and if this keeps up, we'll need to rent a hall for Thanksgiving! I am blessed with an amazing family: Holly, Jeff, Jake, and Morgan Bradley; Emily, Nick, Olivia, Mia, and baby boy Rollins; Lauren Nelson and Riley Rue; and Rob and Morgan Nelson. I love you all.

The person who deserves the most credit for sticking with me is my husband, Doug. He never complains when I spend hours at my desk or when dinner plans fall through because I want to finish one more chapter. He understands my need to follow this passion, and for that, I am eternally grateful. His love reminds me that everything really will be okay.

Thank You

Thank you for reading *Everything Will Be Okay*. I hope you enjoyed Maggie and Ella's story and will consider sharing it with friends and family and leaving a review online. Reviews, especially on Amazon, make a huge difference for authors. If you use Goodreads or BookBub, I'd be grateful for your thoughts there as well. Your support and feedback mean everything and allow me to continue writing books and sharing them with readers.

Check out the latest news from
Christina Edgar Olds:

christinaedgarolds.com

Facebook: Christina Edgar Olds, Author

Instagram: @christinaedgarolds

www.ingramcontent.com/pod-product-compliance
Lightning Source LLC
Chambersburg PA
CBHW071531110726
47908CB00007B/1837